His Unstable Obsession

His Unstable Obsession

Book Two of His Crazy Obsession Series

Ana Denise

Contact Information:
Instagram: authoranadenise
TikTok: author.ana.denise
Facebook: Ana Denise

Front Cover design by: Deranged Doctor Design
Model: Taria Reed from The Reed Files
ISBN: 9798988462927

First Edition: February 2024

Chapter One

Kyla

I smiled before I placed a soft, tender kiss on Ryder's chubby cheek as we continued to sing.

"Happy birthday to Ryder, happy birthday to you."

A chorus of clapping sounded as we gathered to celebrate my son's fourth birthday.

"Make a wish, Ryder," Ryan, my wonderful husband of five years, stated.

He reached over and ran his fingers through

Ryder's curly brown hair. Even though I had endured eight hours of immense, pain-filled labor, Ryder came out looking like Ryan's twin. The only difference was Ryder had a caramel skin tone complexion.

"I wish for..." Ryder began.

"No, silly. You don't wish out loud, or your wish won't come true. Make your wish in your head," Bria said to her brother.

Ryder closed his light brown eyes for a few seconds before he opened them up. I bent over a few inches, allowing Ryder full access to blow out the four candles sitting on top of his zoo-themed vanilla cake. We all cheered again once the candles had been blown out as I put Ryder down on the ground.

Before Ryder was out of my grasp, he took off running with half of the children attending the party.

Ryan and I had put together a birthday party for Ryder at our house. We still lived in the two-story cobblestone, three-bedroom, two-bathroom house. The only changes that had been made were the gray furnishings had been updated, and Ryan's office had been turned into Ryder's animal-themed bedroom.

On that hot spring day, we had transformed our backyard into any four-year-old's dream party. We had an entire carnival set-up, including carnival games and a mini petting zoo.

"What about cake?" I yelled out as I grabbed the cake knife off the table.

"Honey, most kids care more about ponies than a slice of cake," Aunt Lily stated as she wrapped her arm around my shoulder and gave me a tight squeeze.

Aunt Lily and I looked similar with our dark brown complexion and brown siren eyes. The only difference was that her age started showing by the various gray hairs sprinkled around her hairline.

"I knew I should've gone with the pigs," I joked as I sliced the cake into pieces.

Aunt Lily had flown in for Ryder's birthday from Seattle two nights before. Over the last five years, Aunt Lily held true to her word of being active in our lives. Whenever a significant gathering came up or if she was just missing our presence, she would fly out for a few days and spend quality time with us. She still owned her cleaning company, and the business was doing better than ever financially. Aunt Lily's husband, Gerald, had come to visit with her twice since we had reunited. He was not too involved in our lives, but that was fine. The only thing that mattered was that Aunt Lily made visits to see us. For one of our once-a-year family trips, we had gone to visit Aunt Lily in Seattle during the winter. It was an exciting experience to see the state of Washington for the first time. The only issue we encountered was the weather had chilled me to my bones the entire week we visited. I made a mental note as we boarded the plane to fly back home that the next time we visited would be during the summer.

"You two exceeded my expectations with this party. I never had a petting zoo come to my birthday party before."

"Anything for my two angels. I want them to have the childhood I always yearned for but never received."

Aunt Lily looked over at me and gave a sorrowful smile as my mind drifted to my mother. Even though Aunt Lily was a big support system, I still often wondered what it would've been like to have a mother figure in my life growing up. I wondered what it would have been like to know who my father was.

"You are doing a wonderful job raising those two." Aunt Lily rubbed my back in a soothing manner. "Now cheer up. It's a joyful day of celebrating that handsome little guy."

Aunt Lily pointed to Ryder, who was petting a pretty white pony with a toothy grin. Aunt Lily waved at one of our guests in the distance before she excused herself and walked away.

Placing a slice of cake on a plate, I handed the plate to the child in front of me before hands were thrown over my eyes.

"There is only one person who would throw their hands over my eyes while I am holding a knife," I said in singsong as I stood in semi-darkness.

"It is a cake knife. It is not going to hurt a soul."

I removed the hands away from my eyes and

placed the cake knife on the table. I turned around, and I looked at Sabrina, my best friend, whom I considered a sister.

"My goodness, Sabrina, I missed you."

We wrapped our arms around each other, and we squeezed each other tight. Sabrina's favorite apple-scented conditioner danced into my nose, a feeling of déjà vu coming over me. We squealed in excitement, without a doubt drawing attention to ourselves, but we couldn't care less.

Sabrina and I met when I first moved to South Carolina. We were coworkers at Meg's Coffee Shop, and the friendship blossomed right away.

"I missed you too."

My eyes widened as I took in her new appearance. "You cut your hair." I ran my fingers through her strawberry blonde hair, which was now cut into a cute bob that stopped at her chin. "I am loving the new style."

"Thank you. I wanted a change, and I went for it."

Sabrina's hazel eyes twinkled with excitement as she flashed a big smile, revealing her stunning, straight teeth. Gone were the braces she used to have years ago.

I grabbed her hands into mine and gave them a comforting squeeze. "You look amazing. It feels like it has been years since I've seen you."

Sabrina playfully rolled her eyes as a group of children ran past us. They laughed and screamed.

"It has only been a month."

"One month is too long," I pointed out.

Sabrina agreed. "I know. I'm sorry I'm late. My flight was delayed."

"You have no reason to apologize. I'm just happy you took the time out of your busy schedule to come visit."

Sabrina began taking classes at the local community college four years ago and earned her Associate Degree in Communications. She started a blog and became an instant social media celebrity. Two years later, Sabrina was offered the opportunity of a lifetime to become a co-host on a talk show. Following her lifetime dream, she jumped on that opportunity and loved every bit of it. Every other month, she was either in South Carolina or she was in California filming shows. She was in California this month, but made a few arrangements to come into town. Justin, her husband, and Emily, her eleven-year-old daughter, still lived in town full-time.

"There was no way I would miss my nephew's birthday party. Where is he?"

I did a quick scan of the area where I last saw him. Pointing in the direction of where Ryder was petting a tan goat, Sabrina walked away as she called over her shoulder, "I'll be right back."

I finished slicing a few more pieces of cake before walking to the cooler and grabbing a bottle of water.

My phone sounded in my pocket. Pulling it out, I saw I had a text from Amelia, my mother-in-law.

Amelia: I'm sorry James and I are missing Ryder's birthday party. We are in New York visiting Sophia. We will drop off Ryder's gift when we are back in town.

Smiling, I was excited my in-laws were visiting Sophia. Sophia was Ryan's older sister. She was a fashion designer who had been living in New York for a while. Amelia and James had been planning this trip for months, and they were finally able to go visit. They were going to be in New York for a week.

Me: No need to apologize. Enjoy your trip. Take a few scenic pictures for me.

"Finally, Kyla can take a break and relax."

Chelsea approached me as I placed my phone back in my pocket.

Chelsea and I had met through the friendship our husbands shared. Chelsea was a tall woman with wavy blonde hair and crystal blue eyes. She sipped on a wine cooler.

"This momma never gets a break," I responded before taking a sip of my water.

Chelsea and I looked over to where Ryder was giving Sabrina a hug. "Ryder is having the time of his life."

I agreed. "He is a fanatic over animals."

"I remember when he was born. Now look at him. He is four, going on forty."

I widened my eyes in terror as I shook my head. "Wait, wait, wait, Chelsea. You are aging me way too fast. I am not trying to be a grandma with five grandchildren running around anytime soon," I stated, as we laughed at my response.

Chelsea took another sip of her wine cooler. "He is just growing up so fast."

"Yes, he is," floated over my shoulder.

Chelsea looked over my shoulder. "Who told you to eavesdrop on our conversation?"

Turning around, I looked at Ryan.

Ryan hadn't changed too much appearance-wise over the years. He still wore his hair short, receiving trims every month like clockwork.

"I was in earshot. I couldn't help myself, Chels."

Ryan wrapped his arms tight around my waist as he pressed his chest to my back. My heart raced in my chest as my stomach fluttered with butterflies. He placed his head on my left shoulder.

"How is my amazing wife holding up over here?"

"I'm good. Just taking a breather."

I loved that his presence and touch still gave me the feelings I had when we first met.

"I just wanted you to know you did great with this party."

"Don't you mean we?" I asked as I turned to look at him.

Ryan shrugged before he placed a soft, tender kiss on my cheek, sending chills up my spine.

"The only thing I did was swipe my credit card."

Mark walked over. He held a beer and

slipped his arm around Chelsea's waist.

"PDA is not appropriate at a child's party."

Mark was Chelsea's husband and Ryan's best friend. Mark had brown curly hair and green eyes, and he was tall. The dictionary definition of tall, dark, and handsome. Mark and Chelsea were an adorable couple.

"Marky Mark. A kiss on the cheek never hurt anybody's eyes." Ryan gave a playful smirk.

"Not that kiss. The way you are pressed against her."

He winked before he took a sip of his beer.

"A bit of PDA never harmed anybody before, and it won't harm anybody now," Ryan responded as we all laughed.

Ryan placed another kiss on my cheek.

"So, when are you two going to work on a little one?" I asked as I motioned to the children running around the backyard with my hand.

Ryan nodded. "Yeah, I want a niece or nephew to hold and spoil."

"When the perfect time comes." Mark tilted his beer back, finishing it off.

"When is that?" Ryan raised an eyebrow.

Before Mark could respond, my attention was captured by one of my children.

"Mommy. Mommy."

Bria ran to me lightning fast as she wrapped her arms around my leg.

"Yes, Bria?" I looked down at Bria.

I couldn't believe she was now considered a tween at ten. Her big brown eyes stared up into mine as I ran my fingers through her light brown curly hair that flowed down her back.

Bria pointed in the direction of where the bean bag toss game was set up.

"Can Emily stay the night tonight?"

Ryan planted one more kiss on my cheek before Ryan, Mark, and Chelsea excused themselves and walked away.

Looking over to where Emily was, I saw her brown hair flop as she did a small victory dance, and she landed a bean bag in the hole. It was hard to believe Emily was now eleven. Where had the time gone?

"We are going to have to ask her mom."

Bria scanned the yard. Once she found Sabrina, she yelled, "Auntie Sabrina." Sabrina stopped what she was doing and looked in our direction. "Come here."

As Sabrina trotted over to us, I located Ryan, Mark, and Chelsea at the food table, chatting with Justin.

"Yes, sweetie?" Sabrina placed all her attention on Bria as she tucked a strand of hair behind her ear.

"Can Emily spend the night?"

Sabrina placed her hands on her hips playfully. "You haven't seen me in a month, and you don't even give me a hug before you ask me a question?"

Bria smiled widely as she closed the distance between them and hugged her tight. "Hi, Auntie Sabrina."

"How is my favorite niece doing?" she asked Bria.

"I am good." Bria thought for a second. "Wait. I am your only niece."

"Exactly, sweetie. Of course, Emily can spend the night. As long as you promise me one thing." Sabrina stuck out her pinky finger.

"I'll promise anything."

"You have to promise to give her back tomorrow morning."

Bria hooked her pinky finger with Sabrina's. "You have a deal." She ran toward the bean bag toss to tell Emily the wonderful news.

"I love how much they love each other," I admitted as I watched them get excited about their sleepover.

"They might love each other just as much as we love each other."

I couldn't help but agree. "They should. They only grew up with each other."

Sabrina surveyed the partygoers. "Where is Amy?"

Amy was my best friend whom I lived with while we were both in foster care. We were inseparable until Brad came along and tore us apart. Years later, we reunited, and it was as if our friendship had never had a five-year pause.

"Amy couldn't make it today. Alex's cousin had her wedding today."

Alex was Amy's husband.

"That's always exciting to see."

Sabrina and I walked around the backyard,

checking out all the activities that were taking place.

Sabrina, Amy, and I had formed a beautiful bond. Sabrina and Amy had no other choice but to become close. When it was time to plan Ryder's baby shower, they helped me plan the entire event in depth. When I approached my due date to give birth to Ryder, they were both on call to rush to the hospital as soon as I needed them. Sabrina had arrived a lot quicker than Amy since Sabrina was in town the month that I gave birth. Amy traveled from Arkansas. She had barely arrived at the hospital before Ryder made his grand entrance into this world.

"It's even more exciting to experience. It feels as if it was yesterday that I was saying 'I do' to Ryan, and it's been five years."

I tucked a piece of hair behind my ear before I continued to drink my water.

"Tell me about it. Julian and I will be going on for ten years in two months. Time flies when you are with the person you love."

"Time flies when you enjoy life. Congratulations." I rubbed Sabrina's shoulder. "Are you two doing anything exciting for your ten-year anniversary?"

"We considered a night out on the town or a three-day cruise. Nothing is set in stone yet." We had just walked past the dunk tank, where a child tried to hit the bullseye to drop the man in the tank full of ice-cold water.

"Whatever you decide, let me know. I don't

mind babysitting."

Sabrina wiggled her eyebrows. "What if we wanted to do a double date with you and Ryan?"

"Well, a romantic double date doesn't go too well with three children running around."

Sabrina tapped her bottom lip with her index finger, deep in thought. "Can Amelia babysit for us?"

"I don't see a reason why she wouldn't. She loves Emily just as much as she loves Bria and Ryder." Emily has spent the night with Bria at Amelia and James' house several times. They have a blast every single time they stay over. I'm sure it's because they get away with more at their house than they get away with at Sabrina's and my house.

Sabrina looked around the backyard again. "Where are Amelia and James?"

"They are in New York visiting Sophia."

"I know they are enjoying themselves."

Sabrina waved at Chelsea, who was walking towards us.

"Yes, they only see her about three times a year."

"See who?" Chelsea asked, joining the conversation.

"Amelia and James only see Sophia three times a year," I informed Chelsea.

Sabrina spoke up. "Well, let me know the next time they go to visit her. I'm going to have them pick me up a few of her designs. Her work is fabulous."

"Yes, it is. I'll let you know." I took another sip of my water.

"Sophia's work is amazing. Sadly, I cannot afford those price tags at this moment." Chelsea finished off her wine cooler.

"Kyla," was yelled across the yard. Stopping in our tracks, I turned towards Aunt Lily's voice.

"Yes?"

"We need a refill on chips."

Turning around, I looked at Sabrina and Chelsea. "My break is over."

Chapter Two

Brad

I walked down the hall, my nose guiding my movements. I walked into the kitchen, my mouth watering for one thing only. Strong, black coffee.

"Good morning, sleepy head."

I looked over my shoulder at Moriah before I grabbed a cup out of the cabinet. "Good morning. You'd be a sleepyhead too if you slept in an actual bed after sleeping on a slab of concrete for five years."

Moriah was a beautiful Indian with a skin tone of honey. She had light brown almond eyes and thick black hair that hung down her back. A hint of a smile touched her lips as she took a sip out of her cup.

"How are you doing this morning?"

I poured coffee into my cup before I blew on the hot goodness.

"I'm good. How are you?"

"I'm great."

She brought her cup to her plump, red lips before she took a sip.

Before I could respond, Joe walked into the kitchen. He greeted me before he walked over to Moriah and gave her a kiss on the lips. Lucky bastard.

"Joe, what have you been up to this morning?"

Joe washed his hands in the sink as I sat at the dinner table next to Moriah. By the sweat that glistened on his forehead and the wetness on his shirt, I knew he had been doing something physical.

He dried his hands before he went into the fridge and grabbed a carton of orange juice. "Hitting iron. I'm trying to get buff like you."

I smirked. I had gained ten pounds of muscle while I was away, and it was evident in my legs and arms. "That is what happens when you are behind bars. Lifting weights made the days better and go by faster."

Joe was my best friend from high school. I

considered him family. We had become inseparable, and we always leaned on each other for support. Even if we fought, we would allow a few days to pass by before everything was fine between us. I was grateful when he left the army to come back home.

A month and a half ago, I was informed by the warden that there was an important meeting I was required to attend. After being shackled by my hands and feet, I was taken to the courthouse. I sat with a judge and was told that since the evidence on file was tampered with, I would be released early. I was overcome with joy, as that was the best news I had heard in five years. Two weeks later, I was released into society. All I was waiting for was my big fat check from the government for wrongful imprisonment. To no surprise, Joe was the person who picked me up from the state prison in South Carolina.

"I'm so glad you are finally home."

Joe gulped down some of his orange juice as he sat at the table across from me.

"You're only glad because you don't have to travel to see me once a month anymore," I pointed out.

Joe was consistent in his visits to see me. I couldn't have asked for a better friend. For a better brother. My parents had cut me off and stopped all communication the second I was thrown behind bars. It was safe to say my dad held true to the words he had spoken to me years before. He disowned me and hadn't budged on that decision, even until this day. Somehow, he convinced mom to jump on board.

"No, I'm glad, because I missed my brother being on the outside with me."

Moriah's eyes traveled between Joe and me as she clasped her hands on top of the table.

"Thank you for letting me stay here while I get on my feet." I took a hearty sip of my coffee and winced as the hot liquid traveled down my throat.

Joe rolled his eyes. "How many times have I told you I don't want to hear another 'thank you' from you?"

I shrugged. "I know, but I can't help it."

"We're family. That's what family do."

He was more of a family figure to me than my parents. All my other friends, before I went to prison, disappeared into thin air. I hadn't heard from any of them since I was locked up. I had no desire to reconnect with them since I've been out, either. They left me at my lowest low, and I had zero respect for that. I would've kept in contact if the shoe was on the other foot. Even if I hadn't visited regularly, I still would've called and made sure they were fine. Eddie, Daniel, and Vince could go straight to hell on a one-way trip.

"How's the job search going?" Moriah asked once the room fell silent.

"Sheesh, Moriah. Already trying to put me out of your beautiful house?" I joked as I took another sip of my coffee.

Joe and Moriah had purchased a Mediterranean Revival-style house a year ago. It was tan with brown trimmings. It was spacious, with two bedrooms, two bathrooms, and a bonus room.

Joe allowed me to stay with them for a few months while I looked for a job and started making money. The house that I had been living in before I went away was purchased by my parents as a gift for taking over part ownership of the family business. The problem with that purchase was that the house was in my dad's name. The only thing I had to my name was my car.

Moriah grabbed her cup and raised it to her mouth. My eyes zeroed in on the gold wedding ring on her finger. She playfully rolled her eyes as she took a sip of her coffee. A smile appeared. "No, silly. I'm just curious if anyone has reached out to you."

I shook my head. "Not yet. It's not easy getting a job when your resume has a five-year gap."

Joe scratched his head. "Something will come along. Don't let it get you down." I stood, and I went into the fridge. I grabbed a carton of eggs. I cracked six eggs into a bowl. "I won't hold my breath on that."

Moriah tapped her manicured fingers on the table. "Miami is a busy city. People are always hiring."

After asking Moriah and Joe if they wanted scrambled eggs, they both declined. I beat the eggs in a bowl with a whisk.

"I'm going to take a shower, sugar lips." Joe leaned across the table and kissed Moriah's lips.

She beamed as he walked away. "Have fun."

Joe called over his shoulder, "I'll only have fun if you join me."

"You two are cute together," I commented as I poured the eggs into a frying pan.

"Thank you. Joe really completes me."

"How long have you two been married?"

I knew it had been a while, but I wasn't sure exactly how long. It hurt Joe's feelings when I couldn't be his best man at his wedding. It hurt my feelings just as much, but I was happy my best friend had gotten hitched.

"Two years."

"Would you still consider that the honeymoon stage?" I asked.

She shrugged. "It's always been a honeymoon stage with Joe. When I met him, I knew he was the one."

Joe and Moriah had met a year after I had gone to prison. They met in a bar one night when Moriah was having a girls' night with her two sisters. Joe had managed to snag her attention with his pool skills. They exchanged contact information and had been inseparable ever since. A year and a half later, Joe decided he wanted to spend the rest of his life with her and proposed.

I finished scrambling my eggs and moved them to a plate. "I can't wait to experience a love like that again."

"It'll come to you when you least expect it, I

promise," Moriah reassured me.

She excused herself, and she walked out of the kitchen.

Within minutes, I devoured my eggs as my mind wandered over to my conversation with Moriah. There was once upon a time when I had the perfect woman in my life. I had her for five years, and I neglected to see the beautiful soul who decided to love me for me, even when I treated her like garbage. She provided me with a wonderful, smart daughter. A family of my own that I had always desired from a young age. Now she had gone and married the man she had decided to cheat on me with. He was probably the father figure to my daughter, as she had no contact with me these past several years.

Kyla should've been my wife. She was supposed to provide me with my happily ever after. That happily ever after never happened. I was the reason for that. Even though I was sure Kyla was still married, I still wanted to give her a chance. A chance to explain herself. I'd take her back in a heartbeat, as long as she divorced the ass wipe she had married out of spite. I know she only did it to get back at me for all I had taken her through over the years.

After washing my dishes, I set them out to dry. I walked through the beach-themed living room. Seashells and nautical figurines littered the space throughout. I walked down the hallway and headed for my room. It was on the opposite side of the house than the master bedroom. I was grateful for that. I didn't want to hear their sex escapades throughout the night. From how happy Joe appeared to be all the time, I knew it was happening plenty throughout the week. I changed out of my pajama pants and into a pair of gray gym shorts and a white t-shirt with the sleeves cut off. After putting on my black tennis shoes, I threw a pair of khaki shorts and a black shirt into my gym bag. I was going to spend two hours at the gym hitting weights, and then I was going to do some research.

I grabbed my car keys and walked out the door. Thankfully, my car was in my name, so my dad couldn't sell it off. For a day in the middle of October in Florida, it was kind of a cool day at seventy-five degrees. The humidity in the air was surprisingly bearable.

My car roared to life as I double-checked the mirrors. Joe had taken over ownership of my vehicle while I was away and made sure to keep up with the maintenance. I turned my country music up, and I traveled through the congested traffic across town to my favorite gym. I couldn't work out at just any gym.

Once I was parked, I walked along the sidewalk with my bag on my shoulder as I approached the door. Two teenage girls in matching sports bras and workout shorts were about to push the door open when I pulled it open for them.

"Thank you," they said in unison as their eyes roamed over my body as they exited.

"No problem, ladies."

After I checked in with my phone, I made a beeline over to the free weights section. The section already had four other men that made my muscles look puny. This section was where I would spend my entire gym trip with the big dogs. Blowing off much-needed steam with forty-pound weights.

After two hours of an intense pump, I put my weights back on the weight stand. I grabbed my water bottle and chugged it down within seconds. My body was soaked in sweat, my arms felt like noodles, and I smelled of pure must. That was how I knew I had done the deed for the day. Grabbing my bag, I said goodbye to the men working out around me and made a beeline for the locker room. A shower was exactly what I needed to wash the smell of hard work away. Thirty minutes later, I stepped out of the locker room dressed and smelled of mountain fresh soap.

After waving goodbye to the gym attendant, I walked outside into the sunshine. The day was continuing to warm up with each passing second. Florida didn't stay in the 70s for too long during the fall.

After getting in my car, I drove twenty minutes south while music filled the cabin on the car.

I decided to get some fresh air. Where was the best place to get fresh air? At the beach. The salty wind always managed to relax me.

I parked in the overly crowded parking lot and killed the ignition. Even in the fall, the beaches crawled with beachgoers. There was never a time our beaches received any rest.

I walked along the sandy pathway that led to the open beach. The beach was clad with women in skimpy bikinis and men in swim trunks that were a size too small.

I walked over to a lounge chair and an umbrella. I sat once the umbrella was opened and provided shade from the sun. I kicked back and watched the beachgoers lounge on beach towels, sit in beach chairs, or play in the ocean. My heart sank into my chest when I saw a family building a sandcastle. The daughter tossed her head back in laughter as she grabbed another bucket of sand as her parents tried to perfect the castle at hand.

My heart was full of sorrow. I pulled my phone out. Today's visit to the beach had a purpose. I would relax by the water I missed so much while I planned my reunion with my family.

I searched the web for Kyla, and my heart sank into my chest. Thank goodness for the world's obsessive desire to use social media. I was grateful Kyla had gotten back onto social media, so she provided me easy access to her current life. She still looked as beautiful as ever in her profile picture. Her striking smile had my heart doing flips in my chest.

Kyla was now an accountant. They had a son after they had married, and his name was Ryder.

They looked like they were happy with their family picture posted as her profile image. That should've been me who stood beside her, and that should've been my son beside our daughter.

I smirked when I came across a post from last year. Kyla had commented her phone number in response to a comment she received. I now had her phone number.

When the prison guard asked me as I was released, "What are you planning to do with your life now that you have been given a second chance?" I was speechless.

I knew I wanted my family back, but that wasn't the answer he was looking for. So, I responded, "I'm going to channel the good that I learned and make a difference."

We pounded fists as I walked out the door of that hell hole I called home.

Kyla was mine, regardless of whether she had gone to marry the man she thought rescued her from the worst relationship she'd been in. It was time to plot out how to take my family back. Once and for all.

Chapter Three

Kyla

I clutched my purse tight in my grasp and placed it on my right shoulder. My car sounded after I hit the lock button. Walking up the cobblestone steps, I approached the massive door to the two-story building that housed my job. Gone were the days of serving steaming coffee cups and delicious pastries.

Walking inside the building, the scent of hazelnuts entered my nose as my heels clicked in the quiet building. My eyes perused the modern-day décor that accented the entire office.

"Good morning."

I waved my hand at the phone receptionist who sat in the lobby area as I walked by.

"Good morning."

Proceeding down the hallway, I continued to call out good mornings as I walked up the stairs to the second floor. The second floor houses several cubicles. Walking down the pathway, I made my way over to my cubicle as my coworkers chorused their good mornings.

Placing my purse in my drawer, I sat in my mesh computer chair and turned my computer on.

"Hello, Kyla."

Lauren, my coworker and friend, rolled over on her computer chair from her cubicle to my left.

Turning around in my chair, I smiled. Lauren was a gorgeous Hispanic woman with big, doe brown eyes and curly brown, shoulder-length hair. Her makeup was done in flawless strokes but was minimal.

"Hello, Lauren. How was your weekend?"

Lauren shrugged. "It was fine. I went on a date."

"How did it go?" I asked as I clocked myself in.

I was running a bit behind schedule this morning, but I still managed to clock in with seven minutes to spare.

"The date was going great until he declared

his hate for books."

Scrunching my face up, I shook my head. "That was the deal breaker for my bookworm friend."

Lauren and I had small talk since the first day I started with the company four and a half years ago. We went from acquaintances who had conversations while passing in the hallway to friends who hung out outside work. Learning that we had a common love for reading solidified our friendship.

"Oh yeah." Lauren scratched her ear with a pink manicured finger as she rolled her eyes. "I made sure to leave enough money for my portion of dinner and my tip before I excused myself to the restroom."

I smirked. Lauren was the perfect person to walk away from a date with no care in the world.

"At least you paid for your meal."

"It was the least I could do."

Lauren and I stood up. Together, we walked to the breakroom, where we prepared ourselves a hot drink.

"Did he try to reach out to you since you walked out on the date?"

I poured steaming water into a South Carolina cup I had purchased at the local flea market four months prior.

"Ten minutes after I walked out." Lauren poured herself a cup of coffee. "He took the hint once I didn't return his three missed calls."

"I'm sorry that the date didn't go so well."

I opened a tea bag and placed it into the cup. My love for hot chocolate was traded for tea while I was pregnant with Ryder. I still had hot chocolate when the kids wanted a sweet drink during the cold, or I went out for drinks at a coffee shop. Even after Amelia purchased exotic coffee and shipped it from Ethiopia, coffee was still on my despised list.

"It's okay. I'm glad I found out on the first date rather than farther down the line."

Lauren poured the creamer into her coffee.

"Are you getting back on the dating site?" I asked her as we proceeded back down the hallway towards our cubicles.

Lauren looked over at me with a smirk on her face. "I never left the dating site."

Lauren was a beautiful woman with a heart of gold. She would give you her last if you needed it. Unfortunately, she was thirty-four years old and had never been in a relationship that lasted longer than two years. Lauren was picky when it came to the men she allowed to be a part of her life. I couldn't blame her as she preferred to have no company than horrible company. Lauren had no children, but she had the desire to have two children when and if she ever found the perfect man for herself.

"Can I tell you something?" I asked.

We approached our cubicles, and I set my tea on my desk to steep.

"Of course."

Lauren took a sip of her coffee before she

placed it on her desk.

"There is no perfect man in this world. No man will ever check off all your desires. You just have to find that perfectly imperfect man, made especially for you."

Lauren smiled widely as she beamed. "The wise words from a twenty-seven-year-old."

"I haven't been in many relationships, but the relationships that I have been in have been long-lasting."

Lauren winked at me. "You must have done something right to get that rock on your finger."

I looked down at my ring as it glinted in the bright light of the office. For our five-year anniversary, Ryan upgraded my white gold one-carat diamond ring to a white gold two-carat diamond ring.

I replied, "I followed my own advice. Ryan is far from perfect, but he is perfect for me."

"Thank you for the advice."

Sitting down in my chair, I signed into the application we used for work. After taking time off from Meg's Coffee Shop years prior, I took the time to figure out what career path I wanted to take. After having several conversations with people in different careers, I came to realize that I would like to follow in Amelia's footsteps to become an accountant. After Amelia was able to obtain special permission at work, I shadowed her for several months, and I grew to love the career. Once I gave birth to Ryder, Amelia decided to retire and help babysit her grandchildren. Ryder and Bria loved the arrangement, as they were picked up by Grandma after daycare and school.

Removing the tea bag out of my cup, I threw the tea bag into the garbage. I took a sip of my tea as I prepared financial records.

Hours flew by as I was waist-deep in records. I had drunk two cups of tea when the alarm on my phone rang, signaling my lunch break was in ten minutes.

A knock sounded on my cubicle. Turning around, I looked at Lauren. "What's up?"

"I forgot my manners earlier. How was Ryder's birthday party?"

Grabbing my phone, I opened it and scrolled through the pictures I could take of the birthday party.

"Look at my beautiful girl." Lauren cooed as she looked at a picture of Bria with her hands under her chin as she smiled sweetly into the camera. "Look at my handsome guy." Lauren looked at a picture of Ryder petting a donkey. "I cannot believe he is four. I remember the first time I met him. He was the tiniest little thing."

"He was six months old," I pointed out.

Lauren smiled. "Do you remember the first time I held him? He spat up on my brand-new shirt."

Lauren and I laughed at the memory.

"Yes, that was horrible. I felt so bad that I offered to buy you another shirt."

Lauren shrugged. "I couldn't take your

money. I knew right away that he was going to be my buddy."

"Yeah, Ryder favors Auntie Lauren."

"I hate I was out of town on Saturday and missed his party. I have his gift at home. I can either bring it here to work or bring it to your house at the end of the week."

I playfully rolled my eyes. "I want you to bring it to my house."

"I don't want to come over uninvited."

I gave Lauren a pointed look. "You never need an invitation. You are family now."

My phone alarm went off again, alerting me that it was five minutes before lunch.

"Are you ready to go to lunch?"

Lauren shook her head. "I have an appointment tomorrow morning, so I am working through lunch today."

I frowned as I asked, "Do you need me to pick you up anything from Tony's?"

Tony's was a local sandwich shop that was in the center of town. It was a popular shop that many people frequented for lunch. Thank goodness for the hour lunch breaks we were given.

"No, I'm fine. I brought a salad for lunch today."

Lauren walked back over to her cubicle.

Confused, I stood and followed behind her.

"You hate salads." I pointed out the obvious as Lauren sat in her chair.

"I know." Lauren gave a pained expression.

"Why are you torturing yourself?"

"I have five pounds I want to lose."

She smoothed her hands over the navy-blue dress that hugged her figure.

"You don't need to lose a pound. You look amazing."

Lauren winked at me. "Coming from the beauty that looks like she never gave birth to two children."

I looked down at my white sleeveless blouse that was tucked into my knee-length black pencil skirt. "My baby weight came off from a clean diet and exercising five days a week. It took months for that stubborn weight to come off." I changed the conversation back to her. "I don't even see where you need to lose weight."

Lauren rolled her eyes as she smiled at me. "Two weeks of torture, and I'll be fine."

I patted Lauren on the shoulder. "If you say so. I'm going to have lunch. I'll see you later?" I asked her.

"Yes. Don't forget, we have our chat about our book next week."

Hearing the mention of a book excited me. "I brought it to work with me today. I'll read it during my lunch."

"Enjoy your lunch," Lauren responded as I walked back to my cubicle and clocked out.

Grabbing my purse, I walked downstairs. The sun's brightness temporarily blinded me as I opened the door and stepped outside. Shielding my eyes with my hands, I walked to my car, slid inside, and placed my purse on the passenger seat. When I abandoned my BMW, I was doing it to protect my family. I fell in love with the car I had bought and traded it for a newer model. It had been nothing shy of great for me and my family. Starting the car, I drove out of the parking lot and towards the sandwich shop. It was only five minutes from the office, so I was at the sandwich shop in no time.

After parking my car, I walked up the sidewalk to the sandwich shop. There were several tables set up outside to dine under a shaded awning. As soon as I opened the door and stepped inside, the smell of fresh bread wrapped its comforting arm around me. I joined the long line of hungry patrons, ready to bite into a delicious sandwich. As I stood in line, I looked around the spacious restaurant. Several tables and booths were set up inside, and half were already occupied.

Taking my book out of my purse, I read as I waited in line. After five minutes of waiting, I heard, "Next in line, please."

Closing my book, I walked up to the order counter. "Can I have a tuna sandwich on rye and a cup of water, please?"

"Of course." The cashier entered my order into the system. After paying for my order, I walked over to the pickup counter.

Within minutes, my order was brought out and handed to me. Grabbing my cup of water and sandwich, I turned around and walked when I bumped into someone hard. I took a few unexpected steps back as I almost lost my balance. My bag fell to the ground, and my cup of water spilled all over the floor. The water splashed up, wetting my exposed lower leg and black open-toed wedged heels.

Gasping, my mouth dropped open. I brought my hands up to cover my mouth as I looked up at the person I had bumped into. The man's slender body was dressed in a dark blue suit, and his feet were adorned with black, shiny dress shoes. He was an attractive man with arctic blue eyes and brown hair cut into a stylish fade. I could tell he had an important job by how he was dressed.

"I'm so sorry," we said in unison.

Grabbing a handful of napkins out of the napkin dispenser, I turned around. Squatting down, I wiped up the water.

"Allow me, please."

Looking up, our eyes locked for a few seconds. Doing as the man requested, I pushed the napkins toward him as he wiped up the remainder of the spill. I grabbed my bag with my sandwich, grateful the sandwich had been wrapped in plastic. Once the spill was cleaned up, the man walked over to the trash can and threw the napkins away. Turning back around, he approached me.

"I'm sorry about that. I wasn't paying attention." I tucked a piece of hair behind my ear with my free hand.

"No, don't apologize. You are fine. Accidents

happen." The man stuffed his hands into his pants pocket.

Nodding, I smiled. At least he was understanding and not upset.

"Can I buy you another sandwich?"

Shaking my head, I replied, "That would be unnecessary. My sandwich is wrapped in plastic."

The man nodded. "Okay, good. I wouldn't want you to eat off the ground."

Looking around the restaurant, what was on my mind spewed from my mouth. "Why would you want to purchase me a sandwich? I was the one not paying attention."

"I am a gentleman, that's why." The man took his right hand out of his pants pocket and held his hand out to me. "I'm sorry for my bad manners. Let me formally introduce myself. My name is Michael."

I placed my hand in his. "I'm Kyla."

He shook my hand with care. "It's nice to meet you."

"It's nice to meet you as well."

He flashed an award-winning smile at me. "I've never seen you in here before. Do you come here often?" he asked.

"Yes, I do. I usually come with my friend, but she had to work through lunch today."

"Working through your lunch is never fun." He looked down as he pulled his phone out of his pocket. He looked at the screen for a few seconds. "I'm sorry to cut our conversation short, but I must get back to work. My boss is texting me. I hope you enjoy the rest of your day."

"You as well." I waved as Michael waved at me before he headed towards the exit.

Walking over to the closest empty table, I sat. I pulled out my book and placed it on the table. Opening my bag, I pulled my tuna sandwich out. Unwrapping the plastic, I took a bite as I dived into my book. I had just started the book, but I knew it would be great. I'd bet my delectable tuna sandwich on that fact.

Chapter Four

Kyla

"Would you recommend this book to a friend?" Lauren read the question from the book club application installed on our phones.

We were having our book discussion at my house this month. For every book discussion we had, we would take turns hosting at each other's houses. Today, we discussed the book in my living room while snacking on a vegetable platter.

"I would if I had other book friends." I grabbed

a carrot stick and took a bite of it.

"Oh yes. This book is worthy of being read by plenty." Lauren tucked a piece of hair behind her ear before she grabbed a celery stick.

Our book discussion snack this month was very healthy as Lauren was coming to the end of her diet. Next month, it would go back to being not as healthy.

"If you could change anything about the book, what would you change?" I crossed my left leg over my right leg.

"I would only change one minor detail." Lauren brought her thumb and index finger in close range of each other, leaving the smallest space possible that was barely visible.

"What would that be?"

"I would kill the villain."

Gasping, I placed my hand over my mouth. The shock was etched into my face. "You call that a small detail?"

Lauren nodded as she took a bite of her celery.

"That's a big detail. The villain going to jail wasn't enough?"

Lauren shook her head. "He still gets to live."

"Killing him off would've been too easy, though," I pointed out.

Lauren raised an eyebrow. "I guess you wouldn't change anything about the book?"

"Nothing at all. It was perfect."

Just as Lauren was about to respond, footsteps sounded on the stairs. There was no visual of the person coming down the stairs, so it could only be one or both of my children.

"Auntie Lauren," my children chorused once they had stepped off the stairs. Their eyes landed on Lauren, and they widened with excitement.

"Hello, sweeties."

Ryder jumped into Lauren's lap first as he wrapped his arms around her neck. He hugged her with all his might as she ran her fingers through his mass of curls.

"My turn, Ryder."

Bria stood in front of Lauren, waiting for Ryder to finish up his hug with Lauren.

Once their hug ended, Ryder stepped down and walked over to his tablet on the end table. He grabbed the tablet and sat on the carpet. Bria sat on the couch next to Lauren and laid her head on her shoulder as she gave her a tight hug around the waist.

"How are my sweeties doing?"

"Good." Ryder gave a thumbs-up before his attention was captured by his tablet.

"I'm good. How are you doing?" Bria looked up at Lauren.

"I'm great now that I'm seeing you." Lauren pinched her cheek, causing a smile to appear.

"What are you two doing?" Bria looked over at me.

"Having a book discussion about this book." I held the book up for Bria to look at.

Bria's eyes widened. "I love books. Can I read it?"

Lauren smiled. "I knew your mom would get you into reading."

"You can't read this book yet." I took another bite of my carrot.

"Why not?" She presented sad eyes.

"This book is for adults only." Lauren rubbed her back in a soothing manner as Bria continued to pout. "How about this? You and I will go on a trip to the library next time I come over?"

"Yay," Bria cheered as she clapped her hands.

I winked at Lauren, giving her a silent 'thank you' that she deserved. I couldn't wait for Lauren to meet the man of her dreams. I couldn't wait for her to have children of her own to love and spoil to the ends of the earth. For now, my children would benefit from that endless love she had in store.

The doorbell rang, echoing throughout the house.

"Who could that be?" Bria asked me as I pushed myself up off the couch.

"It's mom and dad," Ryan called from upstairs.

"Grandma and grandpa."

Bria gasped as she gave Lauren one more hug before she ran for the door.

Bria unlocked the door and pulled it open after I verified it was my in-laws through the peephole.

"Grandma! Grandpa!"

Bria threw herself at them as she wrapped

her arms around their legs.

"Hello, cutie pie."

Amelia smiled at Bria as she ran her fingers through Bria's hair.

Amelia was still beautiful as ever, with her big green eyes. Her blonde hair started to gray at the roots, and it was pulled back in a low ponytail.

"Hello, love bug."

James leaned down and placed a kiss on Bria's head.

Even though Bria was not Amelia's and James's biological granddaughter, they still treated her as if she were their own. They were all Bria had known her grandparents to be.

"Are you ready?" Amelia asked Bria as they walked into the house. James closed the door behind them. I gave both of them a kiss on the cheek.

"Ready for what?" Bria asked.

Bria walked beside Amelia as she held her hand tight.

Amelia and James had walked into the living room. They said their greetings to Lauren as they sat.

"You and Ryder are coming over to spend the night with us."

"Yay," Bria cheered.

"Pack pajamas and clothes for tomorrow."

Bria took off and ran up the stairs at a rapid speed.

"Slow down, please," I said.

Ryder looked up and noticed his

grandparents. He placed the tablet on the ground as he pushed himself up off the ground.

He walked over to James. "Grandpa."

James scooped Ryder up into his arms and sat him in his lap.

"Aren't you going to say hi to Grandma?" Amelia asked Ryder.

Ryder provided a toothy grin. "Hi, Grandma."

Ryder loved both of his grandparents, but he was Grandpa's boy. Whenever Grandpa was around, he was attached to his side.

"Are we interrupting something?" James asked.

James bounced Ryder in his lap, looking between Lauren and me.

"We were just finishing up our book discussion," Lauren said.

Lauren leaned forward and grabbed a carrot stick.

"Doesn't that sound like fun?" Amelia smiled as she placed her hands in her lap.

Lauren agreed. "It is always fun."

"Thank you for babysitting them tonight. We appreciate it."

Ryan's company was hosting a party tonight. Two years ago, Ryan was promoted from Chief Technology Officer to Chief Information Technology. Due to his holding a superior position, we were expected to attend all the business parties thrown throughout the year.

"No thank you needed. We just want you two to have a wonderful night."

I walked over to the stairs, and I picked up Ryder's bag. Footsteps sounded on the stairs.

Ryan came down the stairs with a smile. He kissed my forehead tenderly before he walked over to his parents.

"Hey, Momma. Hey, Dad."

Ryan gave his mom a kiss on the cheek and his dad a hug.

"Hello, Son."

James patted Ryan on his back.

Bria ran down the stairs as Ryan called out, "Slow down on the stairs, Bria."

"Sorry, Dad."

Bria appeared with her backpack already on her back.

It was music to my ears to hear Bria call Ryan, Dad. She had been doing it for years now. When Brad had gone to jail, Bria had asked about him often. I had told her that he was going away for a long time for hurting mommy. Dad, Grandma, and Grandpa had been said once, and it had stuck ever since.

"At least you get a 'sorry.' She didn't even care to respond to me."

"That's because Bria loves Dad," Ryan cooed in the sweetest voice.

Bria nodded as she stuck both thumbs up in the air. She turned her attention to her grandparents. "When are we leaving?" Bria asked as she walked over to the front door.

"I guess that is our cue to leave."

James stood up, situated Ryder on his hip,

and grabbed Ryder's bag out of my hand.

"I want you two to enjoy your date tonight."

Amelia stood up and grabbed me into a hug before she kissed me on the cheek.

"We will."

Ryan walked them to the door. Once the door had closed behind him, Lauren looked at me. "I love how much you get along with your in-laws."

"They are a joy to be around. Besides Aunt Lily, they are the closest thing I'll ever have as parents."

Lauren gave me a genuine smile before clapping her hands together. "Are you ready?"

"Ready as I will ever be."

Lauren stood up, took my hand, and she led me up the stairs.

For a full forty-five minutes, I was Lauren's human Barbie doll. After I slipped into my dress for the night, Lauren applied makeup to my face.

As Lauren applied the finishing touches to my face, she called out, "You are finished."

She placed the mascara wand back into its container and sat it on the end table.

I stood and walked into the bathroom. My eyes widened as I looked at myself dolled up. I wore a red, off-the-shoulder floor-length ballgown with a side slit that showed off my slender leg. My hair was pulled back into a high, formal bun. My eyelashes were lined with black mascara with a stroke of red eye shadow. Silver earrings hung from my ears, and silver heels were on my feet.

"Wow."

I gasped in awe. I could hardly recognize myself.

"You are going to turn heads tonight."

Lauren winked at me as she clasped her hands together.

"I might draw too much attention."

I turned to the side, and my eyes zeroed in on how the fabric hugged all my curves in the right places.

"That will be fine. You will already be the most beautiful woman at the party."

"That is the most honest statement I've heard in a very long time."

Lauren and I turned around. Ryan stood a few feet from the bathroom door. His eyes danced up and down the length of my body.

"You can stop drooling now," Lauren said.

Lauren tucked a piece of hair behind her ear as I laughed at her comment.

Ryan shot Lauren a look. "How can I stop drooling when you have my wife looking so magnificent?"

Lauren smiled, proud of her hard work. "You are right. Drool on."

I playfully rolled my eyes at Lauren as I placed my hand on the vanity. "It's time to get dressed, Ryan."

Ryan shook his head as he took a step forward. "I'd rather undress you."

Ryan seductively tugged on his bottom lip with his teeth. "Keep you here, locked up in this room all night. Since the kids are with my parents,

I don't want to share you with anyone."

Lauren took a step forward, so she stood in between us. "You are not going to mess up my masterpiece."

Giving Lauren a 'you saved me' look, I walked past her and Ryan and into the bedroom. Ryan would have received his wish if Lauren was not my saving grace at that moment. My dress would have been pooled at my feet by now. Ryan reached out, and his hand brushed against my butt as I passed by him. "Get dressed, Ryan."

Walking out of our bedroom took all the strength and willpower I had in my bones.

Lauren followed me downstairs. "I hope you two enjoy your night."

"We will. I'll let you know all about it tomorrow."

I walked her to the door, where she kissed me on both cheeks.

After walking Lauren to her vehicle, I walked back into my house.

Arms snaked around my waist as Ryan pressed his pelvis against my butt. "You dressed quick."

I placed my hands on his arms as I allowed my body to relax.

"I did. How do I look?"

I turned around, my eyes taking in Ryan. He wore a tuxedo, a red tie, and black dress shoes. I leaned forward, grateful for the extra inches the heels gave me. Only mere inches from Ryan's face, I whispered, "You look phenomenal."

Ryan gave me a sweet kiss on my lips. "Thank you, Mrs. Walker."

"You're welcome, Mr. Walker."

I walked over to the end table and grabbed my phone. After I looked at the time, I said, "It's time for us to head out."

"Do we have to go?" Ryan walked over to where I stood. "I'd rather enjoy this alone time."

"I would love to enjoy a night alone, but I doubt your boss would be fine with us not showing up."

Ryan took my hands in his as I looked into his eyes. "Can I tell you something?"

"You can tell me anything."

"I have the desire to kiss your beautiful, soft lips all night."

I smiled, enjoying the compliment. I leaned forward, only an inch separating our faces. "That will have to wait. Let's go."

After a few more minutes of convincing Ryan to walk out of the house, he locked up the house, and we walked to his silver Audi. Sliding into the car, my body sunk into the leather seats. Right before Ryan closed the door behind me, he leaned in and kissed me.

Thirty minutes later, we pulled into the hotel parking lot. The party was held at one of the extravagant, five-star hotels in the area.

Ryan placed the car in park in front of the hotel entrance. He stepped out of the car, walked over to my side, and opened the door for me.

"Mrs. Walker." Ryan held his hand out to me.

Placing my hand in his, I stepped out of the car. "Thank you."

Ryan handed the keys to the valet, received a slip of paper, and led me inside the hotel. The check-in area was decorated with lavish white furniture, and the walls were adorned with popular paintings. A sign had been placed in the middle of the area, stating the office party was in Conference Room C.

As we walked further down the hall, the soft classical music that played grew louder. We walked in the door of the conference room, and the entire room dripped with elegance, adorned in black and white décor. The room was filled with men who wore expensive suits and women who wore evening gowns. The dance floor was located several feet from the band. Waiters and waitresses walked around the room as they carried trays of hors d'oeuvres and flutes of champagne.

"Hello, Ryan. Hello, Kyla. I'm glad to see you two have arrived."

We turned around and looked at Timothy, the CEO and owner of the energy company. Standing beside the tall, balding man who wore a gray suit was his petite wife. Elizabeth had on a gray ballgown. Her head was full of beautiful gray hair curled into ringlets.

We exchanged hello, and you look amazing as we hugged them.

A waitress stopped in front of us as she carried flutes of champagne. We all grabbed a flute, and I took a sip of the bubbly drink.

"It's imperative that I inform you of how this quarter went."

Timothy took a sip of his champagne as his attention focused on Ryan.

As Timothy and Ryan separated from us to discuss their work finances, Elizabeth and I made small talk.

"When will you bring that accounting expertise to our company?"

Elizabeth smoothed her flawless nightgown with her hands, her gigantic ring glistening in the light.

I chuckled as I smiled. "I learned my abilities from the best."

"Hands-on training is the best learning agent out there."

I nodded as I took another sip of my champagne. "I couldn't agree with you more."

"How are the children doing?"

A waiter walked over to us, who carried a tray of tomato burrata bites. I grabbed a napkin before I grabbed two bites.

"They are doing well. I can say I have my hands full with them, but I wouldn't change being a mom for anything in this world."

I took a bite of a tomato, and my mouth burst with flavor.

Elizabeth took a sip of her champagne. "I remember when my two were little. They used to keep me young and in shape with all the running I had to do to keep up with them."

"You are still in shape."

Before Elizabeth responded, a beautiful Hispanic woman approached us. She wore a red ballgown with her ample breasts on full display tonight. Her black hair was straightened, flowing down her back. Her brown eyes traveled my body before she smiled at me. In her hand, she held a silver clutch.

"Hello, Veronica. You look lovely," Elizabeth said, wrapping her arms around Veronica.

"You look amazing as ever."

Veronica gave Elizabeth a kiss on the cheek.

"Veronica, have you met Kyla before?"

Veronica shook her head. "We've never met."

I plopped the last tomato into my mouth, wiping my hand on the napkin.

"Kyla, this is Veronica. She is the Chief Operations Officer. Veronica, this is Ryan's wife, Kyla."

Veronica and I shook hands. "It's nice to meet you."

Veronica's eyes flickered behind me for a brief second before she looked back at me. "It's nice to meet you as well, Kyla."

An arm wrapped around my waist as a sweet kiss was placed on my cheek.

"Hello, Ryan," Veronica waved her hand adorned with long, red and silver fingernails.

"Hello, Veronica."

Veronica's eyes lingered on Ryan for a few more seconds before she turned her attention to Timothy.

I turned my head to look at Ryan. He smiled at me as his eyes glistened. "Can I have this dance?"

"You know I could never turn down a dance."

"Seriously?" Ryan raised an eyebrow. "Even if it's classical music, you are dancing too and not your usual pop?"

Ryan took a few sips of his champagne.

"I will dance my little heart out to any beat that plays."

We drank the rest of our champagne and set the flutes on a table. Ryan took my hand and led me toward the dance floor.

Smiles were given from Ryan's other coworkers who were on the dance floor. Most of them I was familiar with from knowing them over the years.

Ryan placed one hand on my lower back as he clasped my hand in his. My body pressed against his, and we danced to the band's music. The music flowed from all the instruments, and the melody blended beautifully.

"Have I told you how beautiful you look tonight?" Ryan spoke into my ear as we continued moving to the melody.

"You've only told me a thousand times tonight," I pointed out as I laughed. "But I don't mind hearing it a thousand times more."

Ryan kissed my temple. "Well, you look beautiful tonight."

"Thank you."

Receiving compliments from my husband

lifted my spirits.

"The most beautiful woman in this room."

I placed my head on his shoulder as my eyes fluttered closed. I inhaled his scent. The memories we had spent over the years flooded me with nostalgia.

"The most beautiful woman in this world."

"You know the exact words to make me feel special."

"That's because you are special. You have accomplished something that nobody else in this world could accomplish."

I lifted my head off his shoulder, and I looked into his eyes. "What's that?"

"Provided me with the perfect family I can call my own."

The warm heat of love spread through my body. If Ryan's arms were not wrapped around me tight, I would've crumpled to the floor in a heap. Even after five years of marriage, Ryan still made butterflies flutter in my stomach. He made me feel wanted on the days that I couldn't bring myself to look in the mirror. I couldn't ask for more when it came to my family. "You are perfectly imperfect, and I am glad you chose me to be your soulmate."

Ryan smiled. "I am the lucky one."

We continued to dance as the music flowed through the room.

"I almost forgot to give you something."

Ryan stopped dancing, and he released his hold on me.

I reached to twist my wedding ring on my finger. The anticipation of what Ryan would give me ate at me.

He reached into his tuxedo pocket and pulled out a single red rose. He held the rose out to me.

I took the rose and brought it to my nose. I inhaled the floral scent. "You never cease to amaze me."

Ryan had been giving me red roses since we went on our first date. To this day, he still surprised me with roses.

"You deserve it. You have done nothing but make my world complete."

"I can say the same for you." I stared deep into his eyes.

Ryan had taken me, a shattered woman, and placed me back together. I couldn't have asked for more from him.

The band changed to a song I had heard on the radio recently. We continued to dance to the melody.

"Five years down…" Ryan began.

"Forever to go," I finished off.

Chapter Five

Brad

In three miles, get off on the next exit.

I exhaled as I put my blinker on. After making sure the lane beside me was clear, I transitioned into the exit lane.

I hadn't traveled to South Carolina in over five years. The last time I made the trip, I was on the journey to repair my relationship with Kyla so my family could be whole again. I never wanted our daughter to grow up in a broken home. I had the luxury of being with a family that stayed together, and I wanted the same for Bria.

This time around, my main focus was to tear Kyla's marriage apart. As long as she was in great terms with Ryan, she wouldn't give me a second chance. My goal was to tear them apart so she would come back to me. I would drop down to my knees and beg for her forgiveness. I'd do anything for Kyla to come back to me. This time, I would marry her. I wouldn't make that mistake twice. I would never let her go again. I exited the highway and pulled into the parking lot of the first restaurant I located. Once I parked, I stepped out of my car and stretched. I had driven for hours, and my body was stiff and hungry. The temperature was significantly cooler there than it was in Florida. I'd need to wear a jacket for sure. I walked inside the restaurant, where the hostess seated me, and I ordered a coffee.

It was ten in the morning, and I drove the trip straight through. The only time I had stopped was halfway through the trip to fill the gas tank up and get another coffee. I had been living off coffee for sixteen hours. Exhaustion started to take control over me, and soon, no amount of coffee could keep me awake. I was sure I had bags under my eyes.

Once I filled my stomach with food, I would find myself a hotel, and I would go to sleep.

My waiter sat my coffee in front of me. I grabbed the menu and ordered the first item I found. After being told that my food would be out soon, she walked away.

I took a sip of my coffee. Hurting the roof of my mouth with the hot liquid, I winced in pain.

I left Florida on bad terms with Joe. Who would've known after all these years, one conversation would halt all communication and tear our friendship apart. After I received my check from the government and cashed it, I invited him out for a couple of drinks at the bar.

The pungent haze of smoke swirled in the bar, the chatter of various conversations blending. Music played from the speakers in the corners of the room.

I was at one of the local bars on the main strip, enjoying a glass of whiskey. I hadn't been drinking much since I was released. I drank more when I was under a lot of stress, alcohol being a way to escape stress. I was on my second drink for the night and didn't plan to stop anytime soon.

I pulled my phone out of my pocket and checked the time. Joe should've been there ten minutes ago. I typed out a text when heavy hands dropped on my shoulders.

I turned to see Joe sitting next to me. He signaled for the bartender to come over, and he ordered a beer.

I raised an eyebrow as I looked at him. "You're late."

"That I am."

He received his beer and took a few sips.

"Couldn't pull yourself away from your wife?" I asked as I smirked.

Joe chuckled. "I wish that was the cause of my being late. I had to attend a meeting at work, and it ran late."

Joe still worked for the state of Florida. He had been employed with them for almost six years. They must've been treating him well for him to stay around for this long.

"Meetings are overrated."

Joe took a few more sips before he exhaled his breath. "Tell me about it. We have those meetings twice a month."

I scoffed as I shook my head at him. "I couldn't imagine sitting through meetings that often."

"One day, I won't have to." Joe took a sip of his beer. "That is if I ever work for myself." The smell of perfume permeated my nose. I turned my head and watched two ladies walk by. They waved and winked at us as they tossed their award-winning smile in our direction. "Tempting, isn't it?" Joe asked me.

I finished off my glass of whiskey. "No. I'm all good."

Joe scrunched his eyes as he gave me a crazy look. "What in the hell is wrong with you." A long beat passed before he continued. "Unless something happened behind the prison walls that you didn't tell me about."

Joe and I laughed as I playfully punched his arm. "Ha ha. It sure as hell didn't happen in this lifetime. It won't happen in another lifetime."

"What's really going on with you, Brad?" He

shook his head. "Something isn't adding up for me."

I stared at my empty glass. "What do you mean?"

He pointed in the direction of the ladies. "You could've gotten one of those ladies' phone numbers and romanced her. You're the second-best looking man in this bar."

I gave Joe a knowing look. "Who's the best-looking man?"

"Me, in the flesh," he stated with confidence.

"Well, as long as you believe it. That's all that matters."

Joe shoved me on the arm as we laughed. There was never a dull moment when we went out and had a guy's night. We could say things that couldn't be said in front of Moriah with no repercussions or dirty looks thrown our way.

"So, what warrants this special get-together?"

"Why can't we just get together without it being a special occasion?" I asked as I tried to get the bartender's attention.

"That generally doesn't happen anymore. Our young and careless days are long gone."

The bartender brought over another whiskey for me and a beer for Joe. I took a sip of my whiskey, and my body relaxed.

"You're right. I wouldn't say it's a special occasion, but I do need to speak with you."

"It must be something private if you want to talk to me without Moriah around."

I nodded as I took another sip. "You could say that."

Joe clasped his hands on the table as he looked over at me. "Speak what's on your mind. I'm all ears."

"I want Kyla. So, I'm moving to South Carolina to get her back."

Joe nearly choked on his beer as he placed the bottle on the table. He coughed a few times as I hit him on the back. Once Joe was able to speak, he let me have it. "What in the hell do you mean you want Kyla back?"

I gave him a pointed look. "She's my world. I want her back."

"What is wrong with you?"

I scoffed as I rolled my eyes. I took a gulp of my whiskey because I needed it. The whiskey burned my chest. "Nothing is wrong with me. I just want my girlfriend back. I want my family back."

"Kyla has moved on with her life." He exhaled as he stared down at his beer bottle. "You should do the same and save yourself the heartbreak."

I closed my eyes and slowly rubbed my temples in a circular motion as I took deep, calm breaths. The alcohol had mellowed me out, but Joe was pushing my buttons.

"I'm not giving up on my family. I refuse to give up on my family."

Silence lingered between us as Joe processed the words that came out of my mouth.

"Brad, I love you with all of my heart, but I can't support this."

I gave Joe a knowing look. "You're not supporting anything. I have enough money to cover me for months."

Joe shook his head, giving off a pained expression as he grabbed his wallet out of his back pocket. "That's not what I'm talking about."

I watched as he downed the rest of his beer and tossed a twenty on the bar counter. "I can't be involved in this."

My mouth dropped open. "Are you walking out on me?"

Joe looked at me for a beat too long before he responded. "Yes, I am. If you're going to go this route, I can't sit around and watch you self-destruct. I love you, but I have to say no and walk away."

I laughed at his ridiculous words. "Fine. Walk away. I don't need you." I turned the glass back and drained the rest of my drink. I winced as the liquor continued to burn my throat and chest.

"I hope you get the psychological help you need." Joe gave me a piece sign before he walked out.

I couldn't believe Joe's reaction. Where was my best friend's support? He knew I didn't have anyone else but him. My parents had disowned me. All of our friends had walked away from this relationship. Why was he being a bitch and following suit? Joe wasn't a real friend. He never had been, and he never would be.

A mountain of waffles, sausage, and eggs was placed before me, pulling me away from my memories. Muttering a thank you, I dove right into my food. I devoured my food within ten minutes and downed two cups of coffee.

Once I paid for my food, I returned to my car and drove down the road to the hotel that would be my home for a while.

Walking into the three-star hotel, I approached the check-in desk.

A woman smiled as she leaned one arm on the desk and twirled a strand of hair around her finger. Her name tag attached to her shirt read Kelsey.

"How may I help you?"

"I need a room."

She typed into her computer as she looked at me. "Are you alone, or will you have someone else with you?"

She raised an eyebrow, a twinkle in her eyes.

"Just me."

"Perfect. How long are you going to stay?"

"I'm not sure yet." I shrugged. "Let's start with a month."

After she entered the information into the system, she applied a discount for the extended stay before she swiped my credit card. Once I signed the paperwork, she handed me a key card with the #308 listed.

"Let me know if you need anything."

"Thank you," I responded.

I wasn't 100% sure if she was flirting with me.

She grabbed a business card and scribbled on the back of it before she handed it over. She winked at me and stated, "Anything."

I smiled before I walked back to my car to get my belongings. With a carry-on bag over my shoulder and two suitcases packed to capacity, I strolled through the lobby and headed for the elevators.

Once the elevator reached my floor, I headed to my room, located off to the right.

To my surprise, I entered a room with a king-size bed in the middle. A big flat screen braced onto the wall across from the bed. In the corner was a table for two, a mini fridge, a microwave, and a coffee maker. This was the perfect set-up for my stakeout.

I finished unpacking, and I set all my stuff up. The last thing I did was pull out two photos of us as a family that I had framed and placed them on the table. One photo of us was taken when she was two years old. We had taken her to the zoo for a Saturday trip and took a picture in front of the bird's zone. The other picture was an image I grabbed from Kyla's social media. It was a recent picture of her and Bria that had been taken at a playground. I couldn't believe that I had a ten-year-old daughter. Where had the time gone? Oh yeah, half of her life, I sat behind bars. I couldn't wait until I could take updated pictures with her.

I had plotted extensively since I received my check. I couldn't wait for my carefully formulated plan to unfold.

I was sure we'd be together again as a family by Christmas. I couldn't wait to celebrate and enjoy all the holidays together as a family.

Walking over to the window, I looked outside. My room overlooked the parking lot and had a partial view of the main road. I chose this hotel for a specific reason.

The internet not only told me the lives that people chose to live. It refreshed my memories of where people lived. As expected, Kyla left the house, where she almost died. I didn't blame her. I'm sure she left a pound of flesh on the living room floor. What I didn't expect was that the house where I trailed Kyla several times was where they were living now. I'm surprised they hadn't moved to another state after everything that happened. The hotel was only fifteen minutes from where they lived. I was grateful they didn't live in a gated community like his parents. I could spy on them with ease and move as I pleased in the neighborhood.

I stripped off my clothes and slipped into bed. I'd take a shower once I woke up.

My eyes closed, and I dreamt of reuniting with my family.

Chapter Six

Kyla

"You look exhausted."

Lauren arched an eyebrow as she brought her cup of coffee to her lips. She blew on the coffee a few times before she took a sip.

"I am. I didn't get much rest this weekend."

I moved the tea bag in my mug, attempting to hurry the steeping process as much as possible.

Lauren wiggled her eyebrows at me as she smiled. She did a quick scan of the breakroom before she spoke what was on her mind.

"Too many sexual escapades this weekend?" she whispered.

I shook my head as I playfully rolled my eyes.

"No. We took the kids on a weekend trip to the woods."

She raised an eyebrow.

"You? Camping?"

I nodded as I removed the tea bag from my mug and threw it in the trash.

"Is that so hard to believe?" I asked.

She took a sip of her coffee.

"Yes, there are bugs outside. Not to mention, it's chilly."

Taking a sip of my tea, I winced as the hot liquid burned my lip.

"I didn't see any frightening bugs, and we slept under large, warm blankets."

Lauren added creamer to her coffee.

"I never saw you as the outdoorsy type."

I nodded. "I'm not, trust me. I did it for my kids."

We walked out of the breakroom and headed towards our desks.

"You would do anything for those babies, won't you?" Lauren asked. I sat my tea on my desk before I walked over to Lauren's desk. "Anything and everything." Lauren sat in her chair.

I leaned my hip against the cubicle wall. "Has a lucky man grabbed your attention yet?"

Lauren shook her head. "No. I am starting to

think I'm meant to be single for the rest of my life."

I rubbed Lauren's shoulder. "Don't think that way. Someone is out there for you."

"Do you honestly think that?"

"Of course," I answered with confidence. "It's just going to take several trips around the world to find that special someone designed for you."

Lauren swatted her hand at me as she smirked. "I'm not that picky."

"Yes, you are, but someone will love that characteristic about you and blow your mind." I scratched at an itch on my finger. "What did you do this weekend?"

"Layla and I went on a mini shopping spree at the mall."

Layla was Lauren's younger sister by two years.

I gave Lauren a knowing look. "Are you sure it was a mini shopping spree?"

Lauren shrugged. "I consider four outfits and two pairs of shoes, mini."

"In my definition handbook, that is a mega shopping spree," I pointed out. "A mini spree is more like an outfit."

"I'll share a pair of pumps with you. I bought a red pair." Lauren wiggled her eyebrows.

"You know I don't wear pumps. Wedges are my besties."

"Wearing a pair of red pumps in the bedroom might bring a bit of spice into the marriage." Lauren winked at me as she blew me a kiss.

"You are so inappropriate," I commented as I

attempted to hold back a laugh.

"That's why you love me."

"Oh yes. Are you going to lunch with me today?"

Lauren shook her head. "Not today."

I folded my arms across my chest as I frowned. "The more you cancel our lunch plans, the less I feel like you love me."

"I've only canceled on you twice," Lauren said. "You know I love you. I just have some difficult accounts I have to figure out by the end of the day today, so I'll be working through lunch."

"Okay. Would you like me to bring you a sandwich back?"

"No, thank you. It's a chicken and rice kind of day." Lauren pointed to her lunchbox that sat on top of her desk.

After telling Lauren I'd chat with her later, I worked on financial records. After four hours, my lunch break arrived just in time. I was about ready to pull my hair out, and I needed an hour's break.

Grabbing my purse, I told Lauren that I'd see her later. I walked outside the office and exhaled a deep breath as the sun beamed down on me, cutting through the coolness of the air. Once inside my car, I turned my music up and traveled across town to Tony's.

After I parked my car, I walked into the busy sandwich shop. The aroma of fresh bread always greeted me with open arms. My stomach growled on cue as the line moved up.

"Kyla?" came an unfamiliar voice from behind

me.

I turned around and I looked at a man that looked oddly familiar to me.

I raised an eyebrow as I studied the attractive man before me. "Do I know you?"

"We met a few weeks ago."

Silence settled among us as I attempted to assemble the mystery's missing pieces. I moved up in line before I turned to look at the man again.

"I'm drawing a blank. I'm sorry."

"We literally ran into each other a few weeks ago."

The man pointed towards the pickup counter. "Right over there."

I snapped my fingers as I remembered. He was the attractive man in the nice suit.

"Oh yeah. My cup of water flew everywhere."

He stuck his hand into his dress pants pockets. "I'm still sorry about that. It was my fault."

"You have no reason to apologize. It was my fault."

He shook his head. "Truly, it was my fault."

"Why do you keep trying to take the blame for my mistake?" I folded my arms across my chest.

"I was blinded by your beauty."

I raised my eyebrows, willing myself not to allow my jaw to drop from his compliment. The compliment was far from expected. "How did you remember my name?" I decided to ignore the compliment completely. I did not need any compliments coming from anyone besides my husband.

He smiled. "It's hard to forget the woman that ruffled my feathers right before a hearing."

"You are a lawyer?" I asked as we continued to move up in line.

He nodded. "I've been a lawyer for three years."

Today, he wore a black suit, and his feet were adorned by gray, shiny dress shoes. The success in his career was written all over him.

"That's a great profession."

"Indeed, it is."

He pulled his hand out of his pocket and pointed to the available cashier.

I walked up to the counter and ordered my usual. As the price spewed out of the cashier's mouth, I dug in my purse for my wallet.

"I'll take care of it."

He appeared next to me with a black card in his hand. Before I could object, the cashier took the card and paid for my meal.

"You didn't have to pay for my order."

The cashier handed the card back to him. "I know I didn't, but I wanted to."

"You're paying for my meal, but I don't even remember your name?"

"Michael."

The cashier handed me the receipt. "Thank you, Michael," I said before I walked over to the pickup counter.

After Michael ordered, he walked over and stood next to me.

"I can't believe you didn't remember my

name." Michael brought his hand up to his chest, producing a faux shock face.

I tucked a stray piece of hair behind my ear. I laughed. "I'm terrible for that."

"I thought I left an everlasting impact on you."

Looking over at him, I asked, "Why would you think that?"

He shrugged. "I guess the impact would've been left if your cup of water had drenched me entirely."

"That would've left the impact you were expecting," I agreed as I smiled.

"Shucks. Next time, allow the water to rain all over me, please."

I laughed at Michael's comment, and he joined in with me. "Will do."

Once my order number was called, I grabbed my sandwich and water and turned around before I found an empty table.

"It was nice talking to you. I hope you enjoy the rest of your day."

Walking over to an empty table in the corner of the restaurant, I sat with my food. Pulling my latest book out of my purse, I opened it and dived into the universe I had grown to love from page one. The book that Lauren and I had chosen for our next read was a page-turner.

"Can I join?"

I stopped mid-chew as I tugged my eyes away from my book. Looking up, Michael stood on the other side of the table with a cup and bag in hand. Looking around the restaurant, I spotted a few tables unoccupied. I finished chewing the food in my mouth before I responded. "Umm..."

Before I could get a response out of my mouth, he sat and opened his bag up. He pulled out his sandwich before he took a sip of his drink. "What do you do for a living?"

I grabbed a napkin to wipe my hands and mouth before I closed my book. So much for attempting to catch up on reading on my lunch break. "I am an accountant."

Michael took a bite of his sandwich. "You must love working with numbers."

"You could say that. Some days, I don't know how I come home in my right mind. My brain is mush most days after work."

"Do you enjoy your work?" he asked as he took out a bag of chips.

I took a sip of my water. "Yes, I do."

"That's how you deal with your brain being mush. If you didn't love your work, you'd just find another career that you do love."

I couldn't help but agree with him. "I take it that you love being a lawyer?"

He opened his bag of chips. "Yes, I do. I love keeping the bad guys behind bars."

"Well, that's great to hear."

"That I keep the bad guys away? Or that I love my career?"

"Both."

I took another bite of my sandwich, almost positive my entire lunch break would be spent chatting with this mysterious man.

"I'm passionate about keeping the bad guys out of society."

I looked across the table at him. He ran his fingers through his hair before looking out the window beside us. He took another sip of his drink, his adam's apple bobbing in his throat as he swallowed. He grabbed his sandwich and took a hearty bite before he sat the sandwich down. Why was this man giving me so much attention? Of all the others in this restaurant eating by themselves, he decided to give me his attention.

His eyes met mine as he rubbed the faint stubble on his chin. "Are you okay?"

I cleared my throat, pulling my eyes away from him. "Yes, I'm fine."

"If I didn't know any better, I'd think you like what you see."

"Really?" I raised my eyebrows.

His statement caught me off guard.

He winked. "Yes, because I like what I see."

I laughed at his response as a middle-aged woman and a young girl walked by us carrying their food and drinks. "You are something else."

He smiled as he took another bite of his sandwich. He nudged his head towards me. "Is that author any good?"

I looked at the book that sat in front of me. "Do you enjoy reading?"

He raised an eyebrow. "The real question is, who doesn't enjoy reading."

I gasped. "Simple-minded people, that's who. It's good to know there are other bookworms besides my friend and I."

"As long as I have a bookstore and a gym, I'm a happy man."

I took a bit of my sandwich. "There's no way books and a pair of dumbbells make you happy."

"Believe it, baby, because it's true."

His voice came out smoothly.

I tapped my finger on my lip as I studied him. I couldn't figure it out, but something was different. "I take it that you are single?"

"Very much so. I'm hoping you are as well."

"Why is that?"

"I'd be interested in taking you out."

Michael pulled his phone out of his suit pocket and looked at it for a few seconds. Satisfied with what he saw, he placed his phone back in his pocket.

"That's sweet of you, but I'm in a relationship."

He smirked. "I'll compete with a boyfriend. I'm not afraid of competition."

"Try, husband." I pushed my left hand forward, and his eyes zeroed in on the diamond ring several inches away from his face.

"Darn it." He muttered a few curse words under his breath. "Well, it was worth the try."

Silence settled between us as I continued to eat.

"You never answered my question."

I looked up at him. "What question?"

"Is the author any good?"

Excitement coursed through me. "The author

is fantastic. She grabbed my attention from the first page."

"Can I have a look at the book?" he asked as he wiped his hand on a napkin.

"Sure." I handed the book over, and he took it. He read the back cover before he handed it back over. "I think I am going to check her out."

"You won't be disappointed. I can promise you that."

We continued talking for another twenty minutes about books we had previously read and what books we'd recommend to each other.

I finished eating my sandwich and wiped up any crumbs I had dropped on the table.

"It was nice to talk with you today."

"It was nice chatting with you as well."

He grabbed an unused napkin and pulled out a ballpoint pen from his suit jacket pocket. He scribbled on the napkin before he handed it over to me.

"Use this, please."

Looking at the napkin, I saw his first name and his phone number. I shook my head.

"I can't take this."

I placed the napkin on the table.

"Why not?"

I showed my ring once again. "I'm married."

He shrugged. "We had a great conversation today. I'd love to continue talking."

Should I take the number? Should I leave it? He was a nice man, but a nice man who had already shown his romantic interest in me.

"If I decide to use this number, it'll be as friends."

He held his hands up in surrender. "I'm fine with being your friend."

"Okay."

He picked the napkin up and opened my book. He slipped the napkin inside and closed the book tight. "I have to get back to work now, but I hope to hear from you soon."

"I hope you have a great day."

He grabbed my hand and he placed his lips to the back of my hand.

"You have a great day as well."

With that parting response, he grabbed his trash and threw it away before leaving the restaurant.

I grabbed my book and I opened it. I grabbed the napkin with his phone number and tossed it into the trash. I refused to disrespect Ryan. He was everything I needed, and a man showing me interest wouldn't change anything. He tried, but to no avail.

Chapter Seven

Kyla

"Dining for one?"

I stood at the hostess counter of the mom-and-pop breakfast diner I often frequented. The smell of bacon wafted into my nose as I looked around at the décor collected over the owner's years of traveling.

"No, I will be meeting someone."

The hostess grabbed two menus. "Follow me to your booth."

Walking through the small restaurant, she led me to an empty booth. "Enjoy your breakfast."

Shooting a smile in her direction, I sat in the booth and opened my menu. Even though I ordered the same meal whenever I went there, I enjoyed browsing the menu.

"Is that my beautiful best friend?"

Turning in my seat, I looked at Sabrina. She wore a pink blouse that complimented her strawberry-blonde hair and dark blue jeans.

"In the flesh."

Standing up, I grabbed Sabrina into a hug, and squeezed her tight.

"How are you doing?" I asked as we sat in the booth.

Sabrina opened her menu. "I'm well. How are you?"

"Delighted. Wonderful. I honestly feel like I am floating on a white, fluffy cloud."

Sabrina looked up from the menu. She raised her eyebrow as a smile appeared. "Please, do tell."

Before I could provide the news that was threatening to spill out of my mouth, our waiter walked over. I ordered hot tea, and Sabrina ordered coffee.

"Please, spill the details."

I clasp my hands together. "I don't know. I mean, it's not really news, but I'm so happy."

Sabrina's mouth dropped open. "Are you pregnant?"

I gasped as I shook my head. "Heck no. We

aren't trying to get pregnant. I think Ryder's the last child we are going to have."

Sabrina gave me a pointed look. "Are you sure about that?" I nodded as I closed my menu. "I'm positive. I'm taking my birth control, and there are no plans for another mini, running around."

Our waiter came and delivered our drinks before he took our food orders. I ordered French toast with a side of fruit, and Sabrina ordered eggs with a side of turkey sausage.

"Darn." Sabrina stuck her bottom lip out. She added creamer to her coffee before she took a sip. "I thought I was going to have another niece or nephew."

I sipped my steaming hot tea before I placed it on the table. "Not in this lifetime."

A waitress bustled past us, carrying four plates of food.

"Wait."

Sabrina cradled the cup in her hands.

"Wait, what?"

Sabrina took a sip of her coffee before she looked at me. I clasp my hands together.

"You want another niece or nephew from me. I only have one niece. When are you going to give us another baby to spoil?"

Sabrina shook her head. "You have two nieces."

"I have Julia, but I'm talking about you."

Julia was Amy's six-year-old daughter that she had with her husband, Alexander.

Sabrina sat her cup down and exhaled. "I

don't have the time to have another child." She paused as she looked past me. "I don't even have time for Emily and Justin."

Taking a sip of my tea, I placed my hand on Sabrina's. "I think you make all the time that you can for your family and your dreams." I gave her hand a squeeze. "We do miss you a ton when you aren't in town. I know it's been two years since you have been going back and forth to California, but I cannot get used to not seeing you."

Sabrina smiled as she exhaled. "I know. It's difficult for me to not see my family and friends." She took another sip of her coffee before she continued. "I only have one life. I can only live once."

"Becoming a talk show host has always been your dream."

Sabrina nodded as she placed her coffee on the table. "Yes, it has been. I still can't believe I am living this dream."

"But it's okay to make some sacrifices." I couldn't help but give Sabrina some encouragement.

"Sacrifice is my middle name."

I grabbed a packet of sugar, ripped it open, and added some of it to my tea. "How is your job going?"

"Great. I love my cohost. We get along so well. I wish my best friend would take that initiative, as we discussed years prior."

I laughed as I stirred the sugar into my tea. "That was your initiative." I had blossomed out of my shell, but I wasn't talk show worthy.

Sabrina tucked a strand of hair behind her ear. "Since I cannot have my best friend as my co-host, do you think I can ever get you to come on the show as a guest?"

"Do you honestly think anyone who watches your show would be interested in a married accountant with two children?"

I sipped my tea, the sugar adding just the right amount of sweetness.

Sabrina tapped her finger on her lip several times as she thought deeply. "Probably not, but it's partially my show. I can bring whomever I want on there."

I playfully rolled my eyes. "You have to do what is best for your show and its rating."

"So, a happily married accountant with two children won't have that effect?" Sabrina asked as she smirked.

"Not in the slightest," I said.

Our waiter brought over our food. With no skip in the beat of our conversation, I cut into my French toast.

"I could always suggest a segment on best friends?" Sabrina cut into her eggs.

I ate a piece of French toast, closed my eyes, and hummed my appreciation of the delicious, sweet toast that made my tastebuds happy. "I would be of no interest to your audience. They'd only have interest in me if I had an unusual talent."

"You are an amazing dancer," Sabrina

pointed out before she ate some of her eggs.

I stabbed my fork into a strawberry. "My dancing is not glorious. There are a million other people in this world who can dance better than me."

Sabrina huffed, giving me a pointed look. "If you don't want to be on my show, just say it."

"When I develop an unusual talent, you will be the first person I will call."

Sabrina smirked. "Sounds like a deal."

I placed my fork on my plate. "I forgot to tell you what happened the other day."

"What happened?"

"I ran into a man a few weeks ago when I was at Tony's."

Sabrina wiggled her eyebrows as she smirked. "Was he cute?" She took a sip of her coffee.

"He was attractive, but that's beside the point."

"What do you mean you ran into him?"

Sabrina tucked a strand of hair behind her ear.

"I grabbed my food, and I ran into him. I didn't see him."

"Hm."

She ate a piece of turkey sausage.

"He came into Tony's the other day, paid for my meal, and ate with me."

Sabrina raised an eyebrow. "That's strange."

"I thought the same thing."

"Did you get any stalker-like vibes from him?"

she asked.

I could tell she was concerned. Her playful tone had vanished, and she was serious.

I shook my head. "Not at all. He's a nice man. He likes books just as much as me."

Sabrina gave me a pointed look. "Or he pretended to like books to get closer to you." She winked. "Mommy of two still has it."

I laughed before I took a sip of tea. "Do you think it's weird?"

Sabrina shook her head. "Not at all. He probably did it just to be friendly."

Sabrina and I ate breakfast as we caught up on what had occurred in our lives in the past two months.

After we had paid for our breakfast and left a tip, we walked out of the restaurant and into the sunshine.

"We have to set up a play date for Emily and Bria."

Sabrina pulled her phone out of her purse.

"Our schedule is clear next weekend."

We walked to our vehicles parked next to each other in the parking lot.

"At our house or yours?" Sabrina asked.

"Doesn't matter to me."

Sabrina thought for a second. "I'll host this time. I have a new recipe I want you two to try."

"Sounds like a plan."

Once Sabrina and I decided on a date and time, she entered the information into her phone and sent it to me by text.

After hugging and exchanging parting words, I got into my car and started it up.

I waved to Sabrina as she drove out of the restaurant parking lot. I sent a quick response to Lauren's text that came through during breakfast before I put my car in reverse.

As soon as I pulled onto the main road, a call echoed through the speakers. When the caller's name appeared, I smiled. I swiped my finger across the screen and brought the phone up to my ear. "Hello, Amy."

"Hello, how are you doing?" Amy's voice was sweet and full of energy.

"I'm doing good. How are you?"

I passed by two cyclists in tights, moving their legs in perfect sync.

"I'm great. I haven't heard from you in what seems like forever, and I had to make a call to check on you."

I smirked as I tapped my fingers on the steering wheel. "It's only been two weeks," I pointed out.

"Two weeks too long."

I laughed, the truth evident in that statement. "How are Julia and Alex?"

"They are great. Alex took Julia on an ice cream date, so I am home relaxing. How is the family?"

"An ice cream date sounds wonderful. They're good. They are at home entertaining themselves." Amy hummed. "Where are you?"

I put my blinker on and made sure the left

lane was clear before I got over. "I just had breakfast with Sabrina."

Amy groaned. "That sounds amazing. Going out with your friends, without your children and husband."

"It was amazing. Sometimes, we just need that time away." Amy and I continued talking. We caught up on what had happened since we last talked and reminisced about when we were in foster care.

Amy and I were alike in several ways. We had similar upbringings where we relied heavily on each other for support growing up. That support was interrupted when I conceived Bria, and Brad stopped all communication. That support started again as if no interruption had occurred when Amy had located me after learning I had left Brad once and for all.

After Amy and I exchanged our parting words, I pulled into my driveway.

As my hand touched the door handle, a text sounded.

I opened the text, and my heart sunk into my chest.

Unknown: What would your husband think of this?

I clicked the attached picture, and my stomach turned sour. It was a picture that showed Michael's lips on my hand while at lunch.

I looked around as a sense of fear riddled me. Who could've sent this?

It couldn't be Brad. Brad was locked up, four

hours away. There was no way they'd let him out for what he did to me. Was it a friend of his? Or could it have been an idiot that saw me in the headlines of every news article five years ago that wanted to antagonize me?

Several people sent me weird and frightening messages the first year after everything happened. When I provided the information to Detective Simpson and Detective Black, they determined it was nothing to worry about. Maybe someone wanted to play a cruel joke on me again.

I blocked the sender and erased the message. I refused to allow fear to rule my life again.

"I'm home," I called out as I swung open the door. It was best to keep the text message to myself. I didn't want Ryan to worry about something that would turn out to be nothing.

"Mommy," was chorused by my children as they bombarded me at the front door with hugs and kisses.

Ryan walked around the corner with his arms open wide.

"Did you all miss me?" I asked as Ryan peppered my cheeks and forehead with kisses.

"Yes," Ryder called out.

"Of course," Bria responded.

"We missed you a ton." Ryan gave me a tight squeeze, my favorite cologne surrounding me. "Now, come in here and relax. It's time to watch the movie Ryder picked out."

"What's it about?" I walked into the living room.

"Animals. What else?" Ryder asked with a toothy grin.

We laughed as Ryan went into the kitchen to make popcorn and grab candy.

These were the days I dreamed of.

Chapter Eight

Kyla

"You're going to turn heads tonight."

I placed my hand in Ryan's before stepping out of his car's passenger side.

Ryan wore a dark blue dress shirt that hugged his muscular torso and snug gray dress pants on his hips.

I smooth my hands across my dark blue, tight-fitting, floor-length nightgown. I tucked my hair behind my ear, the silver earrings that Ryan had bought me on display. We were matching, and we looked amazing.

"The only head I'm worried about turning is yours."

Ryan cupped my face before he kissed my forehead, the kiss feather-soft.

"Well, you did that five years ago without even trying."

"You know exactly what to say and do to make me feel loved," I admitted. Ryan was a hopeless romantic.

Ryan handed me a red rose, and I smiled. "You deserve to feel loved every day."

I inhaled the rose, the scent inviting. Ryan occasionally showered me with roses, and it still surprised me when he pulled one out.

Hand in hand, we walked into the upscale seafood restaurant two towns over from our home. The lighting in the restaurant was low and intimate. Classical music flowed through the room, and nautical decor was placed throughout the room.

We approached the hostess stand, where a young woman dressed in all black stood.

"Follow me to your table," she said, once she found our reservations.

We followed the hostess through the restaurant. We approached a table where menus sat on each side, accompanied by wine glasses.

"Your waiter will be with you soon."

"Thank you," Ryan responded as he pulled my chair out for me. I sat, and Ryan sat beside me.

We agreed to dine at Sailer's Fine Dining to celebrate Sabrina and Justin's ten-year anniversary. This was our first time coming to this restaurant, and I was excited to try their cuisine.

I opened my menu and was surprised by the extensive list of entrees. They offered anything you could desire from the sea in three or four variations.

"The double date of the century has started."

We turned around, and Sabrina and Justin walked behind the hostess. Sabrina wore a maroon knee-length evening gown with gold accessories, and Justin wore a maroon dress shirt with black dress pants.

After the hostess stated our waiter would be with us soon, she walked away.

Ryan and I stood, and we greeted Sabrina and Justin.

I wrapped my arms around Sabrina. Her apple shampoo greeted me. "You look stunning."

"You look beautiful," she replied.

We squeezed each other's hands as Justin and Ryan's hug ended.

I hugged Justin, while Ryan hugged Sabrina.

"Happy ten-year anniversary," I said as we sat at our table.

Even though we frequented each other's house often and hung out more than what would be considered usual, we still greeted each other like we hadn't seen each other in years.

Justin beamed as he looked over at Sabrina.

"Thank you."

Sabrina gave his hand a squeeze before she opened her menu.

"How does it feel to be with someone for a decade?" Ryan asked as he opened his menu.

"I don't know how to explain it." Sabrina smiled. "I just know it feels good. It feels like a breath of fresh air."

"We're half a century." I looked at Ryan. "We only have another half to go."

"That other half will fly by like the snap of a finger," Justin said.

"He's right." Sabrina agreed. "I swear it was two days ago that I said, 'I do' to him."

Our waiter walked over. He introduced himself as Samuel.

"What can I get you all to drink tonight?" he asked.

Ryan spoke. "We'll take a bottle of wine."

"Make sure it's sweet, please." Sabrina winked at me.

Samuel looked around the table. "Are we celebrating a special occasion?"

"Yes, we are." Justin wrapped his arm around Sabrina's shoulder and pulled her close.

Sabrina smiled. "We're celebrating our ten-year anniversary."

"Happy anniversary," Samuel smiled. "I'll be right back with your complimentary wine."

I looked at my menu as a hand landed on my knee. I looked at Ryan, and he winked at me as he squeezed my knee.

"Are you two flirting over there?"

We looked up at Sabrina, and she winked.

"Maybe," I responded.

"Yes," Ryan said at the same time.

We looked at each other and laughed.

Sabrina motioned to Ryan. "Well, at least Ryan told the truth." Sabrina looked at me. "What were you doing?"

Justin chimed in. "Kyla told the half truth."

I nodded as I pointed at Justin. "Exactly."

"It is the perfect time to flirt, though," Justin pointed out.

"Why do you say that?" Sabrina asked.

"We are out on a double date. The children are with Ryan's parents."

Amelia and James were honored when we asked if they could babysit. They didn't see watching the children as babysitting. They saw it as hanging out.

Ryan nodded as he caught on to what Justin referred to. "We'll have alone time with no interruptions."

Ryan emphasized the word alone. Sabrina scrunched up her face. "I'm not following."

"We'll go home to an empty house," Justin emphasized the word empty.

Sabrina gasped. "Oh." She looked at Justin and smiled. "Oh."

Samuel came to the table, and he filled our glasses halfway with wine. "Have you decided what you'd like to order?"

Ryan shook his head. "No, we need more

time."

Samuel set the bottle on the table. "Okay, I'll be back in a few minutes."

Once Samuel walked away, we grabbed our glasses and sipped the wine.

"It's delicious," I commented as I took another sip.

"As long as Kyla approves, we all approve," Justin joked.

"Hey, I can't help my picky taste for wine."

Sabrina agreed as she sat her glass on the table. "Trust me, we've tried to break her of her love for the sweet stuff."

Sabrina took me to a wine-tasting event last year that was hosted in town. During the forty-five-minute tour through the vineyard, we were given a brief explanation of each bunch of grapes that we came across. Once the tour ended, we sampled wines created with the grapes we saw. I tasted every wine they offered, and none of the dry wines seemed to appease my taste pallet.

Ryan nodded. "Nothing, and I mean nothing can break her from the sweet stuff."

I cleared my throat. "Enough about my picky wine habits. Let's decide what we want before Samuel comes back."

We looked at our menu and discussed the options we considered amongst ourselves.

Once Samuel came back to take our orders, I order the lobster with a vegetable medley. Ryan and Justin ordered the Mahi Mahi over a bed of wild rice. Sabrina ordered snow crab with mashed potatoes.

"We didn't have time to shop for a gift this year." I grabbed Ryan's hand and gave it a squeeze.

"It's okay." Sabrina looked over at Justin and smiled. "We don't need a gift. We have the gift of love."

Justin kissed Sabrina on the cheek before he agreed. "That is all we need."

"Well, our gift was to pay for our meal but if you insist on not receiving the gift..." Ryan shrugged.

Sabrina gasped as she placed her hand over her heart. "You're going to pay? Are you sure?" She looked back and forth between us.

"Of course we're going to pay. We wouldn't take no as an answer," I admitted.

They smiled as they chorused a "Thank you."

We continued to talk as we waited for our food.

Once Samuel placed our food on the table, we placed our napkins on our lap before we dived into the exquisite cuisine.

The lobster was juicy and delightful, and the vegetable medley had the perfect crunch and bite.

"We had a wonderful time tonight" Sabrina said as we walked out of the restaurant.

Our stomachs were full of delicious food, and we were ready to call it a night.

"We did as well." I tucked a strand of hair behind my ear.

We approached our vehicles that were parked next to each other.

"We have to get together soon. Maybe I can cook on the grill?" Ryan suggested.

Justin nodded. "Sounds like a great idea."

After our parting words were exchanged, we got into our separate cars, and we drove home. Ryan's hand was on my thigh on the drive home as we listened to music.

We walked into the house and left our shoes at the door. We made a beeline for our bedroom.

I walked over to the dresser and took my jewelry off. I looked over my shoulder. Ryan looked at me, his eyes heavy with love. Ryan closed the distance between us just as I placed my earrings on the dresser. He cradled my face as his lips crashed onto mine. Desire pooled in between my legs as my knees went weak with need. It's only been two days since we last touched, and my body yearned with anticipation.

Our bodies became entwined. Our tongues collided and tangled together as articles of clothing were removed and thrown to the floor in a heap.

I maneuvered onto the silky bed spread, our mouths never ceasing to part as Ryan climbed on top of me. Our bodies melded together as our kiss intensified, a need for intimacy deep within. "I need you inside me," I gasped in between kisses.

The only thing separating us from skin-to-skin contact was my bra, panties, and his boxers. Those items of clothing needed to go, now.

"Your need is my command."

Ryan unclasped my bra from the front and threw it to the floor. He lifted my butt so he could remove my panties. He tugged his boxers off, and his erection sprung to life, our eye contact never breaking.

Ryan settled in between my legs. We stared deep into each other's eyes as Ryan reached to tuck a piece of hair behind my ear. His touch was like fire, a hot spark made contact with my ear.

"Ryan."

"Yes?" His voice was raspy.

"Now," I demanded.

Ryan smirked, enjoying the sexual torture he was putting me through. "What is the magic word?" he whispered. His voice dripped with seduction.

Before I could mutter the word 'please', his initial thrust took my breath away. An involuntary moan escaped my lips as I closed my eyes in complete satisfaction and gratitude. This was exactly what my body needed. Thank goodness for birth control pills.

Ryan's lips captured mine. A climax built in my core. He smiled as he licked my lips and my body traveled on a journey of pleasure.

"Ryan." I panted in between kisses.

"Yes?" Ryan looked down at me as he caressed my face. His thrusts never ceased or changed rhythm.

Love sparkled in his eyes. What beautiful eyes he had. "I'm going to..." I said before ecstasy took over and stars blurred my vision. I lost every ounce of control of my body.

Ryan held onto me as my body rocked with gratification. Once Ryan found his release, his body stilled. He laid his body on top of mine, and I rubbed his back in a soothing manner.

"Damn." Ryan exhaled a deep breath.

Our hearts beat in synchrony, my smile never wavering.

"I couldn't agree with you more."

Chapter Nine

Kyla

"The party can finally start." Sabrina stood at the door as she posed. She wore blue pants, a white blouse, and blue heels.

"You look cute," I complimented.

"Thank you." We hugged before she walked into the house. "You, on the other hand, look like you've lounged in the house all day."

I looked down at my gray sweatpants and black T-shirt. "I have lounged all day."

"Let me guess." Sabrina tapped her finger on her lip. "You just finished your book."

I gasped as I brought my hand to my chest. "How did you guess?"

She smirked. "I know everything."

We walked to the living room where Sabrina sat. "What's taking Emily and Justin so long?"

Sabrina shrugged. "They're grabbing some things Emily wanted to play with tonight."

I gave Sabrina a pointed look. "You didn't want to help?"

She scrunched her face up as she shook her head. "I just got my nails done." She held her hands up, the light blue noticeable on her fingers. "I don't want to mess them up."

Ryan walked down the stairs, followed by Bria. Ryan greeted Sabrina with a warm smile.

"Where's Emily?" Bria squealed.

Sabrina folded her arms across her chest and pouted. "What about Auntie Sabrina?"

Bria smiled as she walked over and gave her a hug.

The front door opened and closed.

Emily and Bria's chatter filled the living room as Ryan walked to the front door to help with the items they brought over.

"What time is Lauren coming over?" Sabrina asked as she pulled her phone out and checked the time.

"She should be here in about twenty minutes."

"Well, you better get out of the sweats and

put on something stylish."

Sabrina smiled.

I winked. "I'm going to look hot tonight."

"I can't wait to see." Sabrina directed her attention to the men. "Are you two sure you can handle three energized children for the night?" Sabrina asked as she smirked.

"As long as we have a beer, we can conquer anything."

Julian and Ryan bumped fists.

I placed my hands on my hips. "You need more than just beer. They're hungry."

Ryan smiled. "We're prepared. Pizza and wings are en route."

Sabrina clapped her hands. "It looks like you two have everything under control."

"That we do," Justin agreed.

"Well, I'm going to get ready. If Lauren arrives, let her in, please?"

"Yes, ma'am," Julian called out.

Sabrina and I went upstairs. I wore white jeans that made my legs look long, a peach-colored blouse that went with my skin tone, and white sandals.

Sabrina stroked on a thin layer of makeup before we walked downstairs to find Lauren sitting on the couch. She wore a black jumpsuit and black-heeled boots.

"Hottie at seven o'clock." I whistled.

Lauren smiled as she pushed herself off the couch. She strutted a few feet towards the front door before she stopped and struck a pose.

"Definitely not the old woman of the group." Sabrina winked.

Last week, Sabrina, Lauren, and I hung out at Lauren's luxury apartment. While we ate grilled ham and cheese sandwiches and tomato soup, we talked about our tolerance of alcohol. After we figured out Lauren had the highest tolerance, Sabrina and Lauren almost fainted once they learned I'd never been to a club. Fast forward to this week, I'm being dragged to a nightclub for my first-time experience.

"Old woman?" Julian asked, perplexed.

"Don't even ask," Ryan answered.

"Why not? I'm curious." Julian looked at each of us as we laughed.

"It's an inside joke, babe."

"Oh. Code for the husbands don't need to know?"

"Exactly," Sabrina sang.

I grabbed my handbag off the coffee table. "Let's go, ladies. Who's driving?" I asked. "The Uber that we ordered," Sabrina responded.

I stopped and turned around. "Uber?"

"Yes." Sabrina nodded. "After the night we have planned, we won't be able to drive."

"I agreed to a night out, but I didn't agree to drink."

Sabrina and Lauren exchanged a look.

"Live a little bit? For once?" Lauren asked me as she placed her hand on my shoulder.

"Yeah. Live a little. You'll enjoy it," Ryan interjected.

"Ok, fine. We'll see you later."

We walked out of the house and headed for the Uber that was parked behind Lauren's car. We filed into the backseat and danced to the music our driver played through the speakers as she drove us to our destination.

Twenty minutes later, we pulled into the parking lot. As early as we had arrived, there seemed to be quite a few people there already.

"Are you ready for the time of your life?" Sabrina asked as we stepped out of the Uber.

"Is it really going to be the time of my life?" I asked.

Lauren tossed her hair over her shoulder as we approached the bouncers. "No, but it'll be an experience of a lifetime that you'll never forget."

Once the bouncer checked our IDs and ogled our bodies for a second too long, we walked into the venue. The high-paced music vibrated the walls as we walked down a hallway that led to an open room. Colorful strobe lights bounced around the room, highlighting the many bodies on the crowded dance floor. Others surrounded high tables spread out around the room, and a small crowd was at the bar.

"What do you think so far?" Sabrina asked as she slipped her phone into her clutch. She had just texted Julian to let him know we had arrived.

"It's everything I've seen in the movies."

They laughed.

Lauren clapped her hands together. "Well. Let's go get drinks and see if you feel the same afterward."

We walked to the other side of the room, where we waited in line for drinks.

"What can I get you, beautiful ladies?" the bartender asked.

Lauren leaned against the counter. "I'll have a pomegranate martini."

"I'll have the same," Sabrina called out.

"I'll have a Sprite."

"No, she won't," Lauren interjected.

"She'll have what we're having," Sabrina ordered for me.

The bartender looked at me.

"Live a little," Lauren said in a sing-song tone.

I shrugged my shoulders. "What the hell? I'll take one as well."

"Yay," Lauren and Sabrina cheered. "You got it."

He swiped my card and gave me the slip to sign. He made our drinks as we checked out the scene.

"It'll be a great night," Lauren observed.

"What gives you that idea?" I asked.

"Most of the guys here are with ladies. There's a big chance we won't get hit on tonight."

"That would be great. I don't want to fight a herd of men off tonight," Sabrina said.

Sabrina turned around with her drink in her hand.

Lauren and I grabbed our drinks and walked to the dance floor. Tonight, we didn't plan on leaving the dance floor.

"The music is amazing," Sabrina commented.

"Yes, it is." I swayed my hips as I took a sip of my drink.

Lauren whistled. "It looks like the dancer is ready to dance the night away."

I smiled as I took a sip of my drink. The pomegranate came alive on my taste buds, and I took another sip. "I'm ready to dance the night away."

Hit after hit played through the speakers as we sipped on our drinks. By the end of the fourth song, we had finished our drink.

We made a beeline back to the bar for another drink, and Sabrina bought the next round.

"How do you feel?" Lauren asked me as I sipped my second drink.

My body relaxed, and I gave a thumbs up. "I feel great."

"Are you having fun?" Sabrina asked as she placed her hand on my shoulder.

I smiled. "Yes, I am."

Sabrina and Lauren looked at each other and smiled. "She's tipsy."

I nodded as the beats that played caused my feet to move across the floor with no effort. Tonight, I would be carefree. I would enjoy my night with my friends as I had one too many drinks. I deserved it. I never let loose ever, and Ryan gave me permission to put my mother hat aside and have fun. I had fun I never experienced when I was younger.

I felt light as a feather on my feet as I danced with my friends. The strobe lights moved around as I danced. My body formed a thin layer of sweat as I warmed up. Everything around me slowed down as I moved onto my next drink. Then, everything went black.

Chapter Ten

Kyla

My head pounded as I stirred in my sleep. Why did it feel like someone hit me in the head with a bat one too many times?

A knock sounded on the door. I groaned as I tried to cover my head with my pillow. The sunlight seeped in, and I wasn't welcoming it with open arms. I wanted the sun to go away for twelve hours and come back when my head didn't feel close to an explosion.

The door opened.

"Kyla."

It was Ryan's voice.

I groaned again as I turned over in bed. Maybe he'd get the hint that I didn't want to get up. I wanted to continue to sleep.

He touched my shoulder.

"Kyla."

He wasn't going to let me sleep. I might as well address him.

"Yes?" My voice was raspy, my throat dry as cotton. What had happened to me?

"You need this."

I opened one eye, and Ryan held a bottle of water and a bottle of pills.

I groaned as I pushed myself to sit up. I opened my eyes and winced. The sunlight that came from outside hurt my head. "What happened to me?" I asked as Ryan dropped two pills in my hand and handed me the water bottle.

Ryan smiled. "You have a hangover."

I washed the pills down with half the bottle of water before I handed the bottle back to him.

"A hangover?"

He nodded.

"Have you ever had a hangover?" He asked me.

I shook my head as I raked my fingers through my hair. I looked down, and I was in my night clothes.

"I don't remember too much from last night," I admitted.

He laughed as he sat on the edge of the bed and looked at me. "You really let loose, didn't you?" he asked.

I chuckled as I rubbed my eyes. "I guess so."

I looked around the room. Ryan's side of the bed was made.

"What time is it?" I asked.

"It's almost noon."

I gasped. "How did I sleep this long? Why did you let me sleep this long?"

I pushed the blankets off me, and I stood. I stood too fast, and my head spun.

Ryan jumped up and caught me before I face-planted.

"Kyla, relax. What are you doing?" Ryan sat me down on the bed. "You needed the rest. You had a long night last night."

"When did I get in last night?"

Ryan shrugged. "Around two in the morning."

I exhaled. No wonder Ryan allowed me to sleep. I didn't get in until late.

"I'm sorry."

Ryan raised his eyebrow. "Why are you apologizing? If you are apologizing for having a great night and enjoying yourself, you can save your breath. You deserved a night with your friends, and that is what you received."

I smiled as I squeezed Ryan's arm. "I love you so much."

Ryan leaned forward and kissed my head. "I love you too. Now, take it easy. The children and I have leftover pizza downstairs that we will heat up for lunch if you'd like to join us."

I nodded. "I'll be down once I freshen up."

Ryan kissed me on the cheek before he walked out of the room.

I stood slowly and walked to the bathroom. My eyes widened when I saw how disheveled my hair was. I must've had the night of my life. I couldn't wait to talk to Sabrina and Lauren about it. Once I handled my hygiene, I grabbed my phone off the charger. I had four messages and two missed calls waiting for me.

I had one missed call from Lauren and Sabrina.

Lauren: Good morning sleepyhead.

Two hours later, she texted again.

Lauren: I can't believe you are still asleep. Text me or call me when you wake up.

Sabrina: We had a blast last night. I hope you remember when you wake up. Call me when you can. We have a ton to discuss.

I opened the last message, and my heart dropped into the pit of my stomach.

Unknown: I know what you did last night.

I clicked on the two attached pictures. One picture was of me as I leaned my head against a tall, blonde man. I squinted to see if I could make out who the man was, but his face was obscured. From my outfit and the background, I could tell this picture was from last night. What had I done? Who was I with? Who took this picture? Why didn't I remember the end of my night?

I clicked on the second picture. I looked up at

the man, and I smiled at him as he smiled at me. The man's face was in view. It was Michael. The man I met at Tony's. What was he doing at the nightclub? Why was he there?

I looked around the room as my heart pounded in my chest. This text came in three hours ago. For some reason, this message didn't seem like a random idiot who wanted a rise out of me. This text message, with these images, had intent. This was something Brad would send.

Brad? Why did I keep thinking about him? He was in jail. He received life. He wouldn't have the capability to send these messages.

Who else would send these messages? Who else would continuously send me messages? The messages I had received years back were nothing like this. It would be a harmless message that meant nothing. These messages meant something. It had to be Brad.

Me: When did you get out?

Within seconds, another message came through.

Unknown: Two months ago.

I exhaled. Defeat settled around me as my headache intensified. I didn't understand how he could get out. If he was released, how was I not informed of this before it happened? I wasn't even included in the decision to let him out. I was the one who endured pain and suffering, both physical and psychological. How did his sentence of life turn into five years? How was someone who wasn't even affected by this incident allowed to determine that he could be free and in society again? They had no idea what he was capable of. It made no sense to me, and I doubted it ever would.

Seconds later, another message appeared. I rolled my eyes as I sensed the cockiness that oozed from the text.

Unknown: Missed me?

Me: How did you get my phone number?

I thought I had been careful over the years with handing my information out. In all honesty, I had slacked off on how strict I had been. I was sure Brad was in jail, and he wouldn't see outside prison bars for twenty-plus years. Boy, I had been wrong.

Unknown: Enough small talk. Meet me right now, or I will send these pictures to your husband.

Ryan. I didn't want to stress Ryan with this situation. I didn't even know what this situation was. Or how to explain it. I had to handle it on my own.

Reluctantly, I typed out the message I never imagined I'd send.

Me: I'll meet you, but it must be in public.

Unknown: Perfect.

He attached a maps link. I clicked it, and the location was ten minutes away.

Unknown: I'm waiting.

I closed my phone and tossed it beside me. I put my head in my hands and cursed under my breath. This was real. This wasn't a joke or a game.

Brad was released without my knowledge. He was back in society, and I couldn't do anything about it. What was up with the picture he had taken? Did he go right back to his stalker ways the second he stepped foot out of prison?

I put on a pair of black sweatpants and a blue sweater. I had to get this done so Brad could go away once and for all.

Hopefully.

I walked downstairs, and a chorus of Mommy's up echoed.

I squatted and hugged Bria and Ryder an extra second longer. A bit tighter than usual.

"How are my sweeties doing?" I asked.

"We're good." Ryder gave a thumbs up.

"Do you want to watch a movie?" Bria clasped her hands together. "It's my pick today."

I looked at Ryan, and he smiled. He took a sip from his water bottle.

"Mommy has to go run a quick errand. Once I get back, we can watch the movie."

Ryder stuck his bottom lip out. "I want to watch the movie now."

Ryan raised an eyebrow. "Where are you going?"

I scrambled my mind for an excuse as I stood. "I have to go pick up some things from the store."

Ryan looked at me for a beat too long. Was that excuse feasible? Did we have everything we needed in the house, and Ryan just caught my lie? Gosh, I hoped not.

"Okay. Drive safe."

I smiled as I walked over and gave Ryan a kiss. "I will. I'll be back soon."

I rushed out the door and got into my car. I looked around before I started my car. Why was I doing this? Brad wasn't watching me. He was waiting for me.

As I drove, my heart pounded in my chest. In a few minutes, I'd face the man who tried to end my life. Why did I agree to this?

Oh yeah. Brad gave me an ultimatum and didn't give me a chance. Why did he have this hold on me? Especially after so many years. Oh yeah, I feared him with every fiber of my being.

I pulled into the parking lot, and I saw five vehicles. I breathed a sigh of relief as there were other people here. He couldn't hurt me. Hopefully, he wouldn't try.

I parked in front of the playground area where people could see me.

I stepped out of my car and walked to the front of it. I wondered which vehicle belonged to Brad.

Brad stepped out from by the bathrooms. He stood tall, more muscular than I remember. He wore a pair of khaki pants and a black t-shirt. His face and hair were nicely trimmed. If I didn't know any better, I'd think he was a normal man.

He approached me, and I took a few steps back. I wasn't comfortable with him being close to me.

Brad smiled as he came to a stop. "You look

amazing."

I nodded as I looked around. I was frightened out of my mind. Yet, he wanted to comment on my appearance.

"Are you not going to speak?"

I exhaled as I rolled my eyes. "What do you want, Brad?"

He smiled. "I missed that beautiful voice so much."

This man had the nerve to comment on how much he missed my voice. He had to be kidding me.

"If you don't tell me why you're sending me text messages and pictures, I'm just going to leave."

Brad shook his head. "No, you won't because I'll show Ryan these pictures." He held his phone up for me to see.

I folded my arms across my chest, becoming agitated. "What is it that you want from me?"

"I want to be a family again."

"What?" I couldn't have heard him correctly. There was no way possible he said what I thought he just said.

"I want you, Bria, and I to be a family again."

I took a step back, completely shocked. "You've got to be kidding me?"

The look on his face said otherwise. He shook his head.

"Hear me out. I stopped drinking. I spent five years behind bars figuring out how to get my life back on track. I'm out now, and I've finally done it. Now, all I need is for you and Bria to complete me."

I exhaled.

"Brad."

"Yes?"

I motioned around the park. "I understand you did all of this to make me feel more comfortable talking with you."

He smiled.

"But it still doesn't change the years that we were together. You have to understand the choices I made. I'll never be with you, and you'll never see Bria again."

Brad walked towards me, and I put ample distance between us. "Don't do this, Kyla. Just give me another chance. I want to do this the right way."

"There is no right way, Brad."

Brad stopped advancing toward me, and I stepped back a few more feet. We had walked around my car, and I was beside the driver's door. If Brad advanced towards me again, I'd get inside and escape.

"Yes, there is. All you need to do is divorce Ryan and come back home with me."

Divorce Ryan? Was he insane? How would he think I'd divorce the man who helped heal me from the inside out from all the physical, emotional, and psychological abuse that he caused and put me through?

I shook my head. "No, I'll never do that."

Brad narrowed his eyes as he pointed at me.

"You know I'll never give up on you. You know sure as hell that I'll never give up on Bria."

I looked at the playground. Children ran around with no cares in the world as they played on the monkey bars and went down the slide. Their parents talked and laughed with ease. Why couldn't my life go back to that? I asked the one question I knew I didn't want to know the answer to.

"What are you saying?"

"Let the war begin."

With that parting statement, I opened my door and slipped inside. I locked the doors immediately. My heart pounded so loud, I could hear it in my ears.

What just happened?

Why did it happen?

What was I going to do?

All I knew, Brad wasn't kidding when he said a war was going to ensue. I had to prepare for the battle.

Chapter Eleven

Brad

How could she?

How could Kyla betray me like this? She basically spat in my face, said she'd never be with me, said I'd never see Bria again and drove away.

As I watched her leave the park, I wanted to scream and hit anything I could get my hands on, but I had to keep my cool.

Bria was my everything. Kyla knew that, and I couldn't believe she wouldn't even let me see her. Hell, Kyla still was my everything. For the first year I spent in prison, I held hatred in my heart for her. She took away my child and family, and she wouldn't even let me get those things back. The last four years, I decided to put my pride aside. I wanted to rekindle with her for the sake of our family. All I wanted was those two things back. Nothing less and nothing more.

I didn't understand why she was being difficult. Yes, I stalked her and hunted her down. Yes, I shot her when she wouldn't pack her things up and come back home with me. Yes, I knew she didn't want to be found, but she left me with no explanation. She left me with a shattered heart and a broken home. All I wanted was to get that back. That's all.

Kyla looked amazing today. She looked the same as she did when we were in high school together. The only difference was, she wore her hair longer now. How I wish she would've allowed me to run my fingers through her beautiful strands just one more time. Sadly, she wouldn't let me get close enough to touch her.

When she left, she ripped my heart out of my chest. Who did she think she was?

Even if she didn't want to give me another chance, the least she could've done was let me see Bria. I helped conceive her. She didn't do it on her own. I helped raise Bria for the first four years of her life. I was in the delivery room when Bria made her arrival at 11:53PM as she cried her little lungs out. I cried happy tears as Kyla held our bundle of joy for the first time.

Did she forget all of that? I knew it happened almost eleven years ago, but I couldn't imagine she'd already forgotten about it. I sure as hell hadn't. I knew she hadn't.

I should've continued to raise Bria, but Kyla took that opportunity away from me. Yes, we had our issues. Yes, I had anger issues. Yes, I should've gone to anger management and gotten help, but I didn't. The big picture was our issues didn't involve Bria.

If Kyla wouldn't give me another chance, so be it. I'd just make her life hell in the process to get my family back.

This was just the first step in my plan to ruin Kyla's life and take mine back. She had no idea what was in store for her... and her husband.

Ryan took care of Bria while I was away. No man should ever raise another man's child, and he did just that. By the time I was done with them, they'd need psychological help.

Kyla would think long and hard about the following decisions she'd make. I knew she was thinking about it as she left in her car. Granted, she was seen with the same man twice. They looked more than just friendly when I snapped those pictures. A man kissed her hand, and he was all over her in the nightclub. I wonder what Ryan would think of his wife when he found that out.

I walked to my car, and I got inside. I opened my phone, and I sent out a text.

Me: Time to kick it up a notch. Meet me in thirty minutes at the bar in town.

Chapter Twelve

Kyla

What should I do?

I couldn't let those pictures get out to Ryan. Heck, I didn't think twice when Michael kissed my hand. I thought it was a genuine move. I still thought it was a genuine move, but I had to question everything now. I had to question everyone. How did Brad get that picture? He had to be following me again. How long had he been following me?

He's been out for two months. Has he been stalking me since then? Or did he just come to town?

I had so many questions and not enough answers. I was in for a whirlwind of issues.

What was I to do? I didn't want those incriminating pictures to get out. I didn't even know how the pictures were taken last night. I didn't remember too much of anything before I woke up in bed this morning.

Brad was in the nightclub with us last night. Had Sabrina and Lauren seen them? Or were we all drunk off our butts? Why did I drink so much? I hated I let my guard down. The first time I let my guard down to have fun, I woke up to this mess.

I pulled into the parking lot of a convenience store. I threw my car in park, and I closed my eyes. I hadn't dealt with this much stress in years. Honestly, all the stress I encountered was a result of Brad.

I needed to call someone. I didn't know what to do. I had to call my best friend.

The phone rang three times before it was answered.

"Hey, I'm glad you called."

Amy was cheerful, something I lacked.

"You are? How come?" I sat back as I prepared to talk to Amy. I wanted to catch up with her on this call, as well as confide in her. "I missed you, of course."

I opened my mouth to respond, but no words came out.

"Kyla, are you still there?"

"Yes."

My voice came out faint.

"What's wrong?" Concern oozed from her voice.

I exhaled a deep breath. "It's Brad."

"Please tell me he's dead. He got into it with the wrong person, and they shanked him."

A laugh escaped from within me, catching me off guard. Amy knew exactly what to say to attempt to cheer me up and get me out of my depressive state. She always had a need to defend and comfort me, so she always wanted what was best for me.

"No, that didn't happen."

Amy huffed. I imagined her folding her arms across her chest and pouting. "Well, darn it. Tell me what happened."

"Brad was released."

Amy yelled into the phone. "What? How could this be?"

I shrugged my shoulders as if she were looking at me. "I don't know Amy, I don't know."

Amy told me to give her a second. I could hear her muffled voice before I heard a soft voice respond.

"Is that Julia?" I asked once Amy told me she was back.

"Yeah. We are having a girl's day while Alex is at work."

"Tell her Auntie Kyla says hi." I exhaled. I didn't want to interrupt her time with Julia. "Let me get off the phone. I don't want to interrupt your girl's day with my problems."

"Nonsense. We haven't talked on the phone in a few weeks. I can spare a few minutes for my best friend."

Amy called Julia over.

Julia took the phone and talked to me about how she liked her friends at school. After speaking with her for two minutes, she handed the phone back to Amy. "How did you find this out? Did the prison reach out to you?"

I watched as a silver SUV parked. A young mother stepped out and went to the backseat to retrieve her newborn baby. "No, Brad, reached out to me."

Amy cursed under her breath. "What the hell? What happened?"

I rolled my eyes as I gripped the steering wheel. "Well, I wish I could say it's a long story, but it's not."

I went in depth about the two text messages that I received, the incriminating pictures, and my meeting with Brad.

I closed my eyes and thought over my decision. It was a dumb one indeed, but I wasn't thinking about my safety. I only thought about Ryan's opinion. I didn't want to disappoint him, and I didn't want to drag him into another whirlwind of issues. I'd already dragged him into enough issues to last him a lifetime.

"You need to talk to Ryan pronto."

Amy said the words I didn't want to hear, but

I knew I had no other choice at this point.

"I'll go home to talk to him about it now."

"Good. I don't want you and Ryan not getting along because of Brad. That is what he wants. Don't allow Brad to win. Don't allow him to control you."

I nodded. Amy was right. I couldn't allow Brad to run this show. If it were up to him, my marriage would crash down to a pulp, and he'd feel like he had another chance with me. Not in this lifetime. Not in another lifetime.

I thanked Amy for her words of wisdom. She was right. Brad would want me to keep things away from Ryan in order to have control over me. If I allowed him to control things, nothing positive would come of this situation. Brad would get exactly what he wanted.

"I'm going home to talk to him."

"Good girl. Text me after you talk to him, okay. I want to make sure that my favorite couple is going strong."

I smiled. I looked in the rearview before I backed out of the parking space and headed home. "You always know how to make me feel better."

"That is what best friends are for. I'll talk to you later, Kyla."

After exchanging our parting words, I drove home with purpose.

I walked into the house and made my way to the living room.

"Back so soon?" Ryan asked as he smiled.

"Can we talk?"

Ryan looked at me. He looked at my hands and then stood. "What's wrong?"

I held my finger up to my lips. I pointed upstairs. "I don't want Bria to hear."

Ryan scrunched his eyebrows. He took my hand.

"Bria. Ryder. Mommy and I are going to talk outside for a few minutes. When we come back inside, we're going to watch the movie."

A chorus of cheers traveled before we walked out the back door. We walked to the gazebo, and we sat on the lounge chairs.

"What's going on, Beautiful?"

I looked into Ryan's eyes, and every secret that I held onto spewed out of my mouth. I told him about the text messages with the incriminating pictures. I told him about my meeting with Brad as I showed him the pictures.

"What?" Ryan gasped as he stood. His eyes widened. "Why would you meet this man? He could've killed you."

I looked at the ground. "I know, I know. I'm sorry, I didn't have a choice."

"Yes, you did. You always have a choice. The best choice would've been to ignore him entirely. I know you'd never cheat on me, so those pictures mean nothing to me."

A feeling of relief washed over me. Ryan believed me. He believed me when I said I didn't have any interactions outside of being friendly with Michael.

"What I don't understand is what happened last night."

I shrugged. "I don't understand either. I don't even remember seeing him there last night."

"Do you think you were drugged?" he asked.

I shook my head. "I'm a lightweight when it comes to alcohol. I was just drunk."

Ryan paced back and forth in front of me. "You have to contact Sabrina and Lauren to see if they remember anything."

I agreed. Hopefully, they remembered something and didn't black out like I did.

Ryan was silent as he was deep in thought. "Who is this Michael man?"

I racked my brain for all the information that I had on him. "He's a lawyer. I know him from Tony's."

He tapped his finger on his chin as he continued to pace. "Are you sure he isn't connected to Brad?"

I nodded as I sat back. "I think so. He says he's a lawyer, and he put the bad men away."

Ryan nodded. "Then they shouldn't be connected." He exhaled as he wrung his hands. "I don't like him reaching out." Ryan stopped and looked at me. "How did he get out of prison?"

I shrugged. His guess was as great as mine. I thought he'd spend at least another fifteen years in prison. That's what we were told at the hearing. Something major must've happened for him to get released early. I'd have to call and get information on his release. There had to be an error.

"I just want you to be safe. I want you to feel protected. I don't want you to be afraid. I don't want him to have control over you anymore."

"I wish it were that easy," I admitted.

I was scared out of my mind. I didn't even know why I met up with him today. I must've been running on pure adrenaline this afternoon. I was stupid to meet up with him. He could've hurt me. He hasn't thought twice about hurting me in public before.

Ryan sat beside me and held my hands. "It can be that easy."

"What do you suggest?" I was ready to hear Ryan's suggestions. Any suggestions were better than none. I didn't feel safe in my own skin.

"Keep living life."

I raised an eyebrow as I waited for Ryan to continue, but he never did. He left it at those three simple words. Keep. Living. Life.

"Just keep living life?" I repeated it. It was more of a question than a statement.

"Yes." Ryan looked over at our house before he looked at me. He caressed the back of my hands with his thumbs. "Don't stop living your life because of Brad. He might be all talk this time around."

I shook my head. "I don't think so. I know for a fact that he is serious. He wants me back. He wants Bria back."

"But he must have some type of supervision he requires. He was released early. Maybe he has to abide by rules in order for him to stay in society."

I gave Ryan a pointed look. "The Brad I saw today is the same Brad I was with for five years. If he doesn't get his way, he throws a fit. Once he sets his mind to something, he will not let up until he's able to accomplish that goal."

Ryan looked away, and I could tell he was deep in thought. "I'll buy you some protection."

"A gun?"

Ryan nodded.

"I don't want a gun." My voice raised an octave. I didn't want a gun anywhere near me or my children.

"Okay, fine. No gun." I could tell Ryan was not happy with my decline. "You don't have to have a gun, but I at least want you to carry a knife and pepper spray."

I agreed with those two items.

"I'll go pick those up later."

I smiled, showing him my gratitude. "I'd also prefer you're never alone."

I gave Ryan a pointed look. "You know that's not going to happen."

Ryan smirked. "I know, but it sounded great."

"Thank you."

"You never have to thank me." Ryan released my hands, stood, and kissed my forehead. "Call Sabrina and Lauren. See what they remember. I'm going to start the popcorn."

"What movie did Bria decide on?" I asked as I grabbed my phone from my pocket.

"A princess movie."

I smiled. "Our princess loves princesses."

Ryan agreed. "That she does."

Once Ryan walked inside, I called Sabrina and Lauren on a three-way call.

"Woah, Mommy, are you just waking up?" Lauren asked with a chuckle.

"That's what I was going to say. It's going on two o'clock."

"No, we have a problem."

"What's wrong?" Sabrina asked.

"Is Ryan upset you came home wasted?" Lauren chimed in.

"If that's the case, I can call him and tell him that I liquored you up."

"Yes, we can blame it all on Lauren. The old woman of the group."

Sabrina and Lauren laughed. If I weren't so stressed, I'd join in with the laughter, but I was not in the laughing mood.

"Do you two remember a man with me last night?"

The line fell silent.

"No," Sabrina said softly.

"What man?" Lauren asked.

"Well, Brad texted me this morning…"

"Brad who?" Sabrina blurted out.

Lauren gasped. "Please tell me it isn't your ex that should still be in jail."

"Yes. That Brad." I explained in detail how I met Michael at lunch one day, the two text messages I received, the incriminating pictures, and how Michael was in both the pictures.

"Unbelievable," Sabrina responded.

"How could this be? How did this happen?" Lauren asked.

"Do you two remember a man all over me from last night?"

"We were pretty wasted as well," Sabrina added.

"Yeah, we don't remember anyone."

I exhaled. I was defeated. Nothing, and I mean nothing, could uplift my spirits.

"What are you going to do?" Sabrina asked.

"I'm not sure."

After we said our parting words, I walked into the house. Everyone sat in the living room, waiting for me to join.

Ryan and I exchanged a silent conversation. He knew they didn't know anything either. They were just as drunk as I was.

"Let's watch some princesses," I called out as I sat beside Bria.

I tried my hardest to sound enthusiastic, but deep down inside, I knew my world was about to fall apart.

Chapter Thirteen

Ryan

I couldn't admit it to anyone, but I was frightened. I was frightened for Kyla and Bria's safety. I was even frightened for Ryder, even though I knew he wasn't coming after him. Brad could come after me if he wanted. I wasn't scared of him, but I knew he placed fear into my wife. That was unacceptable.

What was up with this man? Why did he try to get Kyla back with blackmail? He knew she didn't want to be with him. If she wanted him, they would've never broken up. He didn't learn how to treat her like the wonderful woman she is. That was his mistake, and he would never get another chance to be with her again.

What was hilarious was his attempt to catch Kyla in a position that would look fishy to any other man besides me. I knew the woman that I had, and she was no cheater. We weren't together for five years for nothing.

Tuesday morning, I woke up in an empty bed. I yawned and stretched before I went into the bathroom and bathed.

Once I was dressed in black pants and a teal dress shirt, I walked downstairs. The smell of bacon and eggs greeted me.

I entered the kitchen. "Good morning." I walked over to the children and placed kisses on their foreheads.

Ryder scooped eggs into his mouth. "Good morning, Dad."

"Good morning, Daddy," Bria said before she drank her juice.

"Good morning." Kyla's voice was soft as she made two plates of eggs, bacon, and toast.

"Let me grab those for you."

I kissed her forehead before I grabbed our plates of food and brought them to the table.

Kyla sat my cup of coffee in front of me before she sat across the table from me.

We talked as we ate. I watched Kyla closely as the children talked. She looked like her normal self, but I could just sense that she was shaken. She had every right to be, and I hated that. I hated that she didn't feel safe. That was my main objective, to make her feel safe and secure. I instilled this feeling into her, and Brad's release yanked that feeling away from her.

Once breakfast was over, I helped carry the dirty dishes to the kitchen.

"Bria, Ryder. Grab your backpacks. We're running a bit behind," Kyla said as she opened the dishwasher.

"I'll put the dishes in," I said.

Kyla stopped and looked at me, her eyebrow raised. "Are you sure ?"

"Yes, leave. I'll make sure everything is clean before I go to work."

Kyla smiled. "Thank you. I'll see you later."

I wrapped my arms around her, and I squeezed her tight. I didn't want to let her go. I wanted to comfort her until the end of time. At the end of our hug, I tilted her mouth up to mine, and I kissed her. It was sweet. It was tender. It was full of love. "I'll see you later. Call me if you need me. I'll be there at the drop of a dime."

She smiled. The smile didn't quite reach her eyes. "I love you."

"I love you too."

Once the dishes were loaded into the dishwasher, I grabbed my travel cup from the cupboard and poured coffee into it. Coffee was my best friend since I slept with one eye open at night. I walked to the door, where I slipped my jacket on. We only had a few weeks left before the cold weather went away, and I couldn't wait. This winter was brutal, and I was ready for the warm temperatures.

After I locked the house, I got into my car. Once inside, I put my coffee in the cup holder as the car warmed.

I loved my job. I loved what I did for a living, but going to work was hard. Veronica , my coworker, was persistent about how much she wanted me in the last three weeks. She told me every day, and she didn't know how to take no for an answer. I had too much going on to deal with her.

After driving twenty minutes through traffic, I parked my car in front of the massive four-story building.

After turning my car off, I gathered my coffee, phone, and wallet. A knock sounded on my window, startling me. I looked over, and disappointment washed over me.

Veronica stood on the other side of the window. She waved with a bright smile . She brought her hand up that held a coffee.

I rolled my eyes as I exhaled. This woman wouldn't take the hints that were thrown at her .

Veronica knew I wasn't interested in her, but she continued her persistence every chance she got.

I pushed my door open. The cold air greeted me with force. She stepped back and placed her hand on her hip. I stepped out, and I towered over her by several inches.

"Good morning, baby boy," she murmured as she stepped closer to me.

"My name is Ryan," I responded.

I closed the door and locked the car.

She tried to touch me, but I moved out of her reach. I walked towards the entrance.

"You can at least say good morning."

"Good morning, Veronica."

My voice was stern, to the point. Only fifty more feet until I was in the building and around other people. Veronica didn't bother me if there were people around us.

"Yikes. Someone woke up on the wrong side of the bed this morning."

Her comment stopped me in my tracks. I turned to look at her, and she gave me a smirk.

"What? You seem grouchy."

I tapped my finger on my chin several times. "Hmm. I wonder why? Maybe it has to do with you flirting with me and not taking the hint that I'm not interested."

She raised her eyebrow. "What hint? I know you want me just as much as I want you."

Choosing the high road, I ignored her and walked into the building.

The building was older, but the modern-day white décor made it appear new and lively.

The warmth enveloped me as I said good morning to the security guard at the entrance. I waved at the receptionist in the middle of the first floor.

I made a beeline for the elevators, Veronica on my heels. I jabbed the call button, tapping my foot on the floor.

The door to the elevator opened, and I walked in. Pushing the button for the fourth floor, I sipped my coffee. Veronica stepped onto the elevator and stood beside me.

Once the doors closed, she glanced over at me. "Are you okay?"

"Fine." One-word responses were best.

"Are you sure?"

The elevator stopped on the fourth floor.

"Yes."

Once the doors opened, I rushed out of the elevators and headed for my office. I unlocked it and walked inside, closing the door behind me.

The smell of lemon hit me. My office must've been cleaned last night after I left. I placed my coffee on my desk before shrugging off my jacket and hanging it on the coat hook by the door. I plopped down in my chair.

I laid my head on the cool, mahogany desk. I exhaled, trying to calm my nerves.

A knock sounded on the door a few minutes later.

I straightened up and took a sip of my coffee. I fixed my shirt before I called out, "Come in."

Timothy opened the door and walked inside. He wore a gray suit and black dress shoes. "Ryan, we just put together a last-minute meeting. Can you meet in the conference room in five?"

Oh great. Last-minute meetings usually didn't

result in a positive discussion.

"I'll be there."

Timothy walked out of my office with a parting smile and closed the door.

I grabbed my notebook, favorite black pen, and coffee. I walked into the conference room, which had a long cherry wood table that was surrounded by fancy, black computer chairs. The room was already filling up. I called out good morning as I sat in between two coworkers.

I knew I had made the right choice when Veronica walked into the room. She looked at me, and disappointment danced in her eyes. She forced a smile as she sat at the table and talked with a coworker.

Timothy walked in minutes later, followed by Elizabeth. Elizabeth sat at the head of the table where the computer was. She operated the computer as Timothy started the meeting.

After thirty minutes, the meeting came to an end. The room was filled with light chatter. I smiled and waved before leaving the room and headed for my office.

I wasn't inside my office for a good minute before a knock sounded.

"Come in," I called out.

The door opened, and Timothy walked in.

"Ryan. We need to talk."

Timothy's tone was all business. That was never good. The color drained from my face as my mouth went dry. What did we need to talk about right now? The meeting had just ended.

Whatever he needed to talk to me about was serious.

"Yes, Sir." I stood, and I motioned with my hand for him to sit.

He closed the door, and he sat.

I focused my attention on him.

"What is this about?" I asked when he didn't immediately start talking.

"It's about Veronica."

I scrunched my eyebrows. "What about Veronica?"

Timothy moved his hands. "We have a no fraternization policy here."

My heart dropped into my stomach as I grabbed my coffee and took a sip. The coffee was lukewarm. I sat my cup down, and I spoke. "There's no…"

Timothy held his hand up. I snapped my mouth shut. Timothy didn't want me to defend myself. This was not good. "I want to make something very clear with you. Right here and right now."

I waited in silence. There was no reason to speak until I heard what he was going to say.

"When you started working here, you sat with Human Resources. What did Human Resources say?"

I exhaled. I didn't appreciate how Timothy was talking to me. I worked for this company for over ten years. He should've known my work ethic by now.

"There is a no fraternization policy."

"Correct."

Timothy looked around my office.

I tapped my fingers on the desk, willing this uncomfortable and pointless conversation to end.

"I hope this is the last time we will have this conversation."

I nodded. "Yes, Sir."

Timothy stood, opened my door, and walked out.

What just happened? Why did it just happen? What was going on?

Timothy walked into my office and completely disrespected me. He didn't even have the decency to hear my side of the situation. There was nothing going on between Veronica and me, yet he didn't even give me a chance to speak. He said 'we' needed to talk. The only thing that just happened was he talked. I listened.

Timothy had known me for over ten years. He should've known I would never do anything to jeopardize my job. Besides, he knew I had an amazing wife and two children at home. What would I get from a fling at work? That wasn't even my character, and I felt insulted.

I stood and walked to my door. I flung it open, ready to confront Timothy for not giving me a chance to speak.

I took two steps back. Veronica stood at the door with a smirk. She waved and winked before she walked away.

What in the hell? This was serious.

Chapter Fourteen

Kyla

"Mommy, mommy. Over here."

Ryder waved his hands above his head as I held the plastic football in my right hand.

It was a beautiful Saturday morning, no clouds visible in the sky. The sun shined bright, but it was cold. Thank goodness for thick coats. All four of us were in the backyard playing a game of touch football. Ryan and Bria were teamed up, while Ryder and I were on a team. Ryder and I led by a touchdown.

"Catch, Sweetie."

The ball sailed through the air towards Ryder. Bria, who guarded Ryder, had stepped in front of Ryder to catch the ball. Ryder maneuvered around her and caught the ball with ease. Bria allowed Ryder to run through the makeshift goal. He turned around, threw the ball to the ground, and did his victory dance.

"I scored. I scored."

Ryder celebrated as I jogged over to give him a high-five.

"Good job, Ryder."

Bria walked over and gave him a rub on the top of his head.

"Let's go again."

Ryder burst with energy. I'd like to blame it on the pieces of chocolate he had an hour ago before we came outside for family time.

"One more round. The pizza should be here any moment."

Ryan held his hands open as Bria threw the ball to him.

After Ryan hiked the ball, I guarded him as he managed to throw the ball right over my head and into Bria's hands. She ran for their goal and scored.

"Good game, Bria."

Ryder grabbed the football from Bria, and we walked towards the house.

"I had tons of fun."

I smiled. The night prior, Ryder and Bria

argued at the top of their lungs. Bria ate the last cookie, and Ryder wasn't happy about it. After they sat in the corner of their room for ten minutes staring at the wall, they came back downstairs and apologized for their argument. A container of cookies had reappeared after their timeout was over, thanks to Ryan making a quick run to the store. Both children received a cookie, and peace settled among them. The argument between the siblings was solved.

"Can we play tomorrow?" Ryder asked.

I opened the back door for us all to walk in. "Maybe. If you are a good boy."

I walked into the house behind Bria and Ryder. Ryan closed the door behind us. It had been two weeks since I had seen Brad. I hadn't received any more text messages from him since. He hadn't called either. You'd think the silence placed me in a great head space, but it did the complete opposite. I preferred it when Brad was in contact. I could try to gauge what his mindset was or what he was thinking about. When there was silence, I didn't know what he was up to. I was blinded, and I didn't like the feeling. As I grabbed paper plates out of the cabinet, my phone rang.

I pulled my phone out of my back pocket and smiled. Answering the phone, I wedged it between my ear and my shoulder as I walked into the dining room.

"Hello, Aunt Lily."

"Hello. How is my favorite niece doing?"

I smirked into the phone as I separated the plates and placed them in front of our respective chairs. "I'm your only niece."

"Hence, my favorite." Aunt Lily's response caused me to laugh. "So, how are you and the family doing?"

"We are good. We just finished playing football in the backyard."

"Who won?" Aunt Lily asked.

"Ryder and I."

"Woohoo," Aunt Lily cheered into the phone. "Make sure to let Bria and Ryan win the next game. I don't want Bria left out of winning."

Aunt Lily's thoughtfulness never ceased to amaze me. "Okay, I'll make sure of that. How are you and your husband doing?"

"We're great. I just wanted to let you know that we will be going on vacation for a week."

"It's your anniversary, right?"

"Yes."

"How many years have you two been married?"

"Thirty years," Aunt Lily stated.

"I can't wait, I seriously can't." When I imagined my future, I saw us old and gray while we sat in our rocking chairs, watching our great-grandchildren run and play in the yard.

"You'll get there one day, I'm sure." I smiled. I knew I would. I was ready to enjoy the journey. "Enough about my relationship. Where are you two vacating?"

"Hawaii."

"Aloha," I said, full of excitement.

Aunt Lily laughed. "I just wanted to let you know that I will be on vacation, but if you need me, you can call me anytime."

I scoffed. "I will not interrupt your vacation. Just let me know when you arrive."

The doorbell rang as Aunt Lily responded, "I will. I love you."

"I love you too."

As I hung up the phone, I heard Ryan's conversation with the delivery man. Ryan's laugh traveled throughout the house as I called for Ryder and Bria to come into the dining room. As soon as Ryder and Bria were situated at the dinner table, I poured soda into our cups. Ryan walked the pizza box into the dining room and sat it in the middle of the table.

The smell of tomato and cheese goodness filled the room, causing my stomach to growl on cue. Ryan opened the box of pizza as we sat. Ryder sat beside Ryan, and Bria sat next to me. Once we all had our slices of pizza, we dived into the cheesy goodness. We all moaned our satisfaction with the pizza after we had our initial bite.

Bria sat her slice of pizza on her plate and looked at me. "Mommy, can I have a play date soon?"

Ryan interjected before I could respond. "Why do you never ask Dad for a play date?"

I wiped my mouth with a napkin. "I'm pretty sure she asks me because I am the one to take her."

Ryan looked from me to Bria. "I can take you one day."

Bria's eyes widened as she took a sip of her soda. "I'd love for you to take me, Dad."

"Am I just cold turkey now?" I joked with a smirk.

"I want a play date," Ryder interrupted in a loud voice.

After I swallowed the pizza in my mouth, I said, "Inside voices, please."

Ryder repeated himself in a much lower tone.

"I'll contact Sam's mom later today and get one set up."

Sam was one of Ryder's friends from daycare. He had attended Ryder's fourth birthday party weeks prior. Sam's mom and I had to separate their little arms from each other when it was time for them to leave.

Ryan looked over at me. He took a bite of his pizza and swallowed it before he spoke. "How are you feeling?"

Ryan wouldn't come out and mention Brad for the sake of Bria. I appreciated him for that. After taking a sip of my soda, I shrugged.

"I'm okay."

Okay as I'll ever be with my crazy ex on the loose when he should still be behind bars.

"I just wanted to make sure." He took a few gulps of his soda. He smiled before he grabbed another slice of pizza.

"I heard from Aunt Lily a few minutes ago."

Ryan raised his eyebrows. "How's she doing?"

"She's good. Just wanted to let us know that she was going on vacation with her husband."

"What's the special occasion?"

"They are celebrating their thirtieth anniversary."

Ryan whistled before he took a bite of his pizza. "Thirty years is a hell of a long time."

I nodded as I smiled. "Tell me about it."

"Where are they flying to? London? France?" Ryan asked.

"Try Hawaii."

Bria perked up. "Hawaii? I want to go to Hawaii. Can we go to Hawaii?"

"What is Hawaii?" Ryder asked as he picked at his pizza.

Ryan grabbed a napkin and wiped Ryder's tomato-streaked face. "Hawaii is a beautiful state in the middle of the Pacific Ocean."

"Can we go?" Bria asked again.

"Yeah, can we go?" Ryder echoed Bria.

"We can consider it for our next once-a-year trip. Dad and I will discuss it."

Bria did a dance in her chair. "Yay."

Ryan looked at all of us around the table. "A family full of great dance moves."

Bria beamed with confidence. "I learned my dance moves from my mommy."

"Yes, you did," Ryan agreed.

My phone vibrated beside me. I picked up my phone, and my heart dropped into the pit of my stomach.

Unknown: Hello, Kyla, it's Joe. I need to talk to you about Brad. It's urgent.

I showed Ryan the text. His eyes widened as he looked at me.

"We need to call him."

"Dad and I must make an important call right now. Bria, can you clean your brother's hands when he is done eating?"

Bria nodded as she took a sip of her soda. "Yes, I can."

I kissed their foreheads before we walked out of the dining room and out the back door.

The cold air hit me hard. It was definitely cooler now than it was earlier.

I called the phone number. The phone didn't complete its first ring before it was answered.

"Hello."

Ryan and I exchanged a look. "Hello, Joe."

"How are you doing, Kyla?" Joe's voice was warm and inviting.

"I've been better," I admitted.

I introduced Ryan and Joe before the conversation continued.

"I'm sorry to text you with such a drastic message. I've been contemplating this conversation for the past two weeks, and couldn't put it off anymore."

We walked over to the gazebo and sat. I wasn't sure how long this conversation would last, but we had to prepare.

"What's going on?" I asked.

Joe had always been a straightforward man. If he reached out, he meant business.

"It's Brad. I'm worried about you and what he's planning to do." There was a brief pause. "Did you know he's out of jail?"

"Yes, he made me aware a few weeks ago."

Joe exhaled. "I tried my hardest to talk him out of going there."

"Well, thank you for trying," Ryan said.

I nodded, even though Joe couldn't see me.

"He's burned all his bridges with everyone at this point."

I scrunched up my eyebrows. "What do you mean?"

"His parents cut him off when he went to prison."

I gasped as I threw my hand over my mouth. I knew his father was strict, but I never thought the day would come when his mother would disown him. She probably didn't have a choice. He was always a momma's boy.

"Our other friends stop talking to him."

"But you're still in contact with him?" Ryan asked.

"Not anymore. Brad stayed with me when he got out of prison."

"Do you know why he was released early?" I asked.

If anyone knew, it would be Joe. I called the courts last week, and they told me they'd have someone return my call, but I hadn't heard anything since.

"Tampered evidence."

Ryan and I looked at each other. That made sense of his early release. I couldn't believe this. Brad's luck was outstanding.

"Wow." I couldn't think to say anything else.

"Well, now I know you're aware that he's not going to stop until he gets you and Bria back."

Ryan shook his head. "That'll never happen. He's not going to ruin my family because he can't take no for an answer."

"When Brad puts his mind to something, he won't stop."

I knew that for a fact. I was with the man for five years.

"I just felt like he's planning something big, and I want you all to be prepared."

"Something big?"

Ryan looked at me. I could see he was shaken by that comment.

"Like what?"

"I can't tell you what, but from how he talked the last time I saw him, he didn't seem like he was in the right mindset."

My heart dropped into my stomach. I was already feeling defeated, but this call took me to a whole level of depression.

"I have to go, but I had to call you and let you know what I knew."

"Thank you for calling, Joe." I ended the call, and I stared at the concrete. I had no words.

Why would anyone let a psycho out of prison? Brad needed help, and he obviously didn't get the help he needed while he was there.

"Let the war begin."

Ryan's eyes widened at my words, but I wasn't playing. My family's life was on the line, and I wouldn't bow down.

Brad wanted a war, and that was exactly what he was going to get.

Chapter Fifteen

Kyla

"My favorite coworker has finally graced me with her presence."

I clocked in before I turned around in my chair. Lauren leaned against the cubical, her curly hair pulled back from her face with a hair clip. She wore a knee-length white and black polka dot dress that accentuated her curves and white wedges.

"Don't you mean your work best friend?" I

asked her as I smirked.

Lauren looked around before she whispered, "You're my only friend here."

Playfully rolling my eyes, I leaned back in my chair to get comfortable. "If you say so."

"I know so," Lauren sang as she winked at me.

"You look amazing. I love the dress. Is it a new purchase?"

Lauren smoothed her hands over her dress before she smiled her gratitude. "It's new. Layla and I checked out a new boutique in the next town over, and I fell in love with it."

"I can see why. You are killing that dress."

Lauren struck a pose. "Thank you."

"What's the special occasion for buying it?"

Lauren raised an eyebrow. "Does it always have to be a special occasion?"

I shook my head. "Not for you to go shopping, but there's something about this dress. It just screams, I am a special buy to me."

Lauren gave me a knowing look. "Well, I am celebrating my five-pound weight loss."

"That's cause for celebration." I folded my arms across my chest. There was still something she hadn't told me. "Anything else?"

Lauren shrugged as she glanced down at her fingernails. They were painted a dark shade of purple. "I wouldn't say it's a special occasion..."

"Well, spill the details."

The anticipation killed me.

"I went on a date on Friday night."

I gasped as I brought my hand to my chest in shock. "Why didn't you tell me?"

Lauren fiddled with her hands. She exhaled as she twisted her lips.

"I wanted to tell you, but I know you're stressed about Brad."

Brad was on my mind constantly. Since we received the call from Joe, I was more fearful than before. I didn't think that was possible, but there we were. I didn't know what Brad was doing, and that irritated me. He still hadn't reached out, but I knew he was watching and waiting. He was waiting for the perfect time to attack. When was the perfect time? I didn't know, but I had to be ready for whenever.

"Just because I'm stressed doesn't mean I don't want to hear about your date. Tell me all about him, and don't leave anything out."

Lauren motioned with her hands. "Let's go make our drinks, and I'll tell you about him."

We walked to the break room, and she told me about Xavier. She explained how he was a police officer with a daughter and a dog. He was an affectionate person, and no surprise at all, he enjoyed reading books. As my tea steeped in my mug, I observed how Lauren brightened when she told me they went mini golfing for their first date, followed by a hot beverage in the park.

I blew on my tea before I took a sip. We headed towards our desk. "I'm guessing there will be a second date?"

Lauren squealed, drawing the attention of the

coworkers we were passing. "You guessed right. I look forward to the next date."

"Finally, someone to snag Lauren's attention in the right way."

I sat my tea on my desk before I turned to look at her.

Lauren beamed. "Finally."

"It only took twenty men," I pointed out as I walked over to Lauren's desk.

"You were counting?" She raised her eyebrow in suspicion.

I laughed. "I'm just joking."

Lauren laughed. "You're pretty close on that count, though."

"I bet. You are the pickiest woman I have ever met," I pointed out.

"That's why you love me." Lauren took another sip of her coffee before she sat it on her desk. She placed her hands on her hips as she looked at me. "Please tell me you're done with the book?"

I held two fingers up. "I have two chapters left."

Lauren groaned. "I'm dying to discuss it. It was so great."

"I'll try to finish the last two chapters today during lunch."

After another few minutes of our morning chat, we went to our respective desks, and I dived into our work. Lunch had come and gone, leftover tacos from the night before being my lunch of choice as I finished off the last two chapters of the book. After another few hours of work, I only had twenty minutes left of the workday. I sent a quick text to Amelia to make sure we were still meeting up for drinks at Meg's Coffee Shop, my old job that I had when I first moved to town. We were going to meet up to make plans for Thanksgiving and chat about Brad's release.

Amelia: I'll see you in half an hour.

I smiled. Amelia and Aunt Lily had taken over the mom role I didn't have growing up. I couldn't have asked for better women to come into my life. I was grateful to have them both.

When the workday came to an end, I clocked out. Lauren and I headed downstairs and out of the office together once I made sure there wasn't any unwanted visitors in the parking lot. The cool air met my body full force, and I shivered involuntarily.

"Since you finished the book, do you want to discuss it tonight after your time with Amelia?"

"We can discuss it tomorrow during lunch."

Lauren groaned as if she was in immense pain. "I can't wait that long. I might burst at the seams."

I threw my head back in laughter as we approached our cars. "You'll have to burst at the seams then."

Lauren scuffed as she pouted. "Totally not fair."

"I'll see you tomorrow." I wrapped my free arm around her and hugged her tight.

"Bright and early?" she asked.

"Maybe not early, but it'll definitely be bright."

Lauren smirked. "Ryder needs to learn how to get up and get going."

"He's a turtle, just like Ryan in the mornings."

Once our goodbyes were said, Lauren and I got into our cars, and I drove over to my old stomping ground.

As I pulled into the parking lot, I saw Amelia's car.

She stepped out of her car and walked over to me once I had parked. I grabbed my purse, stepped out of my car, and wrapped my arms around her. Her touch was comforting.

"Hey, Pumpkin." She ran her fingers through my hair before we separated.

"Hi, Amelia."

"How was work?" she asked me as we approached the coffee shop. Meg's used to close at two o'clock when I worked there, but their sales had blossomed so well that they now stayed open until nine.

Amelia opened the door, and we walked into the coffee shop. Fresh coffee beans filled my nose. The familiar smell caused me to reminisce about when I met Sabrina and Ryan in this coffee shop. There were groups of people that sat at the tables, chatting away.

Unfortunately, there were no more familiar faces in the shop. Kelsey had sold the shop three years prior and had moved to Florida to live the beach life she had always dreamed of. Scott had moved to Georgia right after the sale to pursue a career in music after his relationship with Vanessa had ended abruptly.

"Financial record happiness," I answered.

Amelia gave me a knowing look. "You mean financial record hell?"

We laughed as we approached the order counter. "Of course, but I can't complain."

Amelia ordered a latte, and I ordered a hot chocolate. Once our order was paid for, we walked over to the pickup counter.

"How were the children today?"

"Angels as always. They are such a joy to be around."

"Really? They tend to be tiny monsters when I bring them home."

Our drinks were dropped off at the counter. We grabbed them as we thanked the barista. We walked over to an empty booth and shrugged off our coats before we sat down.

"That's because I load them up with sugar before they leave."

I gasped in faux shock as I blew on my cup of hot chocolate. "Amelia."

"I know, but I can't help it. They gave me the puppy dog eyes, and I'm sold. I can't bring myself to say no."

I took a sip of my hot chocolate and moaned in satisfaction. The ownership and staff might've changed, but the great taste hadn't. "They have you wrapped around their tiny fingers."

Amelia agreed. "I love being a grandma. For the longest, I thought I would've been well into my seventies before I had grandkids running around."

She took a sip of her latte.

"Really?" I asked, eyebrow raised.

Amelia nodded. "My children have always been invested in their work. I didn't think they cared to start families of their own." Amelia gave me a pointed look. "Until you came along. You changed it all for my son. You allowed him to see what he would miss out on if he didn't put his career aside."

"Yes, that's true." That was one positive aspect I had for Ryan, but I carried a ton of baggage that he didn't deserve. "I love the life we have created, but I feel like Brad won't stop until he tears our marriage apart." I shook my head in anguish.

"Brad can only tear your marriage apart if you allow it to happen. Trust me when I say that. Brad's release might have put a damper on both your spirits, but that is what Brad would want. Don't let him win." I nodded. Amelia was right. Ryan and I had to stay strong, no matter what. "When was the last time Brad reached out?"

I thought back to the day I put my life in danger. The day after the visit to the nightclub that ended in a horrid hangover. I still couldn't remember anything. "A month ago."

Amelia was mid-sip with her latte when she raised her eyebrows and sat the cup down. "Really?"

"Yes."

"I thought he would've been in contact since then." Amelia looked around the coffee shop before she looked back at me.

I tucked a stray piece of hair behind my ear before I fiddled with my cup. "I thought so, too. That's what has me worried. The silence, it just doesn't seem right." Brad's silence further scared me. I was more fearful when it was deadly silent than when he blew my phone up with creepy messages. "I can understand that. I mean, you know him better than any of us." I took a sip of my hot chocolate as two teenage girls walked by. They laughed at something on their phone. I wished I could be carefree and laugh but no, I was worried about my crazy ex.

"Joe just made it seem like he's planning something big."

Amelia took a sip of her latte. "Joe is his best friend. I'm surprised he reached out to you."

"Was."

Amelia gasped. "Was? As in past tense?"

I nodded.

"What happened?"

I explained how Brad had cut his bridges with his family and friends.

"So, Joe gave you a courtesy call."

"Yes. I'm forever grateful for that." I took a hearty sip of my hot chocolate. The drink cooled enough not to burn me.

"We all just need to be on high alert." Amelia tapped her freshly manicured nails on the table, the sparkly white nail polish catching my eye. "In my mind, something big would be to harm you or him trying to take Bria away…"

"I don't want to think about that," I interrupted Amelia.

No, Brad had never caused harm to Bria. Did I think he would start now? No, but I didn't know the mindset that he was in. If he got his hands on her, there's no telling if I'd ever see my daughter again. I couldn't take that chance.

"I know, honey, but we have to be realistic. We know who we are dealing with, and anything is possible."

I placed my hand on top of Amelia's and rubbed it. "You're right. Anything is possible, and we need to keep an open eye on everything. Thank you for meeting with me."

Amelia smiled. "You don't have to thank me. Besides, I can't turn down a latte." I smiled. Amelia loved her lattes.

"So, what do we need to bring for Thanksgiving dinner?"

Amelia clasped her hands together in excitement. Talking about the holidays always put Amelia in a joyful mood. For the next thirty minutes, we went in-depth about what would be on the menu for the day of thanks. We decided to have Thanksgiving at their house this year, as we had it at our house last year. Sophia would be flying in late Wednesday night, and she'd be right back on the plane heading back to New York early Friday morning. We wouldn't meet her boyfriend Gabriel on this trip as he was visiting his family for Thanksgiving, but we'd meet him soon.

As soon as we had finished our drinks, we threw our cups away before we put our coats back on. We had been there for an hour, and it was getting cooler outside as the day was turning to night.

"It's such a beautiful night." We walked outside into the cool, and I breathed in the fresh air.

"Yes, it is. Seems like the perfect night to use that gazebo." Amelia stuck her hands into her coat pockets.

"It's the perfect night for that, but I have to go home and put together Shepard's pie I planned for dinner."

We approached Amelia's car when she turned to look at me. "Something tells me Ryan might have dinner ready when you arrive home."

"What tells you that?"

Amelia shrugged. "A mother's intuition."

I smirked before I wrapped my arms around her. "Well, thank you for tonight."

"No, thank you, Pumpkin." Amelia took my hands into hers, and I looked into her eyes. "If there's one thing I want you to take from our talk tonight, I want you to know we have your back. We won't let Brad harm you or Bria." I held on tight to Amelia's words.

Chapter Sixteen

Ryan

Mark took a swig from his beer. "It's been a while since we've gone out."

"Yeah. Boy, how I've missed going out." I tilted my beer back and gulped half of it down within seconds.

Mark and I had planned our guy's night out two weeks ago. We decided to go to the local sports bar in town. For a Saturday night, the place was packed to capacity. I could hardly move two feet without bumping into someone. Several games played on the huge TVs placed on every available wall space in the restaurant. The room boomed with loud applause whenever a team scored. The energy was elevated tonight.

Mark motioned his hand around the bar. "We need to do this more often. Get away from the ladies for a while. In your case, your lady and children."

"I second that. It'll be just like old times." I loved reminiscing about our days back in college. Those were the days.

"Back in the old days, we were bar hopping on the weekends." Another sip, and my beer continued to disappear.

"You were throwing beers back like a pro while I was surrounded by all the ladies." He smiled as he reminisced.

I laughed. "You were always the lady's man."

Mark shook his head. "I wouldn't say that."

Eyebrow raised, I asked, "Why not?"

"When you didn't show the ladies any attention, they had no choice but to go to the second-best-looking guy in the bar."

Mark smirked as he jabbed his thumbs towards himself.

"Yet, Chelsea seemed to snag your attention and put you in check." I took another sip of my beer before I stuck my hands in the plate of nachos Mark and I shared. They were everything I desired, salty, greasy, and cheesy goodness.

Mark smiled as he nodded. "I'm grateful for

that."

An eruption of cheers traveled through the bar. I turned to look over my shoulder. A group of men stood while they cheered. They high-fived each other.

"Do you want to update me with what's going on?" Mark asked as he grabbed a handful of nachos.

I finished my beer before I waved my empty beer bottle in the air to get the bartender's attention. He grabbed another beer and placed it in front of me as he took the empty one and disposed of it.

"Brad is back, and he's being oddly silent."

Mark widened his eyes. "Oddly silent? Isn't that what you want. For him not to bother your family."

I nodded. "I'd love for him not to bother my family, but I know that's not the case. He's silent for a reason, trust me."

"Woah." Mark held his hand up as he interrupted the spew of words coming from my mouth. "How did he even get out of jail? I thought he went to jail for attempted murder."

"He did, but from what we found out, he got off on tampered evidence."

I grabbed more nachos and tossed them into my mouth.

Mark shook his head as he scowled. "How's Kyla handling it?"

"She's trying to stay positive, but we must prepare for anything. Brad wants them both back, and if I have anything to do with it, he won't ever get the chance." Mark signaled for the bartender to bring him another beer. "Well, if I can help in any way, please let me know. Your family is my family, and nobody is going to hurt my family."

I looked at Mark, and my bottom lip wobbled. I wasn't sure if it was the alcohol or just my emotions getting the best of me, but I was on the verge of crying. I had to keep my cool, in the packed bar. I didn't want anyone to see me cry.

"Are you serious?" I asked.

Mark nodded. "As serious as a heart attack. In whatever way I can help, I'm in. My best friend doesn't fight battles by himself. As long as you want my help, I have your back."

"Thank you."

We stood and grabbed each other into a bear hug. Mark had been my friend for years. I wouldn't trade him for the world.

Once we separated, we drank our beer and ate more nachos.

"There's something else." I stuffed a handful of nachos into my mouth.

"What?"

I took a sip of my beer. "My coworker, Veronica."

Mark raised his eyebrow. "Are you…"

"Hell no," I interrupted Mark.

I didn't even want him to say the words. I'd never disrespect my wife in that manner. Kyla was the best thing to ever come into my life. She gave me two wonderful kids, and she deserved the utmost respect.

"So, what's wrong?"

I exhaled. "She's accused me of coming onto her at work."

Mark looked at me, sympathy in his eyes. "Oh, my goodness. What happened? What did your boss say?"

I chuckled in disgust. "He wouldn't even let me give my side of the story."

Mark raised his eyebrows. "Are you serious?"

I nodded as I took another sip of my beer. "Dead serious."

Another group of people hollered in the corner.

"Do you still have a job?"

I shrugged. "For now, but she probably won't stop until I lose it."

Why was Veronica coming after me? I'd done nothing to her. I was cordial with everyone I worked with.

"Haven't you been there for ten years?"

I nodded. "Yes."

Mark grabbed some nachos as he shook his head. "You would think they'd give you a chance to respond."

I placed my head in my hands and exhaled. "I agree, but I'm not too hopeful right now."

Mark patted me on the shoulder. "You and Kyla are going through the wringer right now. How is Kyla doing with that information?"

I exhaled an exhausted breath. "I haven't talked to her about it yet."

Mark's mouth dropped open. "You need to tell her. Before someone else does."

"I know. I just don't want to add more stress to this stressful situation."

Mark took a sip of his beer. "I know it doesn't seem like it now, but it'll get better. All of this will pass over, I promise. Just stay strong."

The last thing I wanted to be right now was strong, but I held onto Mark's words of wisdom.

Chapter Seventeen

Kyla

I opened the door to my in-law's house. The smell of delicious food filled my nose. I hummed in satisfaction, my stomach growling in response. I carried the pan of green bean casserole into the house and a permanent smile that wouldn't be removed today by any means necessary.

Today was the day of thanks, and I could already feel the thankfulness lingering in the air.

Bria and Ryder ran into the house behind me,

nearly knocking me over. "Stop running," I called out.

They disappeared around the corner as Ryan walked into the house and closed the door behind him with his foot. He carried the pan that held the ham.

Bria and Ryder ran out of the kitchen.

"Stop running," Ryan announced in a stern voice.

They obliged and walked upstairs. In their grandparents' house, they had a playroom that included a flat-screen TV and mountains of toys. Their minds would stay occupied until dinner was served.

"Hey, you two," Amelia stated as we walked into the kitchen. Amelia held a tray of rolls in her hands.

"Hi, Momma."

"Hi, Amelia."

Amelia slid the tray of rolls into the oven before she wiped her hands on the pink apron wrapped around her waist. She pointed towards the kitchen table.

"Put the food on the table."

Ryan and I did as instructed and sat the food in the middle of the table. An extra chair was added to the dining room table, enough chairs for everyone invited to have a place to sit and enjoy their meal. A small table was set up in the corner of the room for Bria and Ryder to eat dinner.

"Is there anything else I can do?"

I was willing to put in all the help that I could

to have Thanksgiving run smoothly.

Amelia tapped her finger on her lip. Moments passed before she spoke. "You can help me finish the mashed potatoes. They should be done boiling any minute now."

"I'll get right on it."

I walked over to the stove and stirred the potatoes before I poked at them, trying to figure out how soft they were.

"Where's Dad?"

Ryan followed Amelia back into the kitchen. He leaned his hip against the island.

"He had to make a quick run to the convenience store."

"What did we forget to pick up from the store?" I asked as I grabbed the pot of potatoes and dumped them into a strainer. We went shopping for all the ingredients we had decided on for the meal.

"Cranberry sauce."

"Cranberry sauce wasn't on our list of items to purchase," I pointed out.

Ryan scoffed as he looked at Amelia. "Momma, you didn't put cranberry sauce on the list on purpose, did you?"

Amelia shrugged her shoulders. "We aren't a fan of it."

I looked over my shoulder at Ryan. He looked at me and smiled before he continued his conversation with his mom.

"Yeah, we aren't, but Dad loves it."

Amelia walked to the fridge and pulled out the

ingredients we would add to the potatoes.

"You're right." She looked over her shoulder at Ryan. "I love it when he proves to me every single year how much he loves that nasty sauce."

Ryan and I laughed. James was the only adult in the family to eat cranberry sauce. Somehow, he managed to convince Ryder last year to try it. Ryder's mouth twisted up into an unrecognizable expression after tasting it for the first time. Even though Ryder was James's sidekick, I doubt Ryder would be tasting it this year.

"My favorite brother has finally arrived," came a sweet voice.

Seconds later, Sophia walked into the kitchen. She was a beautiful, petite woman with dirty blonde pen-straight hair and hazel eyes. She wore a long-sleeved red shirt and plaid jeans. Even for our Thanksgiving dinner, she looked just like the stylish fashion designer she was daily.

"I'm your only brother." Ryan gave her a knowing look.

I watched while I mashed the potatoes.

Sophia smiled as she placed her hands on her hips. "Exactly. By default, you're my favorite."

They chuckled at their back-and-forth banter as they closed the distance between them. They wrapped their arms around each other, and they hugged for what seemed like an eternity.

The sight warmed my heart. Ryan and Sophia were three years apart and loved each other so much. It wasn't common to see the entire family together all the time, but holidays and special occasions brought them together to celebrate and enjoy each other's company.

Amelia bumped my hip. "You talk to your sister-in-law. I'll handle the potatoes."

"Are you sure?"

Amelia nodded. "Of course, I'm sure. Dinner will be ready in an hour."

Their hug ended, and Sophia looked over at me. Her eyes brightened as she waved her hand at me. "Hey, Kyla."

"Hey, Sophia." I walked over to her, and we squeezed each other tight. Her hair smelled of lemons, reminding me of summer.

"How's the New York fashion life treating you?" I asked.

She motioned to her outfit before she took my hands into hers. "Amazing. It's a fast-paced life, but I love the career."

"I know that's a fact."

Sophia gave my hands a squeeze before she pointed upstairs. "I can't believe my niece and nephew have grown so much since the last time I saw them."

"Tell me about it. I can't believe we have a four-year-old and a tween."

Sophia looked over at her brother. "I can believe my brother has a tween," she joked as she winked at him. She looked back at me. "I cannot believe you have a tween, though."

I winked at her. "I would love to say it's the perks of having a child at a young age."

Sophia nodded as we walked out of the kitchen and into the living room. "I won't ever know that feeling."

We sat on the couch next to each other. "You'll be a momma one day." I gave her hand a reassuring pat.

Sophia scoffed as she playfully rolled her eyes. "I know that. I won't ever know the feeling of having a child at a young age. I'll be forty in…" Sophia looked around before she continued. "Two years," she whispered as she held two fingers up in the air.

"You don't look your age at all."

Sophia beamed as her confidence boomed. "Thank you for that wonderful compliment."

The front door opened and closed. Within seconds, James walked into the living room carrying a bag. "My two favorite ladies." He walked over and hugged me as he greeted me and kissed Sophia on the forehead.

Sophia gave James a pointed look as she wagged her finger at him. "You better not tell Mom that."

"Your secret is safe with me." I smirked as I zipped my lips and threw away the invisible key.

James excused himself and walked into the kitchen.

Sophia and I spent the next fifteen minutes catching up. It was great to hear about all the opportunities as a fashion designer. As we continued talking, James, Amelia, and Ryan walked into the living room and sat down. We all joined in one conversation.

The doorbell rang, and I immediately jumped up in excitement. Only two more people were missing from our Thanksgiving dinner, and they had just arrived.

Ignoring all the talks I had told my children over the years, I ran to the door lightning fast. I opened the door and squealed as my eyes landed on Aunt Lily and her husband, Gerald.

"Aunt Lily."

I threw my arms around her neck, and we excitedly jumped up and down. Her signature perfume clung to her skin, and I inhaled it as nostalgia fluttered within.

"Kyla, I missed you," she whispered into my ear as she rubbed my back in a circular motion.

James, Amelia, Sophia, and Ryan walked to the front door to greet our guests as I waved hi to Gerald.

Gerald smiled as he waved back. This was progress. Aunt Lily usually came to visit by herself. Somehow, she managed to talk him into spending Thanksgiving with us.

Aunt Lily grabbed the bottles from Gerald. "We come bearing wine."

She held both of them up to show the bottles they had bought.

Sophia took the bottles of wine from Aunt Lily and kissed her on the cheek. "This is my type of lady."

We all walked into the living room, James closing the door. We entered the dining room after Ryan called for Bria and Ryder to come downstairs.

We sat at the table as glasses of wine were poured for the adults and apple juice for the children. Ryan sat to my left, Aunt Lily to my right.

"Who wants to start off the family tradition?" James said, scanning the table.

"What's this tradition?" Gerald asked.

Ryan spoke up. "We all go around the table and say one thing that we're grateful for before we eat dinner."

Aunt Lily raised her hand. "I'd love to start."

"Go ahead, Lily."

Amelia smiled, waiting for Aunt Lily's response.

"I'm thankful for Tree Branch. Without it, I would've never met my wonderful niece."

Aunt Lily grabbed my hand and gave it a squeeze. She leaned over and kissed me on the cheek.

Tree Branch was the website we used for Aunt Lily and me to locate each other and connect. That was the best decision I had ever made.

"I'm thankful for my thirty years of marriage with Liliana." Gerald took a sip of his wine. "I couldn't have asked for a better wife to love."

We smiled at Gerald's response. Gerald was an introvert, so it was great to have him engage in conversation with us.

"I'm next." James raised his hand in the air as he smiled. "I'm thankful for the gift of life."

We all nodded in agreement. It was great just to sit and be thankful for the life we were given.

"I'm thankful for my career. Designing clothes keeps me sane."

"We know," Amelia, James, Ryan, and I muttered simultaneously, causing an eruption of laughter to travel through the room.

Once the laughter died down, I spoke.

"I'm thankful for my second chance at life. I can't thank anyone else but God for allowing me to live to see another day. If it weren't for God, I wouldn't have had Ryder, and I wouldn't have seen Bria grow into the beautiful almost tween we see today."

Ryan grabbed my hand and gave it a squeeze before he kissed my forehead.

"I'm thankful for the extra daughter I inherited years ago." Amelia looked around the table before she looked at me. "I couldn't have asked for a better woman to have shown my son what love could do to a person."

"Thank you." Amelia's kind words meant the world to me.

"I'm thankful for my mommy and daddy. They're the best parents. They treat me like a princess," Bria called out. Bria tapped Ryder's arm. "Ryder, what are you thankful for?"

The room fell silent. All eyes on Ryder, he looked around the room. "Food."

Ryder's one-word response caused yet another eruption of laughter to echo in the dining room. Ryder was something else.

"Last but I'm hoping not least, it's my turn." Ryan took a sip of his wine before he cleared his throat. "I'm thankful for everyone that has gathered for our Thanksgiving dinner. With how busy Sophia's schedule is, it's rare for us all to gather like this nowadays, but I'm thankful for this family time. Happy Thanksgiving, everyone." Ryan lifted his wine glass in the air.

"Happy Thanksgiving."

We all raised our wine glasses and clinked them together before we took sips.

"Who's ready for turkey and ham?" James called out as he rubbed his hands together.

"What about the sides?" Sophia raised an eyebrow.

James rolled his eyes, a smirk on his face. "Who's ready for turkey, ham and sides?" James repeated, adding on sides.

"Me," Ryder screamed.

"No screaming, Ryder." I turned in my seat, and I shook my finger at him.

We passed the food around the table. I prepared my plate along with Bria and Ryder's plates. After placing their plates in front of them, we all dived into our food. Moans of admiration and satisfaction traveled throughout the room.

"This green bean casserole is to die for. Amelia, did you make it?" Aunt Lily asked.

Amelia pointed her fork at me. "Kyla made it this year."

Aunt Lily looked at me and smiled. "You did great."

"Thank you."

Aunt Lily cut into her turkey and took a bite. "I never told you this before, but you received the cooking gene from your momma."

"Why not from you?" I asked.

"I'll tell you why." Gerald chimed in around a mouth full of food. "She can burn water, and I never thought that was possible."

We laughed at his revelation. Gerald didn't speak much, but when he did, whatever was to come out of his mouth was always unexpected.

Aunt Lily playfully hit him on the arm before she continued talking. "I'm not the best cook. Your mom, though, I can't even explain how amazing her food was."

It was always wonderful to hear great things about my mom. Even though I didn't have any knowledge or memories of her, hearing Aunt Lily talk about her made me feel like I knew her.

Amelia asked Aunt Lily and Gerald about their trip to Hawaii. Gerald grabbed his phone and showed us several pictures. The children's eyes lit up with excitement when they saw the clear, pristine beaches. The beaches here in South Carolina were hours away from us, so Ryder hadn't had the opportunity to go to the beach. The last time Bria had seen the beach in person was before we left Florida six years ago. Our next family trip would be to Hawaii. I couldn't wait until we all could experience a few days of uninterrupted paradise.

A hand was placed on my knee. I turned to

see Ryan looking at me. He had a sincere look in his eyes.

"Can I tell you something?"

"You can tell me anything." I forked mashed potatoes into my mouth.

"I'm thankful for you being my wife. I couldn't have asked for a better woman to love me. You showed me the affection I never knew I needed until the day I locked eyes with you." He looked away for a few seconds. He exhaled before he looked back at me. "I promise to keep you and our family safe." Ryan kissed my forehead several times. I knew Ryan would. I knew he would do that the day I said "I do" to him. The reassurance meant the world to me. We joined the group conversation as we ate.

"Dessert, anyone?" Sophia asked as she carried two pies from the kitchen counter and sat them on the table. One was pecan pie, and the other was pumpkin pie.

"Did you make them?" Gerald asked as I brought in the plates for dessert.

"Yes. They took me about an hour to perfect."

Sophia and I cut the pies into slices before we sat and dug in.

"Sophia. You have to share your recipe." Ryan moaned, his mouth full of pecan pie.

"No way. I won't share my recipe with you." She took a bite of her pecan pie before she pointed at me. "I'll share with my sister, though."

Ryan shrugged. "Works for me. I love it when she cooks for me."

To hear Sophia call me her sister was heartwarming. I finished my pumpkin pie and realized Sophia was the older sister I never had that I always wanted.

After finishing dessert, we moved our gathering to the living room, where we turned on music and played games.

This is what I had always dreamed of. Having fun, joking, and laughing while being surrounded by family. Partaking in holiday celebrations with loved ones near. I couldn't have asked for a better Thanksgiving.

Chapter Eighteen

Brad

Look at them. While they were happy, I sat back in envy   while I sat in my toasty car. I hated to admit it, but I was jealous. Jealous of the man who took my girlfriend away from me. He made her his wife, while I was afraid to make that lifetime commitment.

I now see what a huge mistake I made. I should've married Kyla right after high school, but I couldn't let go of the single life. At nineteen, I was too young to be married. That wasn't considered cool. Looking back, that was foolish of me. I was now twenty-nine, and while everyone else had gone off and married and had kids, I had a daughter I couldn't see and no wife.

My heart wrenched as I watched Kyla closely, yet I couldn't touch her. If only she wasn't so beautiful, I could probably leave her alone. She has a hold on me that I didn't think was possible. She was like a drug. I couldn't get enough of her.

Ryan didn't deserve Kyla. I followed him to work one day and saw how his coworker threw herself at him. He did a wonderful job pretending to be disgusted by her, but I was sure once he got her into his office, he threw her on top of his desk and gave it to her good.

It was nice to see Kyla and Bria while they played touch football in the backyard. It was freezing cold, so I was glad they had thick coats and gloves on to stay warm. For me, it was torturous. I wasn't used to this South Carolina winter, and I shivered my butt off behind the tree across the road as I held a pair of binoculars to my eyes. I made a mental note to purchase a pair of gloves as my hands were frozen by the end of their game.

I couldn't believe how big Bria was. She was turning into such a beautiful young girl. Ten years old. The last time I saw her, she was Ryder's size. How had I missed out on five years of her life? Did she still remember me, or did Kyla brainwash her of any great memories?

I thought my day of investigation was over when Ryan and Kyla came back outside thirty minutes after they went inside. This had to be an important call for them to come outside and sit under the gazebo. This call had to be private for the children not to hear. Who were they talking to? What did they discuss?

After that call ended, they talked for a few minutes before they went inside for the night. I wish I had the audio of that call. It would make my life easier. If only Kyla knew what Ryan was doing behind her back.

My next stakeout led me to the coffee shop that Kyla used to work at. I couldn't believe she was now an accountant. I always knew Kyla was smart. I just didn't allow her to reach her full potential. That was my screw-up.

Kyla met up with her mother-in-law. As they hugged, I could see their love. My heart shattered in my chest. She used to hug my mother just like that. I bet she hadn't had contact with my mother since before I went to prison.

The coffee shop was too small for me to go inside and listen in on their conversation, so I stayed inside my car and just watched. They were only in there for an hour before they called it a night and went their separate ways.

Spying on Ryan and his best friend in the bar was rather easy. The only issue with that setup was that I came with the sports group that cheered every five seconds, so I wasn't able to listen to their conversations. I blended in great with the group, so Ryan didn't even recognize me. Maybe it had to do with the black baseball cap I had tight on my head to shield my face. Ryan looked defeated, and that placed so much joy in my heart.

What didn't bring me joyful cheers was having Thanksgiving dinner alone. My Thanksgiving dinner consisted of dried-up flavorless turkey, stuffing that tasted of day old, and chewy vegetables. Diners could serve up a great cheeseburger, but they needed to give up on the holiday dinners.

Sadly, I couldn't scope out their Thanksgiving in person. It was hosted at his parent's house, and they lived in a gated community. I couldn't get in, so I had to sit back in my hotel room and stalk Kyla's social media from my burner account.

When I scrolled through all the pictures, I couldn't believe my eyes. Not only did their entire family come together for this event, Kyla's aunt and her husband came into town.

Once I learned Kyla had connected with her aunt, I had to investigate. I learned her mother had passed away when Kyla was just a baby. It hurt me that Kyla would never have the opportunity to know her mother or her father. Liliana was the closest relative she had. Kyla was all about family. She would hold on to Liliana tight.

They were a big, happy family. Me. On the other hand, I had nobody. I didn't have any family to celebrate with. I didn't have any friends. The only thing I had was a bank account full of money and nobody to spend it on.

Boy, how badly I wanted to spend that money on my family. Kyla and Bria were mine. All they'll ever be is mine. They could pose and put smiles on their faces with that family now. What they didn't know was that their time with them would come to a screeching halt. I was out of prison. I was capable and willing to provide and take care of them. They had to come back home. They had no other choice.

I had to kick my plan up another notch. In a few months, they'll be back home with me.

I put everything on that.

Chapter Nineteen

Kyla

Lauren sat on the couch and tucked her feet beneath her butt as she threw a blanket over her body.

"This hangout is long overdue."

Lauren and I took an impromptu day off from work to hang out with Sabrina.

"I would have to agree." Sabrina lounged beside me on the chaise.

We were in Lauren's one-bedroom luxurious

apartment having girls' time. We were cuddled up close to the fireplace that gave off a nice, toasty warmth. If it were spring or summer, we'd be in our bikinis as we sat around the pool with a glass of Arnold Palmer. Since it was cold outside, we were stuck inside.

Sabrina, Lauren, and I hadn't hung out since we went to the nightclub that night. What I could remember of our night, we had fun. It was just the end of the night that was a black hole. A black hole for all of us.

"We work around your schedule, Ms. Celebrity," I commented as I winked at her.

Sabrina laughed as she tucked a strand of hair behind her ear. "I wouldn't go as far to say I'm a celebrity."

"Well, you are all over the TV," Lauren pointed out.

Sabrina shrugged. "I'm only on the local channels."

"You interact with other celebrities," I chimed in.

"That's in my job description. That's the reason we have such high views and great ratings."

"How do you like being on TV?" Lauren asked as she rubbed her hands together to generate warmth.

"It's fun. It's exciting." Sabrina smiled, but the smile didn't reach her eyes.

"Why do I feel like there is a but coming up?" Lauren asked as she placed her hands in front of the fire.

I knew Sabrina like the back of my hand, and I could tell something bothered her. I could hear it in her tone, and I was ready for her to come out and say what was wrong.

"Do you ever sit and think about the decisions you've made in life?" Sabrina asked.

"All the time," Lauren responded.

"Of course," I spoke up.

Sabrina nodded before she looked at her nails. To my surprise, her purple nail polish had chips in them. Sabrina didn't allow her nails to have chips in them.

"Sabrina," Lauren called out.

Sabrina looked at Lauren. Worry was etched into her facial expressions.

"Are you okay?" I asked.

Sabrina looked at me. "Sometimes, I'm not sure if I chose the right career."

"Don't you love your job?" Lauren asked.

"I do." Sabrina tucked a strand of hair behind her ears. Her hair had grown about two inches since her last haircut. "I can't express how much I love it."

I was confused. "What's the problem?"

"I feel like it's taking a toll on my family."

I understood where Sabrina was going with this conversation.

"It's the time apart, isn't it?" Lauren asked.

Sabrina nodded as she exhaled. "That's the issue."

I hated to see Sabrina struggle with what she

wanted to do with her career. "I've known you for quite some time. Since I first met you, I knew you were a family-oriented woman."

"How did you know?"

I smiled as I rubbed her back. "The brightness in your eyes when you talked about your family."

"Well, you're right about that," Sabrina said, a hint of a smile appearing.

"But I know you've always wanted to pursue this career."

"That's what makes it difficult for me. On the one hand, I love my job. It's a dream come true. On the other hand, the time away from my family is taking a toll on me. I feel alone even when I'm surrounded by people."

I reached my hand over to Sabrina and gave her a hand a comforting squeeze. "What're you going to do?"

"I haven't decided yet."

"Well, whatever you do, we support you one hundred percent," Lauren said.

Sabrina smiled. "Thank you for allowing me to vent."

"You never have to thank us for that," I responded for Lauren and me.

"How does it feel being back home?" Lauren asked Sabrina.

Sabrina came into town for a week in November to spend Thanksgiving with her family. Thankfully, for the month of December, she only had to film for the first two weeks of the month.

She'd be able to spend Christmas and New Years back home.

"It feels amazing. I missed my family so much."

"Believe me, they missed you too. They came over for dinner a few times while you were out of town."

"You're having dinner without me?" Sabrina shot me a look.

"It's only dinner," I responded as I playfully swatted her hand.

"I'm only kidding. I'm glad there's a friendship without me having to be around."

I agreed. "There's no other choice. Bria and Emily are attached at the hip. Even if you and I weren't friends, we'd still be forced to be around each other."

"You're right about that."

"Where was my invite?" Lauren folded her arms across her chest as she looked over at me.

"When do you ever need an invitation to come over? You usually barge over whenever you feel the desire."

Lauren laughed and smirked as she nodded her head. "That's true."

"Exactly." I winked at her.

"So, what have my girls been up to?" Sabrina grabbed her cup of coffee off the coffee table beside her before she took a sip. "Fill me in on all the juicy details."

"Well, Lauren is head over heels for her new boy toy," I blurted out.

"New boy toy?" Sabrina wiggled her eyebrows. "He must be the perfect package for Lauren."

"Hey, let me tell my story."

"Fine, go right ahead." I grabbed my cup of tea and took a sip.

Lauren told us how she met Xavier. She told us about their first two dates that I was aware of. "Our third date was perfect." Lauren beamed as she brought her hand up to her chest. "Thursday night of last week, he invited me over to his house. We had the perfect night over a romantic candlelit dinner."

"Aww," Sabrina and I cooed.

Lauren blushed as she flipped her wavy hair over her shoulder. "He even cooked my favorite meal."

"He cooked you a medium rare steak and oven-roasted potatoes?" I asked as I sat my cup back on the coffee table.

Lauren nodded and smiled.

"He's a keeper," Sabrina pointed out.

"Are you considering the unspoken L-word?" I asked.

"Like?" Lauren asked, playing clueless.

"No girlfriend. We're talking about love," Sabrina stated as she winked.

Lauren shrugged. "It's still too early in our relationship to tell."

"Oh my gosh. You didn't tell me you made it official." I gasped. "How did you keep it a secret?"

"I wanted to make sure it was real. Besides,

we made it official during dinner. It's only been a week."

"I'm so happy for you," Sabrina stated, her eyes glinting with happiness.

"Lauren finally has the girlfriend title," I gushed in excitement.

Lauren removed her blanket and sat it next to her on the couch.

"Now that we are done talking about me, we need to talk about this book we just finished."

Sabrina exhaled as she playfully rolled her eyes. "I didn't agree to talk about books today."

"How are we friends with her?" Lauren pointed at Sabrina.

I shrugged. "Your guess is as good as mine."

Sabrina, Lauren, and I continued to talk for the next few hours. It was great to get together with my girls and have a great time. We laughed so much that a twinge of pain went through our stomachs from laughing so hard. We smiled so much that it caused our cheeks to ache. The only person missing in action was Amy, but she was here with us in spirit.

When the afternoon rolled around, we exchanged goodbyes.

Sabrina and I walked out together. I looked around the area, and there wasn't anything out of sorts. Honestly, it was too cold for Brad to lurk in the shadows, but I wouldn't put anything past him. Anything he set his mind to, he would do it.

My stomach growled as I left Lauren's neighborhood. Nothing would be better on this cold day than a hot bowl of soup.

I parked and walked inside. For midafternoon, the restaurant was busy. Everyone had the idea of soup to combat this cold winter day.

I joined the line, and within minutes, a bowl of creamy tomato soup sat in front of me. I rubbed my hands together in anticipation as I grabbed my spoon. Once the spoon of soup had cooled down, I scooped it into my mouth, closed my eyes, and moaned in satisfaction.

"Hello, Kyla."

I opened my eyes, and my heart dropped into the pit of my stomach. My hunger was replaced with nausea. Michael stood, dressed in a blue suit, with a bowl of soup in his hands.

He placed the bowl of soup on the table. As he sat, I stood.

"Get away from me," I said.

Michael scrunched his eyebrows as he placed his hands up in a defensive manner. "What's wrong with you?"

"Are you serious right now?" I asked as I folded my arms across my chest.

All noise in the shop ceased. I looked around, and every pair of eyes were on me.

"Yes, I'm serious." Michael nodded. "What's wrong with you?"

I lowered my voice, but I kept my stern tone. "What happened that night at the nightclub? How did..." I stopped my spew of words. I didn't want to mention Brad. Michael didn't even know Brad.

"How did you know I was going to be there?"

Michael was silent, deep in thought. He shrugged. "I didn't know you would be there. I decided to go out after an intense work week and have a great night."

"Why were you all over me?" I asked as the restaurant continued its murmur.

The attention was diverted from me.

Michael smirked as he shook his head. "I should be the one to complain, but I'm not."

What? What did he mean by that? I was confused. I took a step back. "What do you mean?"

Michael motioned for me to sit. "Please sit and eat your soup. It's getting cold."

What in the hell? I was concerned about a night I didn't remember, and he was concerned about my soup getting cold. Who was this man? Was his name really Michael? Was he really a lawyer? Or was everything he told me from the first day we met a lie? Why would he lie? I didn't know him. I didn't know anything about him. He had pushed his interest on me. Not once had I shown him any interest.

I exhaled. Why was he being difficult? What were his intentions? They seemed ill-willed at this point. "What do you mean you should be the one to complain?"

Michael dropped his spoon into his bowl, his chicken noodle soup splashing the table. He gave me a pointed look and his eyes darkened. "Sit down, Kyla."

I looked around. A few sets of eyes were on me. I pulled the chair out as far as it could go, and I sat.

"What do you mean you should be the one to complain?" I repeated.

Michael rubbed the stubble on his chin. "You were all over me that night."

The blood drained from my face as my mouth dropped open. "What? There's no way." I shook my head.

Michael nodded as he ate more of his soup. "Yes way. You had one too many drinks I see." He winked as he took a sip of his drink.

I couldn't believe his words. I refused to believe them. I would never betray Ryan. I would never disrespect him. Something wasn't adding up.

"What are you saying?"

Michael exhaled. "You were the aggressor." He shrugged. "I just didn't want to take advantage of a drunk woman." He looked me dead in the eyes. "So, are you going to play hard to get or finally cave in?"

I became hot all over as I stood, grabbed my purse, and ran out the door.

I couldn't handle this. I couldn't handle this. I couldn't handle this.

Brad wasn't right in the head. Michael wasn't right in the head. But why? What was happening? Why was everything going to crap since Brad was released?

I sped home while I racked my brain. No

matter how hard I tried, I couldn't remember that night. It wasn't often that I let my guard down. I regret it deep in my heart. Brad was there that night. Brad waited until I was vulnerable to take inappropriate pictures. Brad was out to ruin me.

As I approached my house, I saw Ryan's car in the driveway. Why was Ryan home so early? He didn't get off for another few hours.

I parked and I walked inside.

"Ryan, I'm home" I called out as I took my coat and shoes off.

I walked into the living room and Ryan lounged on the couch. He wore sweatpants and a long-sleeved shirt. A crime show played on the TV. "Hello, Beautiful."

"Why are you off so early?" I asked as I sat beside him.

He kissed me on the cheek as he wrapped his arm around my waist. "Something happened."

I looked at Ryan. His expression was hard as stone. He was serious.

"What happened?"

"I lost my job."

Chapter Twenty

Ryan

"What?"

Kyla stood.

She stared at me.

She was shocked.

She had every right to be. Hell, I was shocked.

"I lost my job," I repeated.

I knew I didn't have to. Kyla knew exactly

what I said. I didn't have to repeat myself. Why I repeated myself was beyond me.

Maybe repeating it would help me process the words. I still didn't understand what happened. I doubt I'd ever understand.

I went to work that morning, just like it was any regular day. Since I was confronted by Timothy two months ago, I stopped all communication with Veronica. If I were in the break room having lunch and she walked in, I would cut my lunch short, pack my lunch up, and leave. The only time we'd talk was if it was work-related. I didn't even exchange good morning or have a wonderful weekend with her anymore. I did everything I possibly could to keep my job safe, but when Timothy knocked on my door at ten that morning, I knew my time at the company had come to an end.

Timothy walked into my office, closed the door, and sat. The look on his face was far from cheerful. He looked depressed, and I had never seen him like this before.

"Ryan, we need to talk."

I nodded as I looked down at my desk. This would be the last time I'd sit at my desk in my precious office that I put in overtime to have. I looked up to meet his eyes.

"What do we need to discuss?"

I didn't know why I said we. I was sure the conversation would be one-sided, just like the last one we had.

Timothy exhaled as he clasped his hands

together. He looked around the room as he avoided eye contact with me. He'd never acted like this with me before, so I knew it was my time.

Ten years down the drain.

I took a sip of my coffee as I waited for him to find his words.

"There have been more allegations—"

I interrupted him. "With all due respect, will you let me speak this time?"

I didn't care to hear what he had to say if he didn't hear me out about the allegations. The false allegations.

Timothy shrugged. "The floor is all yours."

Finally.

He would hear my side of the story. He'd hear the truth even if it was too late and his mind was already made up.

"The allegations are false. I have never pursued Veronica, and I never will."

I exhaled. I shouldn't have to discuss this issue. This was not my character, and he knew it. I just didn't understand why he didn't believe me.

"I have a wife I love. I have two children I love. I provide for them, feed them, clothe them, and put a roof over their head with this job ."

I let those words sink in. He had to understand that I'd never do anything to jeopardize my position in the company. "You have to believe me when I say I did not do what I was accused of."

Timothy studied me before he looked away. He nodded before he stood.

"I respect the hell out of you, Ryan."

I nodded, but those words meant nothing to me. The words that followed shattered me from the inside out.

"I wish you the best of luck in your future endeavors. I have to let you go. Pack your things. You must leave."

Kyla looked at me, concern heavy in her eyes. "Why did you lose your job? What happened?"

I looked down in disgust. I hadn't talked to Kyla about what had happened these past two months. She was already going through enough with Brad's release. I didn't want her to have to worry about another issue. I thought I could've solved this issue on my own, but I should've known Veronica wouldn't stop.

"There were false accusations…" I trailed off.

How did I tell my wife I was fired because of Veronica's lies?

Kyla held her hands up. "Ryan, don't beat around the bush. Just come out and tell me what happened."

I nodded. I didn't have any reason not to tell Kyla what happened.

"I was fired because Veronica falsely accused me of coming onto her."

Kyla raised an eyebrow, but she stayed quiet. She looked around the living room before she looked at me.

"Veronica?"

"You met her at the party."

"Oh." Kyla nodded her head. "Wait. Why would she accuse you of such a thing?"

I shrugged. "I don't know. That's what I've been trying to figure out for the last two months."

"Wait." Kyla took a step back. "Last two months?"

Oh boy. I messed up. Royally. I should've told her the first time I was accused, but I wanted to deal with the situation on my own. She didn't need to worry about it.

I nodded. "Yes, two months."

Kyla scoffed as she shook her head. She folded her arms across her chest. "Why didn't you tell me?"

I stood, and I approached her.

"You're worried about Brad and what he's planning next. I didn't think you needed to know about this. I thought I had it under control. I thought I handled it."

She shook her head. "You had it under control, all right." Her voice was sarcastic, but I ignored it. Kyla had every right to be mad. Hell, I was mad at myself. I shouldn't have kept this from her. If things had gone in another direction, this whole thing could've wreaked havoc on our marriage. I didn't even want to think about the alternative.

"I'm sorry for not telling you." I grabbed her hands. "Can you forgive me?"

"I'm not mad at you." She guided us to the couch, and we sat. "I'm mad at the situation. Did you try to talk to Timothy?"

"Yes." I gave her hands a gentle squeeze. "He didn't want to hear anything I had to say."

Kyla was silent, deep in thought. "Why wouldn't he believe you? You're one of his best employees. You didn't have your position all these years for nothing."

I agree. "Exactly. I'm just as confused as you are."

Kyla stood, and she paced. Whenever Kyla paced, she was piecing things together.

"Something isn't right."

More silence.

I smiled as I admired the beautiful woman I made my wife five years ago. How did I get so lucky to have met her? I had gone to Meg's maybe once a week before she started. After I saw her for the first time, I turned that once-a-week visit into an everyday thing. Just so I could see her and talk to her every day. I could tell she was standoffish, but I wanted to find out why. I wanted to know what made her that way. Now I knew everything about her.

"But what could it be?" I asked.

Kyla stopped walking and pointed at me. "She gave you a look at the party, but I didn't think twice about it then." She exhaled. "Now, I think she meant something by it."

I scrunched my eyebrows. "I'm not following."

"Have she ever come onto you?"

I shrugged. Veronica had made small comments over the past year, but I ignored them. I knew that if I didn't entertain her, she would stop.

I didn't think she would resent me for not pursuing her. I never thought this day would come.

Kyla narrowed her eyes at me. "How long has this been going on?"

"She's made comments here and there, but it didn't get bad until two months ago. That's when she falsely accused me."

A lightbulb went off in Kyla's head. She gasped as she shook her head. "I underestimated Brad."

Brad? What did Brad have to do with this situation? What did Brad have to do with Veronica?

"I'm not understanding."

Kyla sat beside me, and she placed her hand on my leg. "Brad doesn't just want Bria back. He wants me back as well."

I stayed silent, waiting for more of an explanation.

"He probably hired Veronica to seduce you, hoping you'd fall for the bait. Then he'd have proof that you aren't the man for me so he could come in and rescue me."

I motioned air quotations.

Kyla's explanation made zero sense, but I didn't admit it.

"Veronica has worked with my company for about three years. She didn't just come around two months ago."

"Didn't you say it got bad around the time Brad got out of prison?"

I nodded. Kyla was right. Veronica's flirting

was harmless until around the time Brad told Kyla he was released. Once Brad's intention was learned, Veronica's flirting turned into a false allegation to Timothy.

"I underestimated him."

Brad managed to get me fired a week before Christmas. The house had been decorated with Christmas lights, and the tree stood six feet tall, yet I didn't feel festive anymore. He was relentless in his fight to get Kyla and Bria back. He just didn't know that I'd never give my family up. He had his chance to be a great father to Bria and a great boyfriend to Kyla. He might've been a great father to Bria, but he was a horrible boyfriend to Kyla. I refused to allow Bria to watch that mental, physical, and psychological abuse again.

Kyla leaned her head against my shoulder. "I did as well."

I wrapped my arm around her shoulder as I thought about our options.

"I can't believe you were fired. What are we going to do?"

I looked at Kyla. "We are going to keep doing what we've been doing."

She gave me a weird look. "We've gone from a two-income household to a one-income household. It's hard to just keep doing what we are doing," she pointed out.

Kyla was right. Kyla had a great income at her job, but I was the main bread winner.

"The wonderful thing is our house is paid off.

Our cars are paid off. We have a huge savings account, and we don't need to make any big purchases anytime soon. We will be fine until I can get a job."

"Will it be hard for you to get another job? With the allegation out there?"

I didn't even think of that. I didn't want to think of the type of damage that could do to my background. I just hoped If I did go for another job and they contacted Timothy, he would be honest about my work ethic. He had to know deep down inside that I'd never do anything to jeopardize my job.

"I hope not."

I refused to sit around the house and do nothing. I wanted to work, I was a workaholic, but it was time to focus. Brad put in overtime to get me fired, but I had to work harder to put an end to his games.

Kyla stayed silent. I didn't like that we were stumped. All because of Brad and his obsession with my wife. Why couldn't he get another obsession? Why couldn't he just leave us alone?

"I think Michael and Brad might be connected."

"Michael? Who's Michael?" I asked.

I remembered that Kyla had mentioned the name before, but now, I couldn't make a connection.

"The lawyer I told you about."

I stayed silent, the familiarity bells not going off.

"The one that bought my lunch a while back at Tony's."

Still nothing.

Kyla pulled up the text messages on her phone and showed the pictures that Brad had sent to her.

"Oh." The man who showed interest in my wife. "It's possible." I shrugged. "Yes, I could see that. Considering every picture Brad had to blackmail you with has this man in it."

Kyla chuckled as she put her head in her hands. "Michael honestly convinced me that he was a lawyer."

I raised my eyebrows. "How so?"

"He convinced me when he said that 'he puts the bad guys away'." Kyla added air quotations as she rolled her eyes.

Ryan chuckled. "He sucked you in with that statement."

"Yes." I nodded. "Yes, he did."

I closed my eyes and imagined what my life was like three months ago. Before Brad wreaked havoc on our lives.

"Brad must've gone through a lot to set all of this up."

Kyla nodded. "Now you know what I had to deal with."

My heart went out to Kyla. She had already gone through enough in her relationship with him. Now, she was going through hell again because they released him early. Didn't they see he was a menace to society? Why were the courts the only ones that didn't see it?

"I do." I kissed her forehead. "I'm going to put an end to it. If it's the last thing that I do."

Chapter Twenty-One

Kyla

Christmas Eve was upon us, and the decorations around me wouldn't allow my festive mood to die down. I checked the time, and the plane should've just landed.

Amy, Alexander, and Julia decided to spend Christmas with my family this year. I'm sure it was Alexander's Christmas present to Amy to spend Christmas with her childhood best friend since we hadn't done that since I was forced out of foster care.

I knew they'd be tired from their three-and-a-half-hour flight from Arkansas. I didn't want them to have to wait around until they could get a rental. I would surprise them when they got off the plane.

Something brushed against my left leg. I turned and looked down. I shrieked as I knelt and wrapped my arms around Julia.

"Hi, sweetie."

I picked Julia up and spun her around. Julia was Amy's twin. The only difference was Julia had green eyes like Alex.

"Hi, Aunt Kyla."

"I missed you so much." I cradled her head on my shoulder. Her strawberry-scented shampoo surrounded me.

"I missed you."

A giggle from close by pulled my eyes away from Julia. I looked into light brown eyes. Light brown eyes that belonged to my childhood best friend.

"I guess I'm chopped liver?" Amy joked as she tucked a strand of her bob-length, red hair behind her ear.

"Amy."

I put Julia down before I ran into Amy's outstretched arms. My emotions took over, and tears streamed down my face as I rubbed Amy's back. It had been two years since we had seen each other. It didn't occur to me how hard it was not to see her until I had reunited with her.

"It's so great to see you."

Amy and I separated. Her face was wet with tears. I grabbed my emergency pack of Kleenex out of my purse. I handed her one and grabbed one for myself.

"I know. It's been too long since we've been together."

I didn't want to go this long without seeing her again.

I looked around Amy, and I saw Alex, loaded down with the luggage.

"Hello, Alex."

Alex sat the luggage down, and we hugged.

"I didn't know you were going to pick us up," Amy said.

I smiled. "My best friend wasn't going to rent a car when I'm more than capable of picking you up."

I wrapped my arm around Amy and held Julia's hand as we walked out of the airport and into the chilly winter. I looked around the crowded parking lot in search of a lurking eye, but I didn't see any. I was grateful for that.

"I'm so excited to spend Christmas together."

I beamed as we walked towards my car in the parking lot. "It's been almost ten years," I pointed out.

"Aunt Kyla." Julia tugged on my hand.

"Yes, Sweetie?"

She beamed as she gave my hand a squeeze. "Did you get me a Christmas present?"

Amy spoke up. "Honey, Kyla might not have

had the chance to buy you a present this year.”

Amy and Alex were aware that Ryan had lost his job a few days ago. We took a look at our finances and figured that my income alone would cover our bills, but we decided to cut back on our spending until Ryan got another job, so we didn't have to worry about dipping into our savings. Even though we decided to cut back, we wouldn't make changes to our Christmas plans.

Julia pouted as she looked at the ground.

“Sweetie, you already opened your presents back home,” Alex chimed in. “Remember, you brought along your two favorite dolls.”

“But I wanted to open presents on Christmas day,” Julia whined.

I chuckled. “Sweetie, I didn't buy you a present.”

Julia scrunched her eyes together.

I gave her hand a squeeze. “I bought you three presents.”

“Yay,” she called out as we approached my car.

“You didn't have to do that,” Amy said as Alex loaded the suitcases in the trunk.

“Yes, I did.”

I couldn't have them over for Christmas and not provide gifts. That would be unethical if it already wasn't.

“I hope you didn't buy us anything,” Alex said as he closed the trunk.

“Well, did you two buy us something?” I asked as we piled into my car. We had a thirty-minute drive to complete, and it would go in a breeze. Any time spent with my best friend always sped by in the blink of an eye.

"Of course, we did," Amy answered as we left the airport.

I laughed. "Well, you know I couldn't go without getting you two something for Christmas."

Amy gasped as she playfully slapped my thigh. "You shouldn't have."

"This is our first Christmas together in a very long time. I couldn't help myself."

Amy smiled as she looked out the window.

"So, are you tired from the flight, or are you ready to get this party started?" I asked as we got onto the interstate.

"When you say party, does this party consist of food? Because I'm starved."

Amy rubbed my stomach for emphasis.

I tapped her fingers on the steering wheel as I looked over at her. "The party does consist of food. For some reason, I thought you were going to request wine."

Amy wiggled her eyebrows. "Having a glass of wine with you sounds perfect."

"What is wine?" Julia asked from the back seat.

Amy and I exchanged a look.

Alex spoke up from the back seat. "Wine is a drink that only adults are allowed to drink."

"Why is it only for adults?" Julia continued with her questions.

Alex responded to her question before Amy

and I dived into what we would do for the rest of the day.

"How does hanging out around a toasty firepit and eating toasted sandwiches sound?"

"Sounds like a dream."

Once we pulled into the driveway, Ryan opened the front door, and my children ran out the door.

Everyone hugged and greeted one another before Alex and Ryan carried their luggage into the house.

The children ran upstairs while we got acquainted in the living room. Amy and Alex sat on one couch. Ryan and I sat on the other couch.

"Thank you for having us over for Christmas," Amy said.

Ryan placed his hand on mine. "You're family. We wouldn't have it any other way."

Alex spoke. "Even with everything going on, you're still smiling."

Ryan and I smiled at each other.

"We have to," I began.

Ryan exhaled. "We know Brad would want us to be sad and depressed."

I agreed. "Brad won't get what he wants, no matter how hard he tries."

Alex wrapped his arm around Amy's shoulder. "Amy has been so worried about you."

Amy looked at Alex and smiled. She leaned her head against his shoulder. "I have been," she admitted.

"But I knew you two would be fine."

I nodded. "We are going to keep our heads up."

Ryan pointed at himself. "I refuse to allow Brad's manipulative ways to ruin what we've built together." Ryan looked at me. "Brad did so much damage while he was with Kyla. I worked hard to undo that damage so she could see how worthy she is." He lifted my chin, and our eyes met. "You are worthy."

My heart. How could this amazing man be so wonderful? He loved me with all his heart, and I loved him with the same intensity.

I leaned forward, and I kissed him. The same fireworks I had felt for the past five years were set off, and I could never get enough of this feeling.

"Aww," Amy chorused as she brought her hand to her chest. "I knew the second I met you that you were the one for my best friend."

"Forever and always. I'll never ever leave her side."

After our heartfelt exchange, Amy and I walked into the kitchen while Ryan and Alex walked outside to start the firepit. The sun had started to set, and it was getting cooler by the second. The firepit would give us the perfect warmth while we enjoyed each other's company. If this was what Christmas Eve had in store for us, I couldn't imagine what Christmas would be like.

Bria, Ryder, and Julia were too excited to fall asleep at a decent hour. Their eyes closed around 11PM, and we were able to bring out the last of the Christmas presents before we all knocked out at midnight.

Bright and early the next morning, Bria and Ryder were in our room.

"It's Christmas. Wake up. Time to open presents."

Bria squealed as she and Ryder clapped their hands. The light snapped on, illuminating the room with unwelcome brightness.

I groaned. I knew it was too early for them to get up, but I knew their excitement prevented them from sleeping another two hours.

I opened an eye, and I looked at the time. It was six thirty. Oh boy, too early to be up for a day off.

Ryan stirred next to me.

"Merry Christmas," I called out as I pushed myself up.

We had only received six and a half hours of sleep, and I needed another two and a half hours to function properly. Caffeine would be our friend that morning.

"Can we open presents now?" Ryder grabbed my hand and jumped up and down.

I yawned and stretched as Ryan rubbed the sleep out of his eyes. "Not until Grandpa and Grandma get here."

Ryder poked his lip out.

"Grandma and Grandpa has arrived," Amelia said as she walked into our bedroom.

"Grandma. Grandpa." Bria and Ryder chorused as they hugged each of them tight.

"Merry Christmas," I said as I looked around

the room.

Thankfully, we didn't have a hot and spicy night last night, and I wore a pair of appropriate pajamas.

"How come you're here so early?" Ryan asked once he sat up in bed.

"Our grandbabies wanted us here as early as possible." James beamed. "We couldn't say no to those faces."

"What about our faces?" Ryan asked as he gave puppy dog eyes.

"We can easily say it to that face." Amelia smiled.

"Present time." Bria jumped from foot to foot.

Ryan groaned. "After everyone's teeth are brushed, then we can open gifts."

Bria and Ryder walked out of the room.

"We'll be down in five minutes," I said to Amelia and James.

Amelia smiled. "Okay, Pumpkin."

"Our children never fail when it comes to waking us up super early for Christmas, do they?" Ryan asked.

"No, they don't."

Ryan and I handled our hygiene before we walked downstairs.

Alex and Amy, who slept in Bria's room, sat on the couch. They were still in their pajamas.

We all exchanged good morning and Merry Christmas.

"How long have you two been up?" I asked Amy.

Amy chuckled as she looked over at Julia. "She woke us up at five thirty."

"Yikes," Ryan responded as we sat.

"We're running on five hours of sleep." Alex held his hand up.

"It's probably more than what you used to survive on back in the college days," Ryan responded.

Alex agreed. "Definitely."

"Can we open presents now?" Julia asked.

Ryder, Bria, and Julia sat beside the Christmas tree, next to their presents.

"Yes, go ahead." Amelia had her phone out, and she was ready to snap pictures.

The adults sat back as the children ripped the wrapping paper off the gifts. The looks on the children's faces as they saw the gifts they had asked for were pure enjoyment for us. Nothing more in this world makes us happier than seeing our children happy. Their happiness completed me.

The adults exchanged gifts, and we opened them. We had all gone simple and purchased each other gift cards to various places.

We all thanked one another before Ryan, Alex, and James worked to open all the toy boxes.

Amelia, Amy, and I went into the kitchen, where we cooked breakfast.

Once we had a heap of bacon, eggs, fresh fruit, and French toast prepared, we sat and ate breakfast. Breakfast was filled with laughter and beautiful memories.

As breakfast came to an end, Amelia helped me load the dishes into the dishwasher.

"What's on your mind?" she asked.

I placed a plate into the dishwasher before I looked at her. "I'm forever grateful that Ryan and I are still positive, even with everything that has been thrown our way." I paused. "Even with Ryan losing his job, we are still afloat. I thought it would've hurt us financially, but we are still making it."

Amelia smiled. "That's what happens in a great, strong marriage, Pumpkin. Nothing, and I mean nothing, can tear you two apart." She handed me a serving spoon. "Even when you have people fighting against you, you still concur in life."

No matter how hard Brad tried to ruin our Christmas, it was the best one yet.

Chapter Twenty-Two

Brad

Sweat trickled down my back, my heart pounding in my chest. Only one set of reps left to go, and I was done with my workout.

Once I pumped my last rep, I placed the dumbbells on the rack.

I grabbed my gym bag and drained my water before I washed up in the shower. After I put on a pair of black sweatpants and a gray hoodie, I exited the gym. The cold air wrapped its tight grip around me, and I shivered.

Hopefully, there were only a few weeks left of this cold weather, and it would warm up. I drove ten minutes before I pulled into the hotel's parking lot. I had been there so long I knew every front desk attendant's name.

I walked into the breakfast buffet, poured coffee, and grabbed an apple. I was on a mission and didn't have time to sit and have a hot breakfast.

Taking the elevator to the third floor, I walked into my room. All my belongings were spread throughout. The room had even taken on my scent. Hopefully, it'll only be my home for one more month. That's all I needed to execute my plan.

I took a sip of the hot goodness out of a paper cup before walking over to my freshly washed clothes basket. I finished my laundry last night before I passed out for the night. I was down to my last pair of warm clothes, and the visit was a necessity.

With the overtime I had put in, Ryan lost his job. It was a relatively easy task on my part. I'm surprised his company had let him go so easily. From what I learned, he had worked for the company for over ten years. Why would they just let a great employee as such go like that?

I folded the clothes I had washed this morning before placing them in a neat pile. I smirked as I rubbed the stubble on my chin. Oh yeah, he was falsely accused of fraternizing with his female coworker. I didn't think Veronica could pull it off so well, but she did one hell of a job. She was the best person to convince me to help me with my plan. I saw her on the company's website and reached out for her assistance. I knew she would be the perfect person to complete the job. We agreed on a thousand dollars if she could successfully get him fired. She told me it would be her honor as he had shot her down more than once in the past. She couldn't wait to get her revenge on him, and she didn't care if she lost her job in the process. She was a trust fund baby whose dad had given her millions. She didn't have to work but worked to get out of the house. Luckily, she didn't lose her job.

When I paid her ten crisp, one-hundred-dollar bills, it was the best feeling I've had in a long time. She had her revenge for being shot down, and I had my revenge since I was the reason Ryan was jobless. I knew he felt hopeless. Now he knew how I felt in prison for five years.

The question was, why was Kyla fine with the reason Ryan lost his job? I knew I'd be upset if I were married to a man who lost his job under those circumstances. What had Ryan told Kyla to cause her not to be angry? It just didn't make sense in my mind.

Christmas was hard to endure. This was the first Christmas I had in years where I wasn't behind bars, surrounded by people who weren't in the festive mood. Instead of returning home and exchanging gifts with my family, I spent

Christmas alone this year. After some hard decisions, I had Christmas dinner at a 24-hour diner. The food wasn't Christmas-worthy, but I was hungry and had to eat.

Even though I had caused Ryan to lose his job, they still had a wonderful Christmas. Kyla picked up that annoying ass Amy from the airport, along with her family. Kyla walked out of the airport with the biggest smile on her face. To see how happy they were as they reunited annoyed me. I couldn't wait to be reunited with my family. That is what I looked forward to the most. I wanted that smile that Kyla had to be the smile she gave me once she realized we were meant to be forever.

I walked over to the grocery bag in the mini-fridge. For the first time in years, my mouth watered for alcohol. Luckily, I had prepared myself for this moment. I knew this time would come. This was a stressful time for me, and alcohol was my stress reliever. I grabbed a red cup and filled it with whiskey. I took a sip and moaned. I missed the taste. I missed the burn in my throat. Boy, how did I go without alcohol for so long?

By force. Absolute force.

One half of my plan to wreak havoc worked somewhat.

Yes, Ryan had lost his job. Even though it didn't cause a strain on the marriage now, I'm sure it would cause a strain on the marriage in the future. There's no way going from a two-income household to a one-income household would not be stressful. I just hoped when Ryan went to look for another job, he wouldn't be able to get one. That would bring me ultimate satisfaction.

On the other hand, the second half of the plan crumpled to pieces. Michael was supposed to cause Ryan and Kyla's marriage to shatter to ultimate destruction. He was the biggest part of this destructive plan. The pictures I took of them together should've been the end of their relationship. Any man who saw his wife with another man on more occasions than one in different locations should've assumed his wife cheated. Ryan, on the other hand, trusted Kyla with all his might. Why hadn't I trusted Kyla in such a manner? If I had, I doubt we would've had as many problems as we did.

I swear, she was the most perfect woman I had ever encountered because no matter her situation, she was still respectful. Even when she and her friends were drunk off their asses, she still didn't do anything inappropriate.

It was simple. I had taken Kyla for granted.

I gulped down sip after sip of my whiskey. I scrunched my face up as I winced. I had to slow down. I had gone from an everyday drinker to a person who hadn't had a drink in over five years. This small amount of whiskey might've been fun and games to me before I went to jail, but now, I'm sure it might put me on my ass.

I set the cup on the table and I sat on my bed.

Ryan should've left Kyla after those pictures

were taken. He was supposed to leave Kyla in a heartbroken heap on the floor of the house they shared, but it seemed like the obstacles I had thrown at them only made them stronger. I didn't need them to be strong. I needed to weaken the walls of their marriage. I needed to do it now so I could get back what was mine. Once and for all.

I wanted to break Kyla down and build her back up. I wanted to redo everything that Ryan had done since I went to prison. I had to do it, one way or the other.

Michael wasn't the lawyer he told Kyla he was. Michael was actually a fast-food worker who aspired to be an actor. I decided to give him a chance and bought him four suits and a few pairs of shoes. Lawyer worthy at its finest. If he succeeded in breaking them up by making Kyla fall for him, he'd get a thousand dollars.

I kind of figured he wouldn't get too far with Kyla when she threw away his phone number the first day at the sandwich café, but I was still hopeful. All I needed was for him to make her fall, cheat with him on Ryan, and then break her heart.

I just hated Kyla figured out something wasn't adding up with him, so he only got paid a hundred dollars, and he could keep the nice clothes I bought him.

I was convinced that he liked her, but I was just hopeful he would've gotten the job done. He failed, but I wasn't mad at him for it. He tried, and that is all that mattered to me.

I walked over to the window, grateful for the

scenic view. Sadly, the trees were bare from the cold weather that time of the year. The trees would blossom bright and lively green leaves in a few weeks when the warm weather rolled in.

In a few weeks, I'd make my journey back to Florida with my family. We would start a new life together, and I couldn't wait for Kyla to live the life she had been missing out on. I couldn't wait for them to have a life where they were spoiled to the ends of the earth. Kyla wouldn't have to work another day in her life. I didn't want Kyla to work, I wanted her home. I wanted her to read a book a day as she relaxed, waiting for me to come home from my long day at work.

Perhaps my parents would be willing to be in our lives again if they learned all had been forgiven. Maybe Kyla was the key to bringing the entire family back together.

My body relaxed, and my mind relaxed, too. I walked over to the bed and I laid down.

It was simple. Plan A didn't work, so I didn't have any other choice but to go to Plan B.

Me: You don't want to come back, but you'll come back one way or another. I will take away something you'll never imagine living without.

Chapter Twenty-Three

Kyla

"Red rose for my Beautiful."

Ryan held out my favorite flower.

I beamed. Ryan always knew how to make me smile, even if it was as simple as a rose. I took it and inhaled its delicate, floral scent. "Thank you."

The new year was only days away. Ryan still hadn't received a job offer but had filled out several applications. Around the holidays, it wasn't as common for companies to hire, but I knew the job interviews and acceptance calls would roll in right after the new year.

Tonight, Ryan and I were out on the town. We walked for an hour as we checked out the small shops. James and Amelia had bought us a gift certificate from a hole-in-the-wall Italian restaurant for Christmas. The dinner was delightful, the best Italian cuisine I'd ever had. It was on my bucket list to come back.

The Christmas lights still hung on buildings, trees, and light posts throughout the area. The Christmas decorations wouldn't be removed until after the new year, and I was happy for it. I was still feeling festive.

Amy, Alex, and Julia left the day after Christmas. I drove them back to the airport, and it was a struggle for Amy and me to tear our arms from around each other. Even though we often talked, seeing her in person was like nothing else. The feeling of that shy girl in foster care came back, and I just needed her to come to my rescue. Before we pried our fingers from around each other, we promised we wouldn't go that long without seeing each other again. Even if it was just a random day trip, we would make it happen.

I twirled the rose between my fingers as I grabbed Ryan's hand. It was a chilly night, and we were clad in our warm clothes. Only a few more weeks to go until we were relieved of the frigid cold weather. I couldn't wait until I could wear a t-shirt and a pair of shorts outside while I sipped on a glass of freshly squeezed lemonade.

"Are you ready to go home?" Ryan asked after we walked into the last shop on the busy strip.

I looked around. There were many others with the same idea as ours tonight.

I nodded. "I'm ready."

We walked back to Ryan's car, and I exhaled once the warmth from the heater blasted us. No matter how many layers we put on, the cold weather still penetrated deep. I placed my hands in front of the heater. My hands had turned into icicles, and they started to defrost.

Ryder and Bria were over at Sabrina's house for the evening. Sabrina planned an indoor camping night where they'd slept in a tent in the living room, eat toasted smores and soup made over an open fire. The kids were so excited to camp indoors that I considered stealing that idea when it was time for us to do another camping trip.

"What are you thinking about?"

Ryan interrupted my thoughts as I looked over at him. In the darkness and the light that illuminated from the dashboard, I could see the outline of his face.

"I'm just thinking about our children."

Ryan chuckled softly. "Isn't it funny that our children are always on our minds, even when we should be focused on us?"

I agreed. "That's the beauty of having children. They rule our lives with just their existence."

Ryan and I continued to talk as we traveled home. Once we arrived, we walked into our house.

We took our shoes and coats off before we walked upstairs to our bedroom.

"I haven't heard this house this quiet in weeks," Ryan commented as he unbuttoned his shirt and pulled it over his head.

I smirked as I removed my earrings. "I don't think it's been this quiet since before Bria and I started coming over."

It was a joy to think about our first visit there. Bria walked in and made herself at home immediately. I loved how she opened up to Ryan. She took to him, and she haven't let up on her love for him since.

"You and Bria made this house a home."

My heart.

How did Ryan know exactly what to say? Ryan didn't consider too much about starting a family until he met me. Love could change a destined course in life.

I smiled as I pulled my shirt over my head and tossed it to the ground.

"For you to take Bria in and treat her like your daughter, I couldn't have asked for more from you."

For Ryan not to be Bria's biological father, he didn't treat her like a stepdaughter. He looked at her as if he was in the delivery room when she made her first appearance in the world. He looked at her as if she was his biological daughter.

"Thank you for loving me, Bria, and Ryder so much."

I didn't thank him as often as I should have. I had to show my appreciation for the wonderful man that I had in my life.

"You don't ever have to thank me."

Ryan wrapped his arms around my waist, and he looked deep into my eyes. "You three are my world, and I wouldn't be the man I am without you all."

I laid my head on Ryan's shoulder, and his scent surrounded me. I'd never get enough of his smell, his mannerisms, or his loving nature. That's what drew me to him when I thought I could never love again. It's crazy what an amazing man can do for your mental stability.

Ryan lifted my chin, and his lips met mine for the softest kiss known to man. The kiss felt like a feather danced across my lip before it was snatched away. I wanted that feather back. I wanted it back now.

I grabbed Ryan's head, and our lips smashed together. The desire within me needed a release. It needed a release now.

We stripped out of our pants before we fell onto the bed. Our lips never parted, but my panting grew louder.

Ryan trailed kisses along my collarbone to my neck as he pinned my hands above my head. The kisses sent chills down my spine. The anticipation. The need. All the foreplay he wanted to do was not necessary right now. I needed contact, and I needed it now.

A text sounded on my phone from close by.

"We need to check that," Ryan said as he released my hands.

I groaned as I shook my head. "No, we don't. Let's ignore it."

Ignoring was the best thing we could do until we received our release. That was most important now. Not a text that we could respond to in thirty minutes.

"We can't." Ryan sat up. "It could be about the children."

Ugh. Ryan was right. Ryan's logical side always trumped my pleasure side. Seriously, what would I do without this man?

I got up and walked over to the nightstand. I entered my passcode before I opened my text messages. My heart dropped into my stomach as I read the text message twice.

Unknown: You don't want to come back, but you'll come back one way or another. I will take away something you'll never imagine living without.

My phone slipped from my grasp. It fell with a loud thump as I threw my hands over my mouth.

"What's wrong?" Ryan rushed to my side.

I lost my balance, and before I fell to the ground, Ryan caught me.

"What's wrong?" Ryan repeated.

I opened my mouth to speak, but nothing came out. I couldn't bring myself to say what I thought the text meant. I didn't want to voice what I knew had ruined my night and would have me on edge for eternity. Why was this happening?

Ryan sat me on the bed before he grabbed my phone off the ground and read the message.

"Is this from Brad?"

I nodded. I stared at the wall. I had no words. I was numb. I couldn't do anything. I was no good use to myself or anyone around me.

"Do you know what this text message means?" Ryan asked.

I wasn't exactly sure what the text meant, but I could imagine it. He was going to come for blood. He was going to stoop to the lowest low to get me back. Brad was stubborn. He'd never give up. He'd never give up until he was able to control my every move again. Brad's obsession with me had gone from crazy to unstable.

"I don't know," I said once I could find my voice. I placed my hand against my pounding chest.

"He's saying he's going to take something away from you. Is his plan to hurt me?" Ryan asked as he looked around the bedroom.

I shrugged. "I don't know."

Ryan gave me a pointed look as he placed my phone on the nightstand. "What do you mean you don't know?"

"I don't know," I repeated. All I could think of saying was 'I don't know' because I didn't know. I didn't know Brad's intentions. I didn't know his thoughts. I didn't know anything. I hated the unknown, and he had me in a whirlwind of the unknown.

"I think we need to call the police."

I stood.

"No," I yelled.

The last thing we needed to do was call the police. If we called the police, we'd be asking for trouble. We couldn't afford that.

"Why not?" Ryan's eyes widened. He looked a bit frightened, and he had every right to look that way.

"If we call them and let them know what's going on, they'll make us give Brad visitation." I paused. Visitation would be the last thing I'd ever want. I'd fear Brad would take her, and we'd never see Bria another day of her life. That was something I wasn't willing to chance. Not now and not ever.

"We don't want Brad seeing Bria. Ever."

Ryan agreed. "Yes, that would be a disaster, but do you have any idea what he means in that text?"

I tapped my finger on my lip a few times as I looked around the room. "He could mean one of two things. Hurt you or kidnap Bria."

Ryan's eyes grew as wide as saucers before his eyes darkened. He clenched his hands into tight fists, and his knuckles turned ash white. "He could come after me all he wants, but I refuse to let him kidnap Bria. He won't even touch a little hair on her head if it's up to me."

I approached Ryan. I held my hands out to

him, and he grabbed them.

"Brad will not get within a few feet of Bria. We will work hard to make sure of that."

Ryan nodded before he released my hands. He walked over to the dresser where his phone was. "I need to call Justin. Make sure the children are okay."

"No." I shook my head. "Don't call Justin. Don't interrupt their fun night with this crap. Brad would want us to drop everything we're doing to hide in a corner, riddled with fear."

I exhaled. A few minutes ago, I was fear-struck, but within a few minutes, my confidence and courage came back full force.

"We aren't going to let Brad win."

Ryan nodded. "You're right. He's not going to win. I'm up for whatever comes our way. Nobody, and I mean nobody, is going to hurt my family."

Ryan's words were reassuring, but deep down, I knew Brad's manipulative ways. We had to stay mindful and safe as we moved around. If Brad put his mind to something, he made sure not to stop until his goal was succeeded. We had to stop Brad in his tracks. We had to do it on our own.

"What did you do to Brad for him to have this obsession with you?" Ryan asked.

I shrugged as I sat on the bed. Ryan sat beside me, and he grabbed my hand.

"I wish I could tell you I did something extravagant to catch his attention, but I didn't."

I thought back to my days in high school. I

was always the oddball, the girl who barely muttered two words to anyone besides the teacher. I went to school with one thing in mind. Learning what had to be learned that day and go home to do my assignments. I wasn't in any cliques or on any sports teams, so I wasn't lucky enough to have friends by default. I didn't actually get a friend until Amy moved into foster care, and we clicked. Then, we were inseparable in school. We'd meet up after every class that we had on that day and talk like we hadn't seen each other in ages. At lunch, we'd talk about the latest shows we loved while eating the disgusting cafeteria food. We knew we wouldn't eat dinner until seven o'clock, and we were never allowed seconds, so we scarfed down the food, regardless of whether we liked it.

One day, while Amy and I ate a chicken sandwich, Brad walked over. He set his food down, and he struck up a conversation with us. Amy gave me a wink across the table, letting me know he seemed genuine and I should entertain what he had to say. When I said I was head over heels for that man, nothing, and I mean nothing, could stop the instant love I felt for him deep within. The following day and up until I was moved out of foster, Amy and I ate lunch with Brad and his friends. They were somewhat considered a group of cool kids, so Amy and I became cool kids by default. Even though we had inherited the cool kid's title, we still mingled amongst ourselves in school. We didn't want fake friends just because of our inherited title.

Brad was the perfect gentleman. He'd walk me to class, he'd buy me extra snacks during lunch, and he'd walk me to my bus at the end of the day. At that time, I was grateful to have met him. I was grateful to have him in my life. Little did I know that he'd turned into an obsessive monster that was out to ruin my life. If I'd known the outcome would've been this, I would've rejected his advances the first day we had lunch together.

"So, you did nothing, and he still became this obsessive freak that can't take no as an answer?" he asked me.

I nodded. "It sounds crazy to me as well. I'd think I was lying if I didn't experience it myself."

Ryan chuckled as he cracked his knuckles. "Well, it's time to tell that obsessive freak to bring it on."

I was silent for a moment as I looked down at my hands in my lap. I couldn't bring myself to understand how such an amazing night was ruined by a dumb text message that Brad sent. I thought back to Brad's mannerisms. At that moment, I knew what he'd do with the two options we had discussed.

"He's going to try to kidnap Bria."

Ryan's mouth scrunched up in disgust. "Not on my watch."

Chapter Twenty-Four

Kyla

"How are you and Ryan doing?" Lauren asked.

We hung out in the gazebo. The weather started to warm up, and the high was seventy degrees. We took advantage by having our book club discussion outside. Due to issues in my life, our book discussions had been pushed back by a month. Our discussion had just ended, and we'd spend the next twenty minutes catching up.

I took a bite of my pretzel stick. "We're okay.

He has three job interviews coming up next week.”

Lauren smiled before she took a sip from her water bottle. “That’s awesome. I knew it wouldn’t take too long before companies would call. Ryan is a hot commodity in the corporate world.”

I smiled as I grabbed Lauren’s hand and squeezed it.

“No wonder I chose you as a friend. You know how to uplift my spirits.”

Lauren smiled. “You need uplifting. You and Ryan are going through the wringer with that lunatic on the loose.”

Lauren rolled her eyes.

All our friends and family knew of the updated, deranged text he had sent last month. We’d kept closer tabs on Bria ever since. We were doing a damn good job of protecting her, without the help of law enforcement.

I exhaled. “You know, I pray that Brad finds it in his heart to let us live our life.”

Bria and I were fine. We didn’t desire anything. Everything we could want and need, we already had. We lived in a nice, clean house that was free from any toxic behaviors. I’d prefer to keep it that way. I looked out to the field across from our backyard. Three squirrels scurried around and played with one another. Those squirrels were carefree. Boy, how I wished I could go back to a time when I could be like that. I couldn’t be carefree with Brad roaming freely.

“What don’t I understand is why he would

want to come back and wreak havoc? Bria hasn't mentioned him in years, and I want to keep it that way."

"Brad doesn't want Bria to forget him. Brad wants to be in his child's life again. That is his only child."

I looked over at Lauren. What did she mean by that? Was she implying he needed to be in her life? Brad's presence would only hinder the progress we'd made since he shot me and left me on my living room floor to die . I couldn't be more proud of how Bria was able to move on with the help of the therapist we provided her.

Lauren held her hands up in surrender. "I'm not defending him. I swear I'm not. I'm just saying that's the reason he wants to be in her life."

I nodded. I could understand her viewpoint of the situation. I'd be out of my mind if I wasn't able to see my child, but if I had psychological issues like Brad, I would understand that not seeing the child would be in the child's best interest . Or maybe not. Brad coming back into Bria's life would only be in his best interest.

Lauren grabbed a pretzel.

"Just keep doing what you are doing. We need Bria protected."

I opened my mouth to respond when a loud "Boo" came from behind us.

We turned to see Bria and Ryder standing directly behind us.

We screamed for their enjoyment before we chased after them. Lauren ran after Ryder while I ran after Bria. At the same time, we caught them. I picked Bria up, spun her in a circle, and tickled her stomach. She laughed uncontrollably as she wiggled in my arms, the sound warming my insides.

"What're you doing, scaring Mommy half to death?"

Bria smiled wide as she pointed at me. "You should've seen your face."

I looked over at Lauren and Ryder. Ryder placed a kiss on Lauren's cheek. The sparkle in Lauren's eyes was pure love. I couldn't wait for her to have children of her own. She was such a great auntie.

"Why do you say I need protecting?" Bria asked.

I looked over at Lauren, and she looked like a deer caught in headlights. How long had Bria and Ryder been behind us? Did they hear our entire conversation, or did they hear the tail end of it? I hoped it was the tail end because I didn't need Bria thinking about Brad. Brad needed to stay out of her thoughts. Bria had nightmares of Brad for six months after he shot me. After those nightmares went away, she still asked about him, but I told her he had gone to jail for a very long time for hurting Mommy. How would I explain to her that he was let out of jail for tampered evidence? There was nothing that I could think to say that could make this all better.

"Because you're a princess, and princesses need 24/7 protection," Lauren called out.

I looked over at Lauren and gave her a silent thank you. I didn't know how to answer that question, and Lauren was on point with her responses. What would I do without Lauren? She saved me.

I nodded to Lauren's answer.

"What about me?" Ryder asked.

"Princes needs protection as well. Just not 24/7 because you are so big and strong," Lauren commented.

"Yay." Ryder clapped his hands.

We walked the children into the house as Lauren announced she'd be leaving so we could get ready for our night. We were going over to the in-law's house for dinner. I looked forward to the meal. It was the first dinner we'd had as a family since the holidays.

Lauren kissed the children on the cheek before she walked out of the door.

"Thank you for rescuing me during that conversation."

Lauren smiled before she kissed me on the cheek. "You don't need to thank me. That's what friends are for. Enjoy your night, okay?"

"I will." I grabbed Lauren into a hug before she left.

Not even five minutes later, Ryan walked through the door and greeted us. Not only had Ryan applied for jobs online, he'd gone to local companies and dropped off his resume. To say he was determined was an understatement. Ryan wasn't stopping until he found a job.

Ryder and Bria ran to the front door and spoke to Ryan before they went upstairs.

"We'll be leaving in thirty minutes. Please clean up your room," I called out before I turned to look at Ryan.

He walked into the living room and smiled. He wrapped his arms around my waist and kissed my lips.

"How're you doing?"

"I'm good."

I smiled. "How're you doing? How was the job hunt?"

"I'm great." His eyes flickered around the living room. "The job hunt went well. I dropped off all the resumes I printed up."

I beamed. "That's awesome." Ryan was a go-getter. He didn't like not having a job, so he searched for jobs every day. I knew by the beginning of next month, he'd have a job. "I love that you don't let anything get you down."

Ryan nodded. "Thank you, the only thing I can do is stay positive." Ryan grabbed my hands and gave them a comforting squeeze. "Let's go get ready now. Mom's making lasagna, and my mouth is watering just thinking about it."

We went upstairs. I changed the children from their play clothes and dressed them in dinner attire. Even though we were only going to the in-laws, I still wanted them to look nice.

I wore a loose-fitting, yellow knee-length dress. I walked downstairs with the children and waited for Ryan to get dressed.

Ryan walked downstairs ten minutes later. He wore a nice pair of dark blue jeans and a yellow T-shirt.

"Mommy and Daddy are matching," Ryder observed, pointing back and forth between us.

"You look nice, Dad," Bria said as she approached him.

"Thank you, Sweetie." He kissed her forehead before he pinched her cheek.

"You look handsome."

Ryan looked amazing in his outfit. He could rock any pair of jeans that he put on. "Did you wear my favorite color on purpose?" he asked as he raised an eyebrow.

I smooth my hand over my dress, the soft fabric smooth on my palms. I tucked a piece of hair behind my ear as I looked up, flashing a smile. "Maybe."

He winked as he walked towards the front door. "Well, it looks amazing on you. My ray of sunshine."

My heart performed a flip in my chest, setting off a multitude of butterflies. I just knew tonight would be great. We had cause for celebration.

Once our shoes were on, we piled into Ryan's car. The twenty-minute drive was filled with genuine chatter and laughter, something I feel we lacked since we became aware of Brad's release.

Once parked outside Amelia and James' house, we followed the children, who ran to the front door. They knocked and rang the doorbell like mad people.

Moments later, the door swung open. Amelia's hair was pulled back into a tight formal bun, her signature hairstyle. She wore a sea foam, flowy dress that touched her ankles.

"I wondered what all the ruckus was, but it's just my grandchildren excited to see me." Amelia grabbed them into a group hug before she kissed them on the cheeks.

James appeared behind her. He wore a white shirt and black pants. "Hey, don't forget they're excited to see me as well."

They were picked up by James simultaneously. He kissed their cheeks as he walked them into the house.

"I guess we're chopped liver." Ryan looked at me and smirked before looking at his mom. "You two used to be that excited to see me."

Amelia placed her hands on her hips. She gave Ryan a pointed look. "I'm still just as excited to see you." She pointed inside the house. "James, I can't account for."

Amelia grabbed Ryan into a hug as we did our greetings. She turned, hugged me, and kissed my cheek.

"You two look beautiful. I love how you're matching."

"It wasn't planned," I mentioned.

Amelia looked between us. "Well, great minds think alike."

"That indeed," Ryan agreed with his mom.

He held the door open for us while we walked

in.

The house smelled heavily of garlic and spices as we walked into the house, causing my stomach to growl. Amelia grabbed my hand and squeezed it as we walked to the dining room. Dinner was in the middle of the table, family style. I looked at the lasagna, garlic bread and green salad.

"Hey, Son." James came around the table and grabbed Ryan into a bear hug. "Hey, Kyla."

He hugged me before he kissed me on the cheek.

We sat down at the table, joining the already-seated kids.

We passed the food around the table. Amelia made Bria's plate, while James made Ryder's plate. Amelia and James did everything for them. What wonderful grandparents they had.

While we ate delicious food, we talked and laughed like old times. I hadn't laughed this much in months. Nothing could ruin the night.

Once dinner was over, I helped Amelia carry the plates, utensils, and cups into the kitchen.

"You clean off, and I load the dishwasher ?" Amelia asked me.

I shrugged. "Sounds good to me."

I dusted the food off the plates into the trash can and handed them over to Amelia.

"How's everything going?" Amelia asked after a minute of silence.

"Everything is great," I admitted.

We hadn't heard from Brad since his bizarre

text. I honestly thought he fell off the face of the earth since he didn't have the opportunity to snatch Bria up. Maybe he gave up, once and for all. I hoped that was the case, but something in the back of my mind told me that might've been a dream.

Amelia smiled as she placed a plate in the dishwasher.

"I'm happy to know that. I was worried this whole situation would've put a damper on your marriage."

"I was worried too, but I'm glad to know that even after everything that has happened, Brad can't break us up."

Amelia placed a cup into the dishwasher. "I think this is the first marriage hurdle that you've come across." She smiled. "I'd like to say you two handled it wisely."

"Thank you."

I handed Amelia another plate.

Amelia placed the plate in the dishwasher before she started the cycle.

"If it's okay with you two, we would love to keep the children tonight so you and Ryan can have some alone time."

My heart warmed all over. "Are you sure?" I asked.

It would be nice to get some alone time with Ryan. We were so invested in spending time with our children we didn't care to get time alone.

Amelia wiped her hands on a dish towel before she placed her hand on my shoulder and gave it a light rub.

"Of course, we insist. You two need some alone time, and that's what you'll get."

I wrapped my arms around Amelia and kissed her cheek. I was forever grateful for my in-laws. I didn't know what I'd do without them in my life.

"Thank you."

Amelia gave me another squeeze before we separated.

"You don't have to thank me. We love having the grandchildren around." Amelia motioned with her hand at the house. "This house is too quiet with only James and I in it. We need the noise to make it lively."

We walked into the dining room. Amelia carried a plate of homemade chocolate chip cookies. Everyone's eyes widened in excitement once she placed the plate in the middle of the table. All at once, our hands grabbed gooey goodness, and within seconds, my mouth was happy with the homemade creation.

After we ate cookies, we said goodnight to everyone as hugs and kisses were exchanged. Before long, we walked out of the house.

"The house is going to be all to ourselves tonight," Ryan said as we walked the pathway to his car.

"Yes. How do you feel about that?"

He stopped in his tracks and turned to look at me. "It feels like a dream come true," he admitted.

He walked to the passenger side of the car

and opened the door.

"Was this your idea?" I asked him once he had slipped into the driver's seat.

He started the car up. "No. It was all Mom and Dad's idea, but I wish I had come up with it myself."

I shrugged as I relaxed my body into the seat. "Well, no matter who came up with the idea, I'm excited about it."

Ryan smiled as he backed out of the driveway. "I know tonight's going to be a night we'll always remember. Just wait and see."

Chapter Twenty-Five

Kyla

"I'll be right back," Ryan said.

My hand stopped in the middle of opening the passenger door. I looked over my shoulder. "Where are you going?"

Ryan drummed his fingers on the steering wheel in a melodic rhythm. "I just thought of the perfect items to set the perfect mood for tonight."

I smiled.

"I can't wait to see what you bring back." I

wiggled my eyebrows.

"You'll be overjoyed. Go inside and get comfortable. I'll be back in a few minutes."

I leaned over and kissed Ryan's cheek before I got out of the car. Like the perfect gentleman, he waited until I had unlocked the house and stepped inside before he drove away.

I locked the door, turned, and placed my back on the door. I slowly slid to the floor.

I loved that man with all my heart. How did he continue to make me feel all types of butterflies? Feeling romantic, I picked myself up off the floor. I went into the kitchen and walked to the pantry. After searching for a bottle of sweet red wine, I placed it in the fridge to cool it off.

My mind went in a million different directions. Tonight needed to be perfect. Maybe light some candles? Have soft music playing when Ryan came back? Maybe I'd be in my birthday suit when he walked through the door?

A shower. That's what I needed to freshen up and get comfortable. I'd be naked when he walked through the door.

I walked upstairs. I peered into the children's room before I shut the doors for the night.

I walked down the hall and into our bedroom. I opened the top drawer of my dresser, and fingered through the lingerie I had bought over the years but only worn occasionally.

Tonight called for skimpy nightwear that could be torn off with a simple tug.

Once I settled for a light pink see-through

nightie that left nothing to the imagination, I walked into the bathroom. I placed the lingerie on the counter and grabbed my makeup remover from the vanity drawer.

I swiped my cleanser on my face before I turned the shower on.

Once the water was hot and steamy, I stepped inside as I thought about our marriage.

Ryan and I had shared some great times over the years. It seemed as if it was yesterday that we vacationed in Bora Bora for our honeymoon, and we were on the balcony of our over-water bungalow. I fit perfectly in his comforting arms. I remembered the time I had a flat tire after I had run over a nail on my way to pick up Bria from school. I had to take her to an appointment. Ryan had gotten off work early to change my tire. I admired how his body looked and how the wet dress shirt clung to his muscular frame as water dripped off his body. I was so thankful for his generosity that I stepped out of the car, wrapped my arms around him, and kissed him with so much passion. The rain rushed down from the darkened clouds that hovered from above, which soaked me to my bones.

Or the day that I found out I was pregnant with Ryder. I had purchased three home tests and was too anxious to drive all the way home before using them. I peed on all three tests at the pharmacy, and they all came back with two lines. Once I had my new reality confirmed for me, I went to the grocery store, picked up baby-themed food items, and prepared a dinner that consisted of baby back ribs, baby peas, and a loaf of bread baked in the oven. Ryan was mid-chew of a rib when Bria handed him a piece of paper that said, 'I'm going to be a big sister soon.'

The look on his face as he cried tears of joy had my hormonal emotions in full throttle. He dropped his rib on his plate as he hurriedly wiped his hands on a napkin, dropped down to his knees, and kissed my stomach several times as he cooed, even though the baby was no bigger than a baby pea.

I couldn't expect more from Ryan. He was the definition of what I dreamt of finding when I was younger. I just had to kiss a frog before I found my king.

Once I was clean, I wrapped a towel around my body and got out of the shower.

"Kyla, did you take a shower without me?" came from the other side of the door.

I smirked. Ryan hated it when I took showers without him when we had the house to ourselves, but I had a surprise up my sleeve.

"Yes, I did."

Ryan opened the door, and I stepped back. He stood in his birthday suit, and I couldn't help but stare. How this man could be this gorgeous was beyond me.

"Care to join me?" he asked as he winked at me.

He turned the shower back on.

His request was tempting, but I wanted to set

the perfect mood. It was time to set things up, and I had ample time to do it while he was in the shower. His tempting request would be denied.

"I have to decline."

Ryan widened his eyes as he stared at me. "What did you do with my wife?" he asked.

I laughed as I swatted at his hand. "Your wife has something to do."

Ryan smiled. "Well, let me get in this shower. I'll be out in a few minutes."

I slapped his butt as he stepped into the stream of water. I walked out of the bathroom and hurried to towel off my body. I had to dress in the lingerie, go downstairs, and grab the bottle of wine and some candles.

Once I was dressed in my lingerie, I walked over to the mirror. I turned and checked myself out from all angles. I looked confident, I felt confident. It was time to create the perfect ending to such a wonderful night.

I walked downstairs and grabbed the bottle of wine, glasses, four candles, and a lighter. Once Ryan stepped out of the bathroom in a pair of gray boxers, he stopped and smiled.

I lounged on the bed in a seductive manner. The bottle of wine and glasses sat on the nightstand. The candles burned, giving off a vanilla scent.

"Is this the something you referred to?" he asked as he dropped his towel and dirty clothes into the hamper.

I nodded as I motioned with my index finger

for him to come closer.

He bit his lip as he approached me. He knelt on the bed, and I grabbed his face. I kissed him deeply as I slipped my tongue into his mouth. The passion in the kiss was apparent, and my insides screamed and yearned for more.

"Do you like the something I planned for us?" I asked.

"Hell, yes."

He crawled to his side of the bed and reached down. He grabbed a plastic bag and pulled out a container of strawberries, whipped cream, and a red rose.

"Wow."

I was impressed. Ryan's idea fitted perfectly with mine. Great minds truly think alike.

Ryan smiled as he handed me the rose.

"Care for a strawberry with whipped cream, madam?"

I twirled the rose between my index finger and thumb before I placed it on the nightstand. "Of course. Care for a glass of red wine, sir?"

I handed the bottle of wine to Ryan. He did the honors of pulling the cork before he poured wine into each of our glasses.

"It feels like my birthday tonight," Ryan commented as he opened the container of strawberries.

"How so?" I sipped my wine before I sat it down.

Ryan motioned to my lingerie before he groaned. "I haven't seen you like this in a while."

He shook his head as he adjusted his boxers. "You're making me excited."

"Well, one of my missions for the night has been accomplished." I crossed my left leg over my right.

"One of your missions?" He looked at me as he gave my knee a playful squeeze. "How many missions do you have planned?"

"That'll be determined by the end of the night."

He smiled as he sipped his wine. He sat the glass down before he opened the whipped cream.

I grabbed my phone off the nightstand and added the perfect finishing touch to our night.

Slow jams.

The R&B melody flowed from my phone as I walked over to the light switch and dimmed it to the lowest setting.

I crawled back on the bed, and Ryan held out a strawberry with whipped cream on it. I took a bite before I moaned. The strawberries had the perfect sweetness.

Ryan growled into my ear as he palmed my butt. "Moan like that again, and you're going to be naked in three seconds."

I whispered. "Maybe I want to be naked in two seconds."

I leaned to his ear and flickered my tongue out before I gave his earlobe a light tug.

Ryan shivered before he adjusted his boxers once more, but it was no use. His erection was visible, and it wasn't going anywhere anytime soon.

Ryan sipped more of his wine. "Is it your plan to torture me? If so, it's working."

I grabbed a strawberry, and I sprayed whipped cream on it before I held it to his mouth. "Would you really call this torture?

Ryan ate the strawberry before he spoke. "Being fed a delicious strawberry by my wife, not so much." He reached out and brushed his hand against my hardened nipples. "You in that lingerie, nibbling on my ear while I just want to pin your arms above your head and make love to you passionately? Hell, yes, it's torture."

I shrugged as I leaned back on my arms, my breasts on full display. "Well, what's stopping you?"

The strawberries, whipped cream, and the wine bottle were cleared off the bed at record speed, and Ryan was on top of me.

His mouth devoured mine, and I moaned into his mouth as his tongue tangled with mine. His hands traveled from my butt after I received a meaningful squeeze to the back of my neck. He held my head as his mouth begged for more attention. I was willing to give him that attention he so desperately needed. He gave me the same attention I so desperately needed.

"Are you still being tortured?" I asked when I came up for air to catch my breath.

Ryan's eyes flickered to my lips. "I'm tortured until this lingerie comes off."

I smiled as I whispered back. "Well, take it off."

Ryan shook his head before he peppered my neck with feather-soft kisses. "If I touched it, baby, I'll tear it."

I gave his arm a squeeze. "I don't mind, as long as you buy me another one."

"Your wish is my command."

Ryan tore the lingerie off me, and his mouth clamped onto my breast as he played with the other.

I threw my head back as I moaned.

"Oh my gosh."

My body had a mind of its own, and I was ready for Ryan to take me on a journey to Pleasure Land.

"How does it feel?" Ryan gave my breast a squeeze before his tongue flickered across my nipple.

I panted. "Amazing, but I need you inside me."

Ryan smirked as he continued to fondle my breast. "I didn't hear you." His gaze darkened. "Say it louder."

I gave him a pointed look. "You heard exactly what I said." I had a pool of desire down low, and I needed him to fill me up.

"I want you to say it louder," he growled into my ear before he gripped my butt with his hand.

"I need you inside of me."

I said it loud. I said it proud. I meant business.

"What's the magic work?" he asked me as he

settled between my legs.

I exhaled. "Ryan…"

He laughed. "Don't Ryan me. I'm in charge right now." His finger danced across my clit, and I shivered under his touch. I was sensitive. Sensitive with need and desire. "What is the magic word?"

"Please," I called out.

"Good girl."

Ryan's boxers disappeared, and he plunged into me. His initial thrust took my breath away. Ryan and I rocked together in unison as his mouth captured mine. Pleasure filled my body as Ryan and I made love to the slow jams that played.

"I… love… you," I panted.

I was close to my climax.

"I love you too," Ryan said, his rhythm never wavering.

He had superpowers because all I saw were stars in my vision as my legs shook with release.

Ryan's release came shortly after, and he stilled. He laid his body on top of mine. I loved the feel of our bodies touching.

He exhaled. He kissed me softly, as our gaze intensified. "I might be obsessed."

We laughed at his comment. "I bet you are."

Ryan rolled over and laid on his back.

I stood. "I have to clean up… again."

Ryan perked up. "Can I join?"

I shrugged. "As long as you promise to keep your hands to yourself."

Ryan smiled as he slapped my butt. "You know that won't happen."

Ryan and I took a shower together. As we showered, we washed each other's backs before we made out under the stream of steamy hot water. We acted like teenagers when we were alone. After we finished our snacks and wine, we fell asleep in each other's arms. Being loved by my soulmate was heaven on earth. Nothing could tear us apart.

Chapter Twenty-Six

Kyla

I turned over in bed, the sun peeked through the window blinds. I reached over and I didn't touch Ryan. I opened one eye to look at him, and he wasn't there.

I rubbed the sleep out of my eyes as I yawned and stretched. The clothes I went to bed in last night were thrown around the room after we had two more love sessions. We were a bunch of horn balls last night and I was surprised Ryan was up already. After all the strenuous exercise we did, I thought he'd still be asleep when I woke up. I was wrong.

The bedroom door opened, and Ryan walked in. He carried a tray of breakfast plates piled high with pancakes and eggs and glasses of orange juice.

"Good morning, Beautiful."

I beamed as I brought up the covers to cover my bare chest. "Good morning."

He sat the tray on the bed before he kissed me on the forehead.

"No good morning kiss?" I asked as I pouted.

Ryan scoffed. "I love you with all of my heart, but I don't want to kiss your morning breath."

I laughed as I winked at him. "You are a mess."

"I'm only kidding." He kissed my lips, a second longer than I anticipated. I love his kisses, I couldn't go a day without them. "Would you care for breakfast in bed?"

I put my hand over my heart. "I'd love breakfast in bed."

Ryan rubbed his hands together. "Awesome. I put a ton of love into this breakfast" Ryan admitted as he pointed at the food.

"Just as much as you put into our love making last night?" I bit my lip, thinking about the intention sessions we had. If we had time this morning, I'd love another round or two before the children came back home.

"Surprisingly, I put more?" Ryan picked up

my clothes and handed them to me.

"Thanks." I took the clothes and I put them on before I sat back on the bed. "I didn't know you had it in you."

"Baby, I can go all night" he boasted.

I smirked as I patted the spot beside me. "I'd love to experience that."

Ryan joined me and together, we ate our breakfast as we talked. Ryan cracked a joke here and there and I laughed uncontrollably as I held my stomach.

After breakfast, Ryan took the dishes downstairs, and I handled my hygiene. Since it wasn't freezing cold outside, Ryan and I could take a nice walk through our neighborhood. We hadn't done that in a while so today would be the perfect day.

"How does a stroll around the neighborhood sound?" I asked as I walked downstairs.

"It sounds perfect." Ryan walked into the living room from the kitchen.

"Well, let's go." I stretched my arms above my head.

We walked to the front door. As we slipped our shoes on, Ryan's phone rang.

"It's mom." Ryan smiled. "I wonder why they're calling so early."

I looked at the time. It was only ten o'clock. It was way too early for them to call. We were lucky enough to get the children back by the late afternoon when they spent the night over there. I shrugged. I was dumbfounded. "Answer."

"Hey mo..." Ryan didn't even get his entire greeting out before he went silent. His eyes widened. "What." Ryan yelled into the phone.

My heart pounded in my chest. Something was wrong. Something had to be seriously wrong. What was wrong with my children? "What's wrong?" Panic had set in.

Ryan looked at me, defeat in his eyes. "Bria's gone."

My heart dropped into the pit of my stomach. My stomach turned sour, and I felt like I would throw up at any second. "What do you mean gone?" Bria couldn't be gone. Bria should be with her grandparents and brother right now.

"They went to a breakfast buffet this morning. Bria had to use the bathroom and she went but she never came back."

I dropped to the floor in a heap. All I felt was the coolness from the tile as my eyes closed. I just wanted to die. How could my child be gone? I couldn't live without her. She was my world. She was my everything. She's the reason I never gave up. She was my saving grace. My saving grace couldn't be gone.

"Hold on mom." Ryan sat his phone on the end table, and he crouched beside me. "Kyla, Kyla." Ryan shook my arm. "Are you okay?"

"No. How can I be, okay? My daughter's gone." I felt numb. How could this happen? How could this happen to me? One second, she was having breakfast with her family and the next, she was gone. Bria didn't vanish into thin air. Bria wouldn't just walk away. Someone had to take her. I knew someone took her.

Ryan expression became unreadable.

A text sounded on my phone. I pulled it out of my phone and unlocked it.

Ryan put his phone on speaker.

"I'm going to call the police" James said into the phone.

"No" I yelled. I lump formed in the back of my throat as I read the text message.

Unknown: Bria's with me. If you want what's best for our daughter, you won't call the police. If the police are called, we'll disappear forever. I'll text you soon with location details. See you soon, my love.

"Why not?" Amelia asked as her voice quivered.

"Brad has Bria" I yelled at the top of my lungs. My worst fear had finally come to the surface. Brad had my daughter, and I didn't know what to do. I couldn't do anything but play by his terms. He had planned this moment for weeks. He waited until the perfect time to snatch Bria and he did it without a skip in beat. He must've followed them to the restaurant. We had underestimated Brad. Why did we underestimate him?

Ryan grabbed my phone and read the text message.

"I'm so sorry" Amelia wailed into the phone.

"I'm going to call the police" James repeated.

"No dad, you can't." Ryan groaned as he paced back and forth in front of me. "This son of a bitch…" Ryan began.

Amelia spoke up. "Ryan, mind your language."

It was of pure respect for Ryan not to curse in front of his parents but Ryan was furious so there was no telling what would come out of his mouth.

"He said we can't call the police, or we'll never see Bria again." Ryan put the phones down and be grabbed a handful of his hair as he sunk to the ground beside me.

"What are we going to do?" I asked. I had no energy to fight with Brad before but I had to muster up the energy to fight with him because he had my world in his hands.

Ryan placed his hand on my knee. He stared at the wall. Amelia and James announced that they were on their way to our house before they hung up.

"I wish we could call the police."

I exhaled a breath as I looked at Ryan. I had no energy to entertain for that stupid idea. He looked at me and we stared at each other.

"What?" he asked.

I chuckled, even though I found nothing funny. If Brad said something, he meant business. It was time to stop underestimating him. "Why in the hell would you suggest something so stupid?"

Ryan shook his head as he moved his hand off my knee. "My suggestion isn't stupid. It's the smartest thing we could do in this situation."

"I can't do this right now." I pushed myself to stand and I walked into the kitchen. I had to separate myself from him. I was beyond stressed, and he wasn't making it better.

"Can't do what? Be logical?"

I rolled my eyes as I turned to look at Ryan. You'd think he'd get the hint that I had nothing to say to him for the time being, but he was right here. Irritating the hell out of me. "The logical decision wouldn't be to call the police. I don't want my daughter to fall off the face of this earth."

Ryan a step back as he placed his hand over his heart. "So, now she's only your daughter?" he asked.

This conversation went downhill quickly.

"Well, you aren't acting like her father right now" I commented.

Ryan pointed at me. "You're so wrong for that. I'm only trying to help."

"If you want to help, you'll understand that Brad isn't playing games right now." I planted my hip against the counter as my mind drifted in a million different directions. "He has my daughter and I have no idea where he could be." Salty, wet tears streamed down my cheeks. I tried to control my sobs, but it was useless. I felt hopeful. I took deeps breath as I gripped the counter. Was the room spinning? Was it getting smaller? I swear the kitchen wasn't this small when I moved into this house. It wasn't even this small a minute ago.

Ryan placed his hand in the middle of my back. "Kyla, you must calm down. You're going to have an anxiety attack."

An anxiety attack was surely underway. I wiped my wet face with my hands, but it was no use. The tears wouldn't stop.

Ryan exhaled a breath as he grabbed a handful of tissues. He handed them to me, and I wiped my face. "We should've gotten a restraining order on him."

I scoffed as Ryan led me to the dining room where I sat on a chair. "A piece of paper won't stop him. That's why I left Florida in the manner that I did. We had no other choice but to leave."

"I just don't feel like this is the correct way to confront Brad. I don't want any of us getting hurt over this situation."

There was no right way to go about this situation. This situation shouldn't even be a situation. It wouldn't be a situation if Brad was never let out of prison.

"Bria is the only person I'm worried about." I wiped my eyes as my tears continued to fall. "I don't care if I get hurt in the process." I would go to the ends of this earth to bring Bria to safety, even if it meant getting hurt in the process. I was prepared for anything as soon as the news was delivered to us.

Ryan was silent. He was too silent. I didn't know what he was going to say but I prepared myself for the worst. "Let's just think logically. We need to call the police."

I pushed my chair back. The chair legs screeched across the tile floor. I slapped my hands on the table as I looked Ryan in the eyes. "I'm going to handle this on my own. I don't need your help" I yelled. I was furious and Ryan didn't make it any better.

Ryan stood and approached me. "You know you can't handle this situation alone."

I gave Ryan a pointed look. "Oh, I know I can deal with it alone." I folded my arms across my chest. "Remember, you weren't there when he shot me and left me to die."

Ryan took a step back like I had slapped him with my harsh words. The expression on his face changed from defeat to sadness. My words stung.

Before Ryan could respond, Amelia, James and Ryder walked into the dining room. Amelia grabbed my hand and walked me over to the couch. James and Ryder stayed in the dining room with Ryan.

"That conversation was too heated. We needed to separate you two."

I cried as I paid my head on Amelia's shoulder. "I just don't know what to do" I cried out.

Amelia ran her fingers through my hair and she rocked me back and forth. "Honey, I know you don't know what to do." Amelia kissed my forehead. "James and I feel responsible that she was with us when it happened."

I shook my head as I looked at Amelia. "It's not your fault." Defeat washed over me. It wasn't anyone's fault but mine. I couldn't believe I said the most hurtful thing to Ryan that I could muster inside. I knew my words had stung. Ryan didn't deserve it, he just wanted to avoid any confrontations, but I knew confrontation was inevitable. "It's my fault."

"It's not any of our faults." Ryan walked into the living room, followed by James and Ryder.

I stood and I rushed over to him. "I'm sorry for what I said." I wrapped my arms around his neck. "I didn't mean it."

Ryan rubbed my back. His touch was comforting. "I know you didn't, Beautiful."

James spoke up. "We're just on edge right now."

Amelia agreed as she grabbed my hand and gave it a squeeze. "We just need to work together to get Bria back."

"Where is Bria?" Ryder asked.

Ryder. My heart shattered into a million pieces. He didn't understand what was going on. I was glad he didn't understand but obviously, he wanted to know where his sister was. I didn't think it would be appropriate to talk to Ryder about how Bria's father, who's been in prison for the past five years, got out early and kidnapped her.

"She's at her friend's house" I responded. His little brain just needed to know that his sister was with one of her friends from school and she'd be back in a few days. We'd be a big, happy family again with no worries. If only we were lucky. If only the plan that we'd come up with would provide us with great results.

"Ryder, why don't we go up to your room and

play some games?" James asked him.

"Yay." He clapped his hands. "I love games."

Ryder and James walked upstairs. "Did you respond to the text message?" Amelia asked once James and Ryder were out of earshot.

"No, not yet." I grabbed my phone from the end table. "What should I text back?"

Amelia grabbed my phone. "May I?" she asked.

I nodded. "Of course."

Ryan and I stood close as Amelia typed out the message. "How does this sound?" Amelia asked.

"It sounds convincing" Ryan responded.

"Yes" I agreed. "Anything that'll keep Bria safe."

Ryan tapped his index finger against his lip as he paced the living room floor. "We might need some help with this situation."

"You know James and I are game."

"No." I shook my head as I looked at Amelia. "We just need you to be here for Ryder."

Ryan nodded. "Yes, we need you two to stay back."

"But…" Amelia started.

"No buts" Ryan responded as he held his hand up.

"I have the perfect person in mind" I responded. I was positive Brad would work alone in this situation. He had burned every bridge that he had so he had no other choice. Just because he worked alone didn't mean we had to work alone. We had friends and family that loved us and would back our every move.

Ryan and I nodded at the same time. It was evident, we had the same person in mind. "It's settled. Now, we just wait for a text message back."

It was hard to sit around and wait for the next move, but we had no other choice. It was time to play the waiting game. We were on Brad's time and Brad's time was what we would wait for.

I opened my phone and looked at the text sent.

Me: I promise, no police. Let me know where to meet you two. It's time to sit down as a family and talk everything over.

I hoped it would work. If it didn't, I'd forever regret my decisions.

Chapter Twenty-Seven

Kyla

A rundown motel. This didn't seem right. The address he sent over had to be incorrect. Brad would never stay in a motel. He thought they were icky and didn't stand up to the standard's he had in mind. He always stayed in a four or five-star hotel, no exceptions. This text had to be incorrect.

Unknown: It's time to meet, my love. Meet us here in thirty minutes. Don't be late.

He attached a link.

Unknown: Also, don't bring anyone else besides your husband. He needs to find out the truth. He at least deserves that.

Ryan scoffed. He folded his arms across his chest. "He said bring your husband as if I wasn't already coming."

"The 'find out the truth' seems off to me," Amelia pointed out.

James nodded. "Yeah, this man seems deranged."

We sat in the living room. We waited seven long hours for this text message to come through. It was an agonizing four hundred and twenty-three minutes, but the text had finally arrived. Now, it was showtime.

Mark stood and rubbed his hands together. "So, let's get this party started."

"Wait, we have to think about this." Amelia stood and held her hand out. "He only wants Kyla and Ryan to come."

James stood and agreed. "Mark, you'll have to go in a separate vehicle and arrive shortly after they do."

I looked around the room. My heart pounded in my chest. This was intense. This was about to happen. I didn't know what would result from this trip to this motel, but I couldn't think straight. Was Ryan and I about to walk into an assassination? I knew he hated Ryan. He had no other choice since Ryan is the only man who'll ever own my heart. Brad had that chance, and he ruined it with his dysfunctional ways. What would he try to do to me? Would he try to make me his girlfriend again? Or worse, his wife?

My mouth went dry. Brad was a loose cannon. This couldn't be good. Maybe we were making a terrible mistake. I'd hate for my decisions to result in anyone getting hurt.

"Should we even bring Mark? What if Brad knows who he is?"

"Even if he does know who I am, he's only looking for you and Ryan to arrive together."

It still didn't feel right. What if Brad already knew our plan? What if…

"How about I arrive five minutes after you all arrive?"

Ryan and I exchanged a look before we agreed on that option. If he arrived after we had made our transition to the room, Brad would be focused primarily on us. He wouldn't worry about who else was . Or would he? I swore. Second-guessing myself wouldn't help the situation, but I'd do anything to protect my child, even if that meant placing myself in harm's way.

"What is the room number?" James asked.

Ryan shook his head. "Brad didn't prove that yet."

Amelia tapped her finger against her lip. She placed her hands on her hips as she looked at us. "He's smarter than I allowed myself to think."

A room number would provide us with the perfect ambush tactic. He purposely left that information out. Brad was smart, all right, in a psychotic, demented sort of way. No way in hell did I think he was crazy when I said yes to being his girlfriend. If only my young, naive, teenage self would've known what twenty-seven me knows now. I would've run for the hills and never looked back. Why did I allow sweet talk and flirtation from a young, attractive man to force the walls down that I'd spent years building?

"I'm sure he won't share that information until we arrive."

I ran my fingers through my hair. This was a horrid situation I couldn't see myself out of, but I had no other choice. This had to be done. Once and for all. Hopefully. If I were lucky.

If we were lucky.

"How far is the motel from here?" Ryan asked.

I clicked the link to the motel. "Twenty-five-minute drive."

James clapped his hands together. "Well, it's time to get the show on the road."

We all nodded except for Amelia. She stood back, her hand over her mouth as her eyes brimmed with tears.

"I don't want you two to do this," she muffled out.

My heart broke as Ryan walked over to Amelia. He cradled her head on his shoulder. "Momma, everything is going to be okay."

I nodded, but I didn't believe Ryan's words. Anything that involved Brad was not okay. We just had to say whatever we had to say to make sure we could leave our house and track Bria down without them coming along what had to be done.

"Please don't get hurt." Her tears drenched Ryan's black shirt.

"We won't."

Ryan gave his dad a hug before he turned and looked at Mark and Ime. "Are you two ready?" He asked.

"Ready as I'll ever be," Mark said.

"I was born ready" I said. That statement wasn't anything but true.

"Well, let's head out." Ryan led the way to the front door.

"Text me the address. I'll leave five minutes after you two do."

I quickly sent Mark the address as we walked out of our house. Before I closed the door, I gave our house one last look. Just in case I didn't come back, I needed to look at our house one last time. We created so many great memories there, and I just hoped after this trip, we'd be able to make more.

Ryan held the door open for me to get into his car. Once we were inside, we looked one last time towards our house. James and Amelia stood outside. Amelia's head was on James' shoulder as he waved to us.

"I hope we're making the right decision," he said.

I gulped in an attempt to remove the lump in the back of my throat, but it was no use. The lump was there to stay.

"I hope so, too," I responded.

I hated I didn't sound as optimistic as I should have, but this was a dangerous situation.

We drove in silence for the first twenty minutes. When we were almost there, we called Mark on the phone.

"Have you two arrived yet?" he asked.

"Not yet."

I reached over and placed my hand on Ryan's knee. The closer we got, the more my heart pounded in my chest.

"We're almost there, but if my thoughts are correct, he'll be watching when we arrive." We turned onto a road lined with trees. I knew we were right down the road, only minutes from seeing Bria. Only minutes from coming face to face with Brad… again. "We'll tell you the room number as soon as he texts us the information."

We pulled into the parking lot of the rundown motel, and I was disgusted. The parking lot was littered with trash, but there were several cars in the parking lot. How could he bring my daughter to such a horrid place? I didn't want to think about what was done in the room she was held hostage in before they arrived. From the looks of things, it could've been anything and everything disgusting I could imagine.

As soon as we parked, a text message came through.

Unknown: Room 114. Leave everything in your vehicle, especially your phones. I'm watching you.

Ryan and I exchanged a look before we looked around the parking lot. Our daughter was across this parking lot. We had to get to her now.

"Room 114 Mark. We have to go now. We can't take anything with us."

"Okay, I'll be there soon. Please, be safe."

Ryan hung up the phone before we grabbed the door handles and opened the door. We stepped out and looked around. Brad had set the stage perfectly. This was the type of place that people didn't want police to frequent.

We closed the doors.

Ryan walked over to my side of the door, grabbed my hand, and we walked across the parking lot. Room 114 was within arm's reach.

I grabbed the doorknob and turned it. I peered inside. It was a cheap, basic room with a ratty full-size bed with terrible bed linen. The mini fridge looked old and dingy. A big black TV on a table stand and an old, wooden table with one plastic chair that looked like it was on its last leg. Literally.

I opened the door all the way, and Ryan and I walked inside. The room was empty. Nobody was in there.

Ryan walked over to the bathroom in the far corner of the room and peered inside.

"They aren't here."

The door opened, followed by a chuckle. Ryan and I turned towards the door and froze in place. Brad walked in, and he wore all black. He had a gun in one hand. He walked further into the room, and a tear-streaked Bria walked in beside him. The look of terror was evident in her eyes. Oh, how I wished I could take all the terror she felt inside away. My heart dropped into my stomach as we raised our hands above our heads. This was a trap. Brad purposely had us enter first so he could trap us in this terrible motel room with no way to escape.

A smirk touched his lips. He looked over at Bria. "Don't move," he growled in a low tone.

I could sense Ryan was about to say something, and I slapped his hand. Now wasn't the time to come at Brad for his tone with Bria.

Brad looked at Ryan and me. He rubbed the overgrown stubble on his chin.

"Hello, Kyla."

"Are you not going to address me?" Ryan asked.

I looked over at Ryan, terror in my eyes. Why wasn't he keeping his mouth shut? There was no reason for him to initiate conversation with the mad man that held the gun.

Brad chuckled. "Hello, Ryan."

"Mommy. Daddy. I'm scared," Bria cried out.

Steam left Brad's ears as he bent down and spoke in her ear. "How many times do I have to tell you that he's not your dad? I'm your dad, and you're going to stop disrespecting me."

"Brad, she just doesn't..." I began.

"Yeah, yeah, yeah." He waved the gun around as he interrupted me. "She would remember me if you had brought her to the prison to see me. Or if you hadn't left me for this asshole to start an entire new life without me."

"She had no other choice," Ryan interjected.

Brad stared at Ryan. He stared for a good minute before a devilish smile appeared. "How would you know? Were you there when we met? Were you there when we fell in love? Were you there when she lost her vir…"

"My daughter is in the room. Can we not talk about that," I interrupted Brad.

Was this room getting smaller? Was the air supply shrinking?

Breathe. Keep breathing. Don't let him know you're scared out of your mind. Don't have a panic attack.

"Don't you mean our daughter?" He placed his hand on her head, and she squirmed. She was uncomfortable, and she had every right to be. I hated that she was in this situation. She didn't deserve it. Hell, none of us deserved this.

Time to get down to business. No more playing games. "Why did you want to meet with us today?"

His eyes brightened. He wrapped his arm around Bria's shoulder and gave her a tight squeeze. "I want us to be a big happy family again."

My mouth dropped open. I looked at Ryan. He was just as shocked as I was. A big happy family? Again? Was he out of his mind or was he out of his mind?

He took a step closer. "Before you say anything stupid, I want you to know something."

I stayed silent. Ryan stayed silent. The only noise in the room was Bria's whimpers and the whining fridge.

"You will either tell this asshole your marriage is done and over with, or you'll say goodbye to Bria forever."

With that statement, Bria's whimper turned into a full-blown cry.

"Stop it now, Bria," Brad said in a stern voice. She continued to cry. "Keep crying, and you'll go back into punishment."

"You aren't going to pun…"

Brad brought the gun up and aimed it at Ryan. "You don't tell me what I can and can't say to my daughter."

I was frozen in place. I should've known how this was going to play out. I was stupid to think anything positive would've come from this. Now, we were in a room with no phones to call for help. All we had was the ratty, old phone in the corner, but we couldn't reach it from where we stood. I put us in danger. I should've listened to Ryan and gotten the police involved.

"I tried my hardest to break you two up, but even with the people I hired to get the job done, you two still wouldn't leave each other alone."

Brad's admission of hiring Veronica and Michael was all we needed to know what we thought was correct.

He gave a devilish grin. "Now I have to break

you two up myself so we can go back home to Florida." He exhaled a breath. "I don't even know why I wasted so much money and time on those dumbasses I hired."

I looked over at Ryan, and I could see the defeat in his eyes. I knew Ryan like the back of my hand. I just hoped Brad couldn't see it. Brad feasted on other's weaknesses.

"So, are you coming home with us, or will you say goodbye forever?" Brad asked.

I wanted to drop to my knees and plead with Brad, but I knew he wanted an answer. Nothing else I had to say would change his mind. Once his mind was made up, there was no convincing him otherwise.

"Brad…"

"No, just give me an answer." He looked at the watch on his wrist. "It's about time for us to leave. If you are leaving with us."

I stayed silent. I couldn't find a word to mutter. There was no way in hell I'd leave this motel with Brad. I didn't understand how he could just kidnap Bria and give me an ultimatum. A ridiculous ultimatum, nonetheless. If I wanted him, I wouldn't have left him. Yet, he spent five years in prison and didn't change. Not one bit.

Brad exhaled a breath. "Well, I take the silence as you are not coming with us. It hurts my feelings that you won't come back home with me, but I can't force you. It's time to say goodbye to Bria."

Bria tried to run towards us, but Brad

wrapped his arm around her body. "No, you won't get to touch them. Go outside and wait for me there."

Bria didn't budge. She just looked up at Brad as tears fell out of her eyes.

"Now," he yelled.

Bria looked at us one more time before she opened the door and closed it.

I didn't want Bria outside by herself. I just hoped Mark was outside taking her to safety.

"Now, it's time to start shooting. Kyla, you're first. I want Ryan to watch you die."

Time moved in slow motion as Brad moved the gun from Ryan and pointed it right at me. My life flashed before my eyes as I watched Brad's finger move towards the trigger. I knew since he didn't kill me the first time, he would make sure the deed was done before he escaped this time.

A scream escaped my lungs as I closed my eyes. I couldn't bear to watch the bullet travel its merry way to kill me.

I popped an eye open when I heard a scuffle ensue. I threw my hands over my mouth as I watched in terror as the scene unfolded. Ryan and Brad fought over the gun, a loaded gun. A loaded gun that could go off at any second. A loaded gun that could take any of our lives. This couldn't be happening.

Curse words spewed from their mouths as they fought. I tried to move my body with all my might, but my feet wouldn't budge. I was frozen in place as fear coursed through me.

Two loud, piercing pops went off, and I screamed in terror. Both men dropped to the ground as the sound of metal clattered to the floor. The gun fell next to Brad's side.

I rushed to grab the gun out of Brad's reach before I dropped to Ryan's side. Ryan's shirt was saturated in his blood, and his face winced in pain. The entry wound was in his lower stomach.

"You're going to be okay. Stay with me. Please, don't leave me," I pleaded. "Call 911," I yelled out.

Mark opened the door and said, "They're already en route."

I shooed him away as I didn't want Bria to see this scene. This was horrific. I didn't even want to see it.

I applied pressure to Ryan's wound with both hands. I had to stop the bleeding. I needed to stop the bleeding. It should've been me that had been shot. Ryan didn't want to do this. Yet, I dragged him into this mess, and he had gotten hurt.

Tears streamed down my face as time moved by fast. If this bullet was deadly, I'd never be able to live with myself. I just hoped that Ryan would be okay.

"Stay with me, Ryan. Please don't leave me. I can't live without you. Our children can't live without you."

Everything was a blur. Time continued, but my life felt like it was on pause. I didn't know people were in the motel room until I was physically picked up and dragged away from

Ryan's side. The last thing I saw was Ryan's eyes closing as medical staff surrounded him.

Chapter Twenty-Eight

Kyla

I sat on the metal waiting room chair. My body trembled. The smell of antiseptic irritated my nose. My foot tapped the floor repeatedly. What was going on? What was taking so long? Where were the updates I was promised on the way over to the hospital?

I rubbed my blood-stained hands together before I buried my face in them. This couldn't be happening. I was sure I was stuck in a horrible nightmare I couldn't wake up from, no matter how hard I tried.

"Kyla. We got here as soon as we could."

Amelia's voice pulled me out of my thoughts.

I looked towards the entrance. Amelia and James rushed into the emergency waiting room.

I ran towards Amelia and threw myself into her arms.

"I'm so sorry," I cried as tears fell from my eyes. "I thought we could've solved this on our own—"

"Kyla, calm down," Amelia interrupted my spew of words as she placed my head on her shoulder.

She soothingly rubbed my back as tears from her eyes fell into my face.

"Yes, Kyla. Please calm down," James said as his voice wavered.

He tried to stay strong, but I knew it was only so much he could bear.

"I can't live without Ryan," I wailed into Amelia's chest.

The last time I saw Ryan, his eyes had closed. They wouldn't let me near him as they worked to stop the bleeding. I couldn't believe Ryan was shot. It all felt like a nightmare that I couldn't wake myself up from.

"Pumpkin, you won't have to."

She rubbed my back, and I melted into her chest.

"This is all my fault."

If I would've gone to the police, none of this

would've happened. Ryan wouldn't be hurt. It was evident Brad still had control over my decisions. I hated him with a passion for that.

"Honey, you two did what you thought you had to do. Ryan's going to be all right. He won't leave you and the children. I can promise you that. Ryan's a fighter. He will pull through." Amelia was silent for a few moments. "Just like you pulled through."

We walked over to a set of chairs and we sat. Amelia and James sat on opposite sides of me. I leaned my head against her chest and continued to sob.

I never imagined Ryan would be in the same predicament I was in years ago. I was positive it would be the last hospital trip we would've made due to a gunshot wound. Sadly, it was a trip down memory lane. The only difference was Ryan was shot. All because of me. I was the reason he clung to life in an operation room.

"What was the last update you received?" Amelia asked.

I sniffled as I looked around the emergency waiting room. We were the only ones in the waiting room. "Ryan's been in emergency surgery since he arrived."

"Where's Bria?" Amelia asked.

"She's with Mark. I don't want her to see Ryan in this state."

I didn't want her to see me in this emotional state. That would further traumatize her, especially after whatever she endured with Brad.

Bria would definitely need counseling again after the ordeal she had to deal with. Even though it was only a few hours, I'm sure she had a whirlwind of emotions to trample through with that man.

Amelia continued to rub my back as James sat on the other side of me.

"I'm so sorry." Tears continued to escape my eyes.

James placed his hand on my back. "You don't need to apologize. This situation isn't your fault. Brad placed you into a corner and you did what you thought was best for Bria."

I nodded but deep in my heart, I knew Ryan wouldn't be hurt if we would've called the police and allowed them to handle the situation. Granted, I was hopeful we could've handled the situation like civilized adults, but I hoped deep in my heart that he wouldn't resort to violence. Some people just wouldn't change, no matter what.

Every five minutes, either Amelia or James would walk to the check-in desk to ask if there were any updates on Ryan's surgery. Each time, they were told he was still in surgery, and they'd tell them as soon as he got out of surgery.

The waiting game ate me alive as I stared at the wall in a daze. The waiting room was getting smaller. It was closing in on me. It was significantly smaller than it was twenty minutes ago, even thirty minutes ago. How long had I been sitting here? Two hours? Almost three?

"Can the family of Ryan Walker come to the desk?"

I grabbed Amelia's and James' hands. Placing one foot in front of the other, we walked twelve steps before we stood in front of the triage nurse.

"Ryan just finished up his surgery."

The nurse typed into the computer that sat in front of her.

"Is he okay?" Amelia interjected as she placed her hand on her chest.

"Can we see him now?" James raised his eyebrows, waiting for an answer.

"Was the surgery successful?" I asked. The anticipation killed me inside. I needed answers and I needed them now.

The triage nurse continued as she gave us a tight smile. "The doctor is coming out right now."

A tall, slim balding man that wore scrubs walked out.

We approached the doctor.

"Hello. I'm Dr. Aaron."

"Hello, Dr. Aaron. How was Ryan's surgery?" James took control of the conversation.

Dr. Aaron looked at the three of us before he spoke. "It was touch and go for a while." Dr. Aaron smiled. "The surgery was successful."

I exhaled in relief as the three of us hugged. Tears of joy brimmed in our eyes and streamed down our cheeks.

"When can we see him?" Amelia wiped her face with her hands.

"You can come to see him now. He's in recovery ."

We followed Dr. Aaron through the door he'd come from. The smell of antiseptic intensified as we walked down a long, white hallway with small rooms lining each side.

A nurse's station sat tucked away in the far corner. We passed the station before Dr. Aaron led us into Ryan's room.

Ryan was in a hospital bed, his eyes closed. He was hooked up to several machines that beeped periodically.

"Is he going to make a full recovery?" I asked as Amelia and James sat in the chairs on Ryan's left side.

"We expect him to. He's lucky the gunshot didn't damage any internal organs. We'll keep him here for a few days so he can heal and get the proper care he needs."

"Thank you for your hard work, Dr. Aaron," James chimed in.

"You're welcome." Dr. Aaron looked over at Ryan before he looked back at me. "I'll give you some time. He should wake up in the next hour or two. When he does, just give the nurse a buzz. He might need more pain medication. I'll bring in another chair."

"Thank you," Amelia called out before she placed her hand on Ryan's.

I walked closer to the bed. Ryan looked out of place in a hospital bed. He was too young to be in a place like this. I couldn't help but think he wouldn't be in this predicament if I didn't come into his life.

"Pumpkin. You can't blame yourself for this."

I looked up. Amelia drew me out of my thoughts once again.

"How did you?" I began.

"Momma knows everything." She motioned with her hand. "Come here. Sit next to your husband. I want you to be the first face he sees when he wakes up."

Amelia stood, and I sat in the chair. I softly placed my hand on top of Ryan's hand, which was at his side.

Amelia sat in the chair the doctor brought into the room. The only sound in the room was the beep of the machines. The machines that monitored my husband's vitals.

An hour later, Ryan's hand twitched in mine. I opened my eyes to look at him. I had closed my eyes as it was well after two in the morning. I was exhausted mentally, emotionally, and physically. I looked at his face and could see he began to stir.

"He's waking up," I said.

"I'll call the nurse." Amelia stood, walked to the other side of the bed, and pressed the button to call.

Ryan continued to stir.

"I'm right here, handsome."

Ryan's eyes fluttered open to the sound of my voice. He looked me in the eye.

"I'm right here."

Ryan cleared his throat before he looked around the room.

"Where am I?"

His voice was raspy.

James stood and approached the other side of the bed. "You're in the hospital. Do you remember what happened?"

Ryan was silent for a few moments. After what seemed like an eternity, he nodded. "I remember everything."

"I'm so sorry this happened to you. You were right. We should've gone to the police and asked for this assistance. I should've never thought that..."

Ryan interrupted my spew of words. "Beautiful, I don't want to hear you blame yourself. You didn't force me to go with you to that motel. I could've called the police. Yes, you would've been livid with me, but I thought it was best for us to handle it on our own."

I raised Ryan's hand and kissed it before I carefully placed it back down. "Thank you for being okay."

Ryan smiled. "Thank you for being one of the many reasons I have to live."

The nurse walked into the room. She introduced herself as I moved out of her way, and my heart softened. Ryan was the man of my dreams, and tonight, he proved he would do anything to protect me. If it wasn't for Ryan reacting as quickly and in the manner that he had, we wouldn't be here to speak our truths. We would be in body bags on the way to the morgue. Once the nurse gave Ryan more pain medicine, she left the room after telling us to call if he needed anything.

I sat beside Ryan. I rubbed my thumb across the back of his hand and looked into his eyes. His eyes translated how much he loved me.

The feeling was mutual.

"We'll give you two some time alone," Amelia said as she walked over and kissed Ryan's forehead.

"Are you sure you two want to step out?"

"Yes, you two need some time to talk. We'll be right outside."

James walked over and gave Ryan a pat on the shoulder.

Once Amelia and James walked out of the room, I looked at Ryan.

"Where's Bria?"

Even though Ryan was in the hospital, he was worried about our daughter. "She's with Mark and Chelsea. Mark was right outside the door when everything went down."

Ryan smiled. That was wonderful news to share. "Perfect. I'm glad she's safe."

"How're you feeling?"

"My stomach hurts, but I feel okay."

"The pain medicine should kick in soon," I pointed out.

Ryan nodded. "Enough with the small talk, though. We need to talk about what happened."

"I know."

I moved my hand to my lap. I stared down at my hands. Ryan's blood was still there, staring back at me.

"I know it's all my fault."

"I didn't ask for you to stop rubbing my hand, did I?"

"No."

I grabbed Ryan's hand and rubbed it with my thumb.

Ryan smiled. "That's better."

Even with a gunshot wound, he was still in a good mood.

"I just feel like I dragged you into a life you had no idea about," I admitted.

Ryan shook his head in disgust.

"I could've walked away the day you told me about him, but I didn't. I stuck around. I stuck around because nobody would prevent me from being loved by the love of my life or loving the love of my life."

I closed my eyes and exhaled. My emotions were getting the best of me. Ryan loved me, and he loved me to the ends of this earth. He continued to prove it to me every day.

"I love you so much, Ryan. I don't know what my life would've been like if I hadn't found you."

"You mean if I hadn't found you?" he asked as he smiled. "I had to be persistent. You had those walls up high. If I hadn't been persistent, you never would've given me the time of day,"

I nodded. He was right, but I had every right to be. "Now, you saw firsthand why."

"Yes, I did."

"I can't believe you saved my life." A tear escaped my eye as I hurried to wipe it away. "I could never repay you for that. You saved our lives." Ryan gave my hand a squeeze. "Repay me by continuing to be my wife. My life without you flashed before my eyes when he pointed that gun at you. I don't ever want to experience that again."

I grabbed Ryan's face and kissed him. It wasn't just a regular kiss. It was sensual. Our lips moved in sync, a rhythm they were only aware of.

"When I sat in the waiting room, I wasn't sure of the severity of your injuries. I wasn't sure if you'd survive, but you fought. You fought for us, and you fought for our family. You complete me. You're my other half."

Ryan wiped the tears that continued to stream down my face. "Don't cry, I'm fine." He kissed my forehead. "Besides, we're bonded permanently now."

"What do you mean?"

"This wound is going to leave a scar. We'll have matching scars."

I chuckled at Ryan's positivity about the situation. I'd been self-conscious of my scar, so I avoided two-piece bathing suits like the plague. Ryan's positivity on the situation encouraged me that I should be grateful I still had my life. If I wanted to wear a bikini, I could do so proudly.

"Forever and always?" I placed my pinky in front of him.

He grasped my pinky with his. "You're my

one and only. Forever and always."

Chapter Twenty-Nine

Kyla

"Tell me your secrets. You're glowing."

I turned in my chair and looked at Lauren. She leaned against my cubicle, hands on her hips as she assessed me with her eyes. She wore a navy blue floor-length dress that flattered her body.

I smiled. "I'm happy. I'm in love."

Lauren winked at me. "I can tell. I'm in love, and I don't shine as bright as you do, though."

Lauren, still in a relationship, was a huge surprise. They'd been together three months, and the relationship was going strong. Lauren might've found her man.

I pressed my hand to my chest and beamed. "Thank you."

Lauren motioned for me to walk with her. I followed her as we called out good morning to our coworkers as we walked past them.

Today was my first day back to work after being off for three weeks. Ryan was feeling strong enough to do some interviews and fill out more job applications. I missed him, but I knew in eight-and-a-half hours, I'd be with him again. Time couldn't go by fast enough.

Once we were inside the break room, Lauren gave me a pointed look.

"You got some, didn't you?" she asked with a smirk.

I laughed at Lauren's question. Lauren had no filter.

I nodded a smile that could be seen a mile away. Lauren wrapped her arms around me and jumped in excitement.

"I knew it. It's written all over you." Lauren beamed. "Was it good? Was it great?"

"Lauren," I hissed as I looked over my shoulder. Thankfully, none of our coworkers had walked in and heard our conversation.

"What? Don't be shy now." Lauren poured herself a cup of coffee.

"It was fantastic," I squealed, doing a victory

dance.

Lauren clapped her hands once she did her own happy dance.

Lauren poured the creamer into her coffee. "I knew the little irritation wouldn't do too much harm to you two."

The little irritation. That's what Lauren called Brad. Personally, I liked that reference. He was an irritation nonetheless, and his ego and psychotic ways made him appear small.

"I'm glad it didn't, but it did throw us some obstacles."

I never imagined Ryan would lose his job, but I saw it as a prime example that everything happens for a reason. If a crazy woman who was out for extra cash could cause him to lose his job, then the job wasn't meant for him. Lauren stirred her coffee before she took a sip.

"You two have always been my favorite couple."

I scoffed. Folding my arms across my chest, I said, "You only say that because you love our children."

Lauren thought for a moment. She nodded. "There might be a bit of truth in that statement. I love those little angels."

"Trust me, they love you too."

Blood didn't always make you family. Family didn't have to be blood.

We walked back to our desks. Lauren sat her coffee on her desk before she gave me her attention.

"Brad's psychotic plan to take me back nearly broke us, but Brad's journey to ruin my life brought us back together."

Lauren caressed my shoulder. "It sounds like the perfect love story you'd read about in a romance book."

I wiggled my eyebrows. "It sounds like a book we need to read so we can have a book discussion."

Lauren sat in her chair as she wiped her forehead, removing imaginary sweat. "Yes, please. We're overdue for a book. I'm having major book withdrawals."

I missed work. I missed Lauren and her overdramatic ways. She always made my day eventful, and it passed by quickly. I couldn't have asked for a better coworker and friend.

"I'll task you with finding a book. Just let me know which one you want to read, and I'll order it."

Lauren giggled. She turned in her chair, went into a drawer, and grabbed her purse. She rummaged through it before she pulled out a book.

"Already purchased."

Lauren smirked as she handed it over.

"You move fast, don't you?" I asked, eyebrow raised.

The cover was adorned with a beautiful woman, her aura screaming confidence.

"I'm not a book fanatic for nothing. I just need you to open it and get to reading. I'll host our next book discussion. I plan to make these cute little finger sandwiches. I just found the recipe on the internet, and I'm dying to try them."

I turned the book over and perused the blurb. "I'll get to reading."

"Goodie." Lauren clapped her hands excitedly. "Let's try for two weeks."

"I'll have it finished by then."

It took a bit for me to get back into my daily groove of work, but once I dived back into the world of examining financial records, I was right back at home.

My first week back flew by with ease. I had no hiccups, and I was fine being knee-deep in work. Life was finally returning to normal.

Since it was Friday night, Amelia and James had suggested they watch the children so Ryan and I could have a date. At first, I was hesitant to say yes. They had done so much for us in the three weeks that Ryan recovered that I couldn't bring myself to say yes, but they insisted. Amelia's words rang true.

"I want you two to have alone time together. You're still recovering from a hard situation."

I couldn't have asked for better in-laws. They were so involved in all our lives, and we appreciated them.

I parked my car in front of the house. With a pep in my step, I walked into the house and kicked my shoes off. Tonight, Ryan told me he would take me out to a restaurant but didn't specify which one. It would be a surprise, and I was ready to go on our date with blinders on.

After putting away a few items that were out of place, I walked upstairs and headed straight for the shower.

Once the water was steaming hot and my clothes were in a pile on the floor, I hopped in and washed away the stress of my workday. Today, I encountered an account that was off by $10,000, and I worked an hour overtime to find the mistake. Lauren had offered to stay and find the discrepancy since she knew Ryan and I had a date. She didn't want me to stress, but I told her I would handle it.

"You're still in the shower?"

Ryan's voice pulled me out of my thoughts as I turned in the steaming water to rinse off the front of my body. The hot water beat on my neck and chest, and it felt great.

"Yes." I thought for a second, a flirtatious smirk touching my lips. "Do you want to join me?"

"I thought you'd never ask." His voice boomed with confidence.

The shower curtain opened, and Ryan stepped in behind me. His hand grazed my butt. I looked over my shoulder and winked at him.

He grabbed the sponge that hung in the shower and lathered it up with rose-scented body wash. The soft material grazed my back, and my eyes fluttered closed.

"How does that feel?" Ryan whispered in my ear, causing my body to shiver.

"Amazing."

Ryan's lips touched the side of my neck as he pressed his body against mine, his erection pressed against my butt.

He wrapped his arms around my body. I melted into his hold as he reached between my legs and found my clitoris.

I sucked in a breath as his rubbing intensified. A shriek escaped my lips as my body lost all control. My legs became weak and buckled underneath me.

Ryan held me up as the stars cleared away from my vision, and reality set in.

I turned and reached for his erection, but Ryan stopped my hand.

"Not now." His eyes stared into mine, and I couldn't tear my eyes away from him.

"Why not?"

"Your pleasure was my priority. Right now, we must get ready for dinner. We have reservations in an hour."

I gasped as I switched places with Ryan in the shower. The water streamed down his body as he closed his eyes and ran his fingers through his hair.

"What about—"

"I'll be fine until tonight," Ryan finished for me as he grabbed his rag and the bar of soap.

After getting one more luscious eyeful of Ryan's naked body, I stepped out of the shower and wrapped a towel around my body.

If the restaurant we went to required reservations, I had to dress to impress. Once I dried off, I walked out of the bathroom.

I headed for the closest. I fingered through the mass of dresses, and my eyes zoomed in on a tan, formal gown with a thigh split.

The shower turned off, and I looked towards the bathroom. I'd never seen this dress before, and it was in my closet.

"Ryan."

"Did you find your new gown?"

I scrunched my eyebrows together. Ryan never went shopping. He was allergic to the activity.

"You bought me a gown?"

Ryan opened the door, a towel wrapped around his waist. Water trickled down his body, and I looked at his torso. Even though he still had a bandage on his abdomen, he still looked amazing as ever.

He smiled as he walked further into the room. "Of course. Tonight is going to be perfect."

"It's stunning." I picked the dress up by the hanger and examined its beauty. "You had help picking it, didn't you?"

Ryan nodded as he walked into the closet and pulled out a pair of black pants and a tan dress shirt.

"It's Sophia's design."

My mouth dropped open. "You had Sophia send a dress for me?"

Ryan was quiet for a few moments. "I had her make this dress specifically for you."

My heart softened at Ryan's effort. He was

doing everything in his power to make this date for us to be a success.

"I can't wait to put it on." I took the dress off the hanger. Ryan placed his clothes on the bed and helped me pull the dress over my head. The dress fit like a glove.

I walked over to the full-length mirror, and my mouth dropped open. There was no doubt that this dress was made for my body.

I pulled my hair into a high, formal bun, placed gold, dangling earrings into my ear and a gold bracelet on my wrist. I spritzed myself all over with sweet, scented perfume. Once I slipped on a pair of silver heels, I smoothed my hands over the silky fabric before I placed my hands on my hips and struck a pose.

"How do I look?"

Ryan's eyes traveled the length of my body. "Like a million bucks." Ryan whistled as he finished putting his dress shoes on. "My sister did great."

Ryan walked over to me, snaked his arms around my body, and pulled me close. The intimacy of us being pressed together, fully clothed, was beautiful. He nuzzled my neck before he kissed my forehead. He went to his side of the bed and opened the drawer. He pulled out a single red rose before he handed it over to me.

"A rose for you."

I inhaled the scent, grateful Ryan hadn't changed one bit since the shooting. Grateful he hadn't changed since the day we said 'I do' to each other.

"You sure know how to make me smile."

"You deserve to smile, every day."

He took my hand and led me downstairs.

After I grabbed my purse, Ryan led me to his car. He opened the door and helped me inside before he closed the door and walked to the driver's side.

As Ryan drove downtown, we listened to pop music at a low volume while we talked. It felt great talking while he drove. Ryan's hand on my knee during the car ride solidified how much he cared about me and wanted this date to be perfect.

We approached a standalone, two-story building. A ship giving off steam was located on the massive building.

"I've heard wonderful things about this place," I commented as Ryan stopped beside the valet attendant in front of the restaurant.

"Now, you get to experience it for yourself."

Ryan stepped out of the car. He walked over to the passenger side, where he opened the door. With his hand extended, I placed my hand in his and stepped out. After Ryan handed over his keys and received a valet slip, he opened the door to the restaurant and guided me inside.

The smell of the ocean entered my nose, reminding me of home. The restaurant was dimly lit, giving off a romantic aura. Ryan led me to the hostess stand, where he gave our last name.

Once the hostess located our reservation, she led us through the nautical-decorated restaurant.

We sat in the booth the hostess led us to. I sat my rose on the table and looked over the menu.

Our waitress, Wendy, came to our table and greeted us before she took our drink orders. Once she walked away, I looked at Ryan.

"Thank you for taking me out tonight."

He looked up from the menu, a sparkle in his eyes. "You haven't even eaten dinner yet."

I shook my head. "I'm not thanking you for dinner, even though I'm totally eyeing the lobster pasta."

Ryan raised an eyebrow as Wendy brought our sweet tea to the table.

"I'm thanking you for all the effort you placed into our date night." I paused to take a sip of my tea. "You went out of your way to get this beautiful dress made for me. You took me to a restaurant I've been wanting to try for months now. You're putting in all the effort I've been wanting out of you, and I couldn't expect more from you."

Ryan smiled as he placed his hand on mine. He gave it a soothing rub. "You're my dream come true. You're my Heaven on Earth." Ryan's voice quivered a bit, letting me know he was getting emotional.

I placed my hand on top of his, giving it a tight squeeze. I wanted him to know that he could take his time.

"I promise that I'll always put in effort. I will always love you the way I promised you that I would when you and I said 'I do' to each other. Every day won't be sunshine and rainbows, though."

"I love you, and I'll forever love you. Flaws and all."

Ryan smiled before he stood, leaned across the table, and grabbed my face in his hands. He locked his lips with mine, a feeling of love blanketing me. Ryan's tongue danced with mine, and I was sold. This man loved me. I loved him. We would do anything and everything to make sure our marriage worked. We were living happily ever after.

Chapter Thirty

Kyla

A constant tap on my arm pulled me out of my sleep. I was sleeping so well I didn't want to get up.

"Wake up, Kyla."

Ryan's voice was soothing. Usually, I didn't mind hearing his voice, but this morning was different. I was exhausted, and I didn't want to get up. I could lay in bed all day if I could.

I moaned no as I turned over, snuggling

under the covers.

"Don't tell me no, Beautiful." Ryan nibbled on my ear, further pulling me out of my sleep. "Today is the day."

The day to sign the adoption papers had arrived, officially making Bria, Ryan's child. Six weeks had passed since Luke called us with the wonderful news. Over the past few weeks, we'd met with Luke to get everything in place. It was going to be a great day. Ryan had gotten a job in the next town over, and he was making more money than he was making at his last job. The switch in employment was the best thing he could've done, even though it was out of his control.

We took the day off from work to get everything finalized. Too bad I couldn't sleep any longer, no matter how much I wanted to.

"I'm getting up." I fluttered my eyes open, and Ryan's face came into view. He kissed me on my lips. "Don't kiss me. I have morning breath."

Ryan shrugged his shoulders as he smirked. "I happen to love your morning breath. Get ready. Breakfast should be ready in five."

"You're gross." I laughed. "I'll be down."

Ryan left the room, and I pushed the covers off my body. I sat up in bed, an uneasy feeling causing my stomach to feel sour. I walked into the bathroom, where I handled my hygiene, dressed in a pair of black pants and a coral-colored blouse, before I walked downstairs.

I entered the dining room, where Ryder and

Bria ate breakfast. Ryan had cooked pancakes, eggs, and sausage.

"Good morning, Mommy," Ryder and Bria called out in unison in between bites of food.

"Good morning." I kissed them on their foreheads before Ryan handed me my plate of food.

I sat at the table. I grabbed my fork and dug into my food when the smell of eggs caused my stomach to turn.

I threw my hand over my mouth. I ran out of the dining room and upstairs to the bathroom before I dropped to my knees and emptied the contents of my stomach.

"Kyla, are you okay?" Ryan's voice quivered with worry as he approached the bathroom door.

"I think so." I flushed the toilet as I pushed myself up.

"Can I come in?" he asked me.

I shook my head as if he could see me. I walked to the sink and turned the water on. "I don't want you to see me like this."

Ryan opened the door and peeked inside. "If you aren't feeling well, I don't need you to be alone. What's wrong?"

I washed my hands with soap. I looked in the mirror and looked into Ryan's eyes. "I just wasn't feeling the best this morning. I think the feeling has passed."

Ryan nodded. "I'll take the children to school once they finish breakfast. Take it easy, please."

I wiped my hands on a paper towel. "I will."

Ryan walked out of the bathroom. I walked out of the children's shared bathroom and down the hall into my bathroom. I brushed my teeth once again before I went downstairs.

My stomach growled as I walked into the empty dining room. My untouched plate of food was still waiting for me. My nose crinkled in disgust, the smell of egg overpowering. I walked over to the garbage, threw away my eggs, and dived into my pancakes and sausage. Once my plate was clean and my stomach was full and satisfied, I placed the dirty dishes into the dishwasher and started the cycle.

I walked over to the couch, plopped down, and grabbed my book. I was five chapters into the book, and I was hooked. I knew it wouldn't take me long to finish the book .

Twenty minutes later, Ryan walked into the house.

"How are you feeling?" he asked me as he sat beside me on the couch. He wrapped his arm around my shoulder before he kissed my cheek.

I closed my book and looked at Ryan. "I'm feeling better."

"Good." He smiled before he pulled his phone out of his pocket to look at the time. "We have thirty minutes before leaving to go to the courthouse."

I gave him a knowing look. "What do you have in mind?"

"Fun between the sheets." Ryan wiggled his eyebrows.

I playfully swatted Ryan's arm as we laughed together.

Ryan grabbed my face and kissed me before we stared into each other's eyes.

This is what I lived for. Happiness in our marriage. The ability to be playful and have fun when necessary. The ability to be serious and take care of responsibilities when necessary. A good marriage couldn't be found. It had to be created.

I opened my book, and Ryan grabbed his laptop off the end table . I read my book for the next twenty minutes while Ryan worked on a project. Even though he just started with his new company, they had already assigned him projects. He had a deadline to hit with a project, so a few minutes here and there was helpful.

The butterflies fluttering in my stomach intensified as we traveled across town to the courthouse. In less than an hour, Bria would be Ryan's daughter.

Once we went through security, we took the elevator to the third floor.

Hand in hand, we sat outside of the courtroom. At any second, they would call us inside. Once we left that courtroom, our lives would change forever.

Exactly seven minutes later, Luke walked out to get us. He wore a dark gray suit with gray dress shoes.

We stood at the same time as Luke approached us.

"It's nice to see you again, Luke." I shook his hand before he shook Ryan's hand.

"It's a pleasure." He clasped his hands together as he looked back and forth between the both of us. "How are you healing up?" he asked Ryan.

Ryan smiled. "I'm feeling better and better each day."

"That's wonderful to hear." Luke pointed toward the courtroom. "This court hearing makes it final. Are you two ready?"

"Yes." I was a bunch of nerves and excitement.

Ryan nodded as he stuffed his hands into his pockets. "This has been a long time coming."

"Let's get to it."

The court hearing took an hour and a half. It was an agonizing ninety-six minutes, but once we signed the adoption papers and the ink was dry on the paper, my emotions got the best of me.

I burst into tears as Ryan wrapped his arms around me. He ran his fingers through my hair as he rubbed my back.

Luke stood nearby, smiling as he clutched his briefcase.

Once my hug ended with Ryan, I walked over and hugged Luke. Ryan found the best attorney to handle our case.

Ryan and I walked out of the courthouse, holding hands.

"I think we should have a celebration tonight."

We sat in Ryan's car, and I opened the visor

and wiped at the smeared mascara under my eyes. I made a mental note to pick up waterproof mascara the next time I went shopping.

Ryan pulled out of the parking garage, and we headed back towards our house.

"I think that sounds like a wonderful idea."

"Let's stop at the store. We have to pick up a few things for tonight."

"How about we stop and have lunch first?" Ryan asked as he patted his stomach. "I'm starving."

"Sounds like a plan." I placed my hand on his knee.

We went to a hole-in-a-wall taco shop where we chowed down on crunchy, delicious tacos. I shared some of my chicken taco with Ryan while he shared some of his steak . We went to the grocery store once our stomachs were full and satisfied.

We spent twenty minutes walking around the grocery store like we were teenagers in love. We walked down each aisle, looking for ingredients for that night's dinner. We held hands, picked up various items, and discussed everything that came to mind.

While I put all the food away, Ryan went to pick up the children from school. I walked Bria's cake upstairs to our bedroom, so she didn't see it when she came home. The cake wouldn't be revealed until after dinner. I couldn't wait for this celebration. It was a great day, and we had much to be thankful for.

Since we were cooking Bria's favorite meal, cheeseburgers and fries, I wouldn't have to start cooking until thirty minutes before dinner time. Extra time to myself meant more time to devour my book. I read through another chapter by the time the children arrived.

I lounged under the gazebo, nose deep in a book, when I was bombarded by a bunch of kisses on my cheeks and arms wrapped around my shoulder.

"Hey, Sweeties. You snuck up on Mommy." I closed my book and basked in the attention.

"Did we scare you?" Ryder asked, a smile threatening to appear.

I nodded. "You frightened, Mommy."

"Yay." Ryder cheered before he took off running around the backyard.

"How're you enjoying your book?" Bria asked as she sat beside me.

I examined the cover of my book. "It's a great read. It's keeping me on the edge of my seat."

Bria tucked a strand of her hair behind her ear. "That's how I feel about the book Auntie Lauren and I found at the library."

Bria was a mini-me, starting her love for books early. My love for books started when my relationship with Brad went sour. Books were my only escape from leaving my life for the time being before and diving into someone else's universe.

"I'm glad you're enjoying it. When you finish that one, how about we visit the bookstore and buy you two books?"

Bria's eyes brightened. "I'll be able to get books of my own?" Bria covered her mouth, her eyes full of excitement.

Lauren had taken Bria to the library to start her reading journey. I thought it was time for her to have some books of her own.

"Yes."

Bria wrapped her arms around me as she cheered. "Thank you, Mommy."

"Anything for you."

Bria ran around the yard with Ryder. Ryan came outside. He had changed out of his court clothes, and he now wore a pair of shorts and a T-shirt, and he threw the football to Bria and Ryder.

In just a few hours, we'd announce the news to Bria. I couldn't believe my life was finally complete. It took years for this time to come. There were plenty of ups and downs, but I wouldn't change anything I've encountered on my journey. Without those trials and errors, I wouldn't be the woman I am today.

Once dinner time approached, I closed my book and walked inside. There were only a handful of chapters left to read.

I washed my hands and went to work preparing dinner. Within minutes, the house filled with the smell and sound of delicious meat sizzling.

By the time the burgers and fries were done, the dining room table was surrounded by my loved ones as Amelia and I walked in carrying the burgers and fries.

We passed food around and enjoyed each other's company as we ate our food.

Once dinner was almost finished, I looked across the table at Ryan. After catching Ryan's attention, I winked at him. He nodded as he wiped his hands on a napkin.

"I'll be right back."

Ryan carried the cake into the dining room a minute later. Ryder and Bria gasped at the view of sweet goodness as Amelia, James, and I gave an emotion-filled smile.

Ryan set the white cake, decorated with colorful balloons, in front of Bria. The cake read, 'Bria, will you be my daughter?' in a simple script.

"Bria." Ryan sat beside her. "I know I've been in your life for several years. I've already taken on the father role since I married your mom."

Silence settled upon us. I brought my hand to my chest as tears welled in my eyes. Ryan was just as emotional as I was.

I looked over at Amelia and James. They had wide smiles as they started to tear up. James placed his hand on top of Amelia's on the table and gave it a soft squeeze. I looked over at Ryder's eyes zeroing in on the cake, his mind filled with sugary fantasies.

Ryan took Bria's hand, and he continued, his voice full of emotion. "I know I'll never replace your birth father. I just want to protect you for the rest of your life."

Tears dropped onto my cheek as I sniffled. I grabbed a napkin and wiped my eyes.

"Will you do the honor of being my daughter?"

Bria looked around at all of us, tears brimming in her eyes. She looked back at Ryan and nodded. "Yes. You've always been my dad."

She wrapped her arms around his neck.

We all clapped and hollered out sweet congratulations. Amelia and James smiled as they grabbed their napkins to dry their wet eyes. The only dry eye in the room was Ryder's.

Ryder pulled his eyes away from the cake to look at us. "What's going on?" he asked.

We all exchanged a look. Ryder wasn't aware that Ryan wasn't Bria's birth father, and I didn't think he'd understand the concept.

"We are celebrating a happy time," James responded.

Ryder nodded. "Okay. Cake time," he called out.

We laughed at Ryder's desire for cake.

Amelia and I stood. We cleared the plates, and Ryan cut the cake. By the time we returned to the table for cake, Ryder wore a frosting mustache.

"My complete family," I said as I dug into my slice of cake.

Nothing else in this world could break me now.

Epilogue

Kyla

The salty breeze whipped through my hair as I adjusted my body in the lounge chair.

Bria rushed over to me, her hair dripping with salty ocean water. Her purple one-piece bathing suit clung to her body. "Mom, you have to come in the water with us."

I shielded my eyes from the sun and looked past her. Ryan and Ryder splashed each other with water before they took off swimming.

I contemplated getting wet in the ocean with my family or finishing off the mystery book I couldn't get enough of. I closed my book and placed it in my bag at the last possible second.

"Why not. Let's go." I stood, grabbed Bria's hand, and ran with her towards the ocean. I wore a light blue bikini for the first time in years. I felt comfortable enough in my body to show off my battle scar. The only thing the bikini couldn't hide was the seven pounds I had gained.

The cool water rushed over my body as we swam to where Ryan and Ryder were.

Ryder and Bria had spring break that week, so Ryan and I decided to take the week off to have a family vacation in Hawaii.

The sun was shining bright, and the sky was free of clouds. We'd been there three days so far, and we'd been having the time of our lives. I was happy Bria suggested we take a family trip there. Hawaii was paradise on Earth.

After swimming for thirty minutes, Ryan and I got out of the water. My eyes danced across his toned torso to his battle scar. It healed beautifully, and I was glad he had no issues with it.

We walked over to our lounge chairs and sat.

"I didn't think I'd love it here this much." Ryan tucked his hands behind his head as he crossed his feet.

"It's by far the best vacation destination we've chosen." I placed my hands on top of my stomach and relaxed. This was life. Vacationing with my family once a year was a special family tradition we started, and it was important to me. It was important to us.

Something had been weighing heavy on my mind, and I needed to confirm it. It would eat at me for our trip if I didn't confirm it now.

I stood. "Meet me back in the room in fifteen minutes."

Ryan raised an eyebrow. "Where are you going?" he asked as he sat up in his chair.

"I have to pick something up. Fifteen minutes, okay?"

Ryan nodded. "Okay. I'll see you in fifteen."

I kissed Ryan before I grabbed my bag and walked to the resort's mini-store. After combing the aisles, I finally located the small family planning section. Once I grabbed the pregnancy test, I checked out at the counter and made the trek back to the room. As I walked along the sidewalk, the bright sun pierced my skin and warmed my body. In a few minutes, I could confirm if what I'd been feeling these last few weeks was a baby or just my body going through weird changes.

I slipped the key into the door and stepped inside our two-bedroom villa. The smell of pineapples wafted into my nose from the air fresher stuck inside the wall of each room .

I sat my bag on the dining room table before entering the bathroom. I followed the instructions on the pregnancy test, and I waited in silence.

Time ticked slowly as I paced the living room of the villa. The test sat on the bathroom sink, and only a few minutes were left.

The beep of the unlocked front door sounded, and my family walked in. Ryder was the first to walk in, and he had a pout on his face, and his arms were folded across his chest.

"What's wrong, Ryder?" I asked him as I squatted down to his level.

"I didn't want to get out of the water." His little lip poked out more as he looked down at the ground.

My phone's alarm went off signaling that the time was up. The test was ready.

"We'll go back out there in a little bit. How does ice cream sound?" I ran my fingers through his wet curls.

His pout turned into a toothy smile. "Yay, ice cream." Ryder tapped his finger on his lip a few times, deep in thought. "I want Cookie Monster."

I pinched his cheek before I kissed him on the forehead. "You can have any ice cream flavor you want."

"Can I get a big bowl?" Ryder stretched his arms out as far as they would go.

I was about to respond when Bria's question stopped me before I could get a word out.

"Mom, what's this?" Bria called from behind me.

Ryan's eyes immediately looked at Bria. I turned, and she held the pregnancy test.

"Bria, hand that over."

I didn't expect her to go into the bathroom and find the test. Lo-and-behold, she found it, and

Ryan had seen it. I wasn't sure if I was pregnant, but I hadn't shared my suspicions with him either.

Without looking at the result of the test, I enveloped my hands across the tests. I looked up, and my eyes met Ryan's.

I was the first to speak. "Can we talk in the bedroom?"

Ryan nodded slowly, as if he were in shock.

After telling the children we would go for ice cream after we talked, we walked into the bedroom. I closed the door behind us.

"So, while the kids are out of earshot, I'd like to talk to you about something."

"Are you pregnant?" He jumped right to the question that was on his mind.

The anticipation had grown with each passing second before we had even walked into the room.

"I haven't been feeling a hundred percent for the last few weeks." I shrugged. "I might be."

Ryan's face softened as he looked down at my stomach. I had gained some weight, and my stomach had been poking out more than usual. He placed his hand on my stomach. He smiled as he looked at me.

"The answer is in your hands. Read the results."

I exhaled as I opened my hand so Ryan could see as well. I looked down at the results and burst into tears.

***

“Just a few more minutes,” I said into the phone.

We had news to share with our friends and family, and we decided to do it on a video call. We couldn’t wait to get home to share this wonderful news.

“What’s going on?” Lauren asked as she flipped her hair over her shoulder.

“Yes, tell us what’s going on. We need to know,” Mark responded as Chelsea swatted his arm.

“Be patient,” Chelsea scolded Mark.

She looked into the camera and gave an apology for her husband’s impatience.

“It’s okay.” I giggled as Ryan bustled behind me.

“Who are we waiting for?” James asked as Amelia elbowed him.

“Stop being impatient. You don’t have anything else to do for the night,” Amelia told James as he did a faux eye roll.

For some reason, the men were impatient today. They weren’t okay with the wait, but the ladies did a great job calming them down for me.

“We’re just waiting for Sabrina and Amy,” I said as Amy’s image popped up on my phone.

“I’m here, I’m here. I’m sorry, I just got home. I hope I didn’t miss anything.” Amy sounded out of breath, like she ran an entire mile to get on the call.

"You haven't missed anything. We haven't started yet." Ryan walked by and smiled into the camera before he walked into the bedroom Bria stayed in. He called for the children to come out.

The children came out and came to a stop in the living room. They looked at the cardboard box in the middle of the living room.

"What's that?" Ryder pointed at the box.

Ryan placed his finger to his lips, telling Ryder to be quiet.

Sabrina's strawberry blonde hair appeared on the screen, and my stomach filled with butterflies. "I'm here. You can start. I just finished filming for the day."

"Perfect. I want to thank you all for taking time out of your day to come on this video call tonight. So, we have some news to share with you all. We thought it was best to share it with everyone at the same time. So, without further ado..." I turned the video from my face to show Ryan and the children surrounding the box.

"Ryder, can you do the honor of opening the box?" Ryan asked as he stepped back.

Ryder lifted the corners of the box, and two balloons popped out. One was white, and the other was black. Scrawled across the white balloon was black writing, and scrawled across the black balloon was white writing.

"Can you read the balloons for us, Bria?" Ryan asked her.

"Start with the white balloon," I called out.

Bria grabbed the white balloon and read the

words. "Baby Walker is baking in the oven." She grabbed the black balloon. "He or she will be here by the end of the year."

The video erupted in cheers as Bria's mouth fell open.

"You're having another baby?" she asked.

I nodded. "You'll have another brother or sister."

Bria ran over to me and threw herself into my arms.

"I can't believe we're going to have another grandchild," Amelia exclaimed as she placed her hand over her mouth.

"Another grandchild to spoil." James raised his hands above his head in celebration.

Mark cleared his throat before he spoke up. "I believe I can speak up for all of us on this call. We're so proud of Mom and Dad for the new baby we'll meet. We can't wait to spoil our niece or nephew. They will be spoiled rotten just like those two."

Ryder and Bria beamed as they were spoiled to a fault by everyone around them.

Congratulations and I'm so happy for you continued to be thrown out randomly as the four of us enjoyed our joyful celebration with our family and friends.

This baby reveal couldn't have gone better. Baby number three wasn't planned, but I was ready to meet him or her with open arms. They were a blessing.

OTHER TITLES BY ANA DENISE

His Crazy Obsession Series

His Crazy Obsession

His Unstable Obsession

Dangers in Love Series

Dangers in Love

Lost in Love

Thank you for reading!

Please add a review on Amazon, Goodreads, or TikTok and let me know what you thought!

Reviews are extremely helpful for authors, thank you for taking the time to support me and my work. Don't forget to share your review on social media and with hashtag #HisUnstableObsession and encourage others to read the story too!

Ana Denise was born and raised on the Treasure Coast of Florida in 1999. She considers her family and friends to be most significant in her life. Growing up, she has always been fascinated with reading and writing short stories. Following her passion, she has decided to become a romance author after obtaining a Bachelor's Degree in Business Administration.